INDIAN PRAIRIE PUBLIC LIBRARY DISTRICT

3 1946 00521 05

W9-BCV-968

3-18(27)

2012

HEADHUNTERS

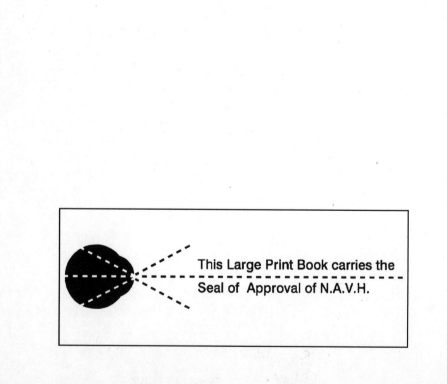

This Large Print Book carries the
Seal of Approval of N.A.V.H.

HEADHUNTERS

JO NESBØ

Translated by Don Bartlett

THORNDIKE PRESS

A part of Gale, Cengage Learning

GALE
CENGAGE Learning®

Detroit • New York • San Francisco • New Haven, Conn • Waterville, Maine • London

INDIAN PRAIRIE PUBLIC LIBRARY
401 Plainfield Rd.
Darien, IL 60561

GALE
CENGAGE Learning®

Translation copyright © 2011 by Don Bartlett.
Originally published by agreement with the Salomonsson Agency in Norway as *Hodejegerne* by H. Aschehoug & Co. (W. Nygaard), Oslo, in 2008. Copyright © 2008 by Jo Nesbø.
Thorndike Press, a part of Gale, Cengage Learning.

ALL RIGHTS RESERVED
This is a work of fiction. Names, characters, places, and incidents either are the product of the author's imagination or are used fictitiously. Any resemblance to actual persons, living or dead, events, or locales is entirely coincidental.
Thorndike Press® Large Print Thriller.
The text of this Large Print edition is unabridged.
Other aspects of the book may vary from the original edition.
Set in 16 pt. Plantin.

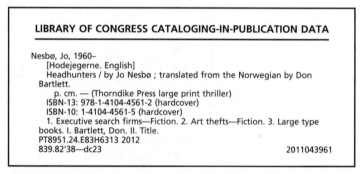

LIBRARY OF CONGRESS CATALOGING-IN-PUBLICATION DATA

Nesbø, Jo, 1960–
    [Hodejegerne. English]
    Headhunters / by Jo Nesbø ; translated from the Norwegian by Don Bartlett.
      p. cm. — (Thorndike Press large print thriller)
    ISBN-13: 978-1-4104-4561-2 (hardcover)
    ISBN-10: 1-4104-4561-5 (hardcover)
    1. Executive search firms—Fiction. 2. Art thefts—Fiction. 3. Large type books. I. Bartlett, Don. II. Title.
    PT8951.24.E83H6313 2012
    839.82'38—dc23   2011043961

Published in 2012 by arrangement with Vintage Anchor, an imprint of Knopf Doubleday Publishing Group, a division of Random House, Inc.

Printed in the United States of America
1 2 3 4 5 6 7 16 15 14 13 12

HEADHUNTERS

Prologue

A collision between two vehicles is basic physics. It all comes down to chance, but chance phenomena can be explained by the equation Energy × Time = Mass × difference in Velocity. Add values to the chance variables and you have a story that is simple, true and remorseless. It tells you, for example, what happens when a fully loaded juggernaut weighing 25 tons and travelling at a speed of 80 kph hits a sedan weighing 1,800 kilos and moving at the same speed. Based on chance with respect to point of impact, construction of bodywork and the angle of the two bodies relative to one another, a multitude of variants to this story are possible, but they share two common features: they are tragedies. And it is the sedan which is in trouble.

It is strangely quiet; I can hear the wind rushing through the trees and the river shifting its water. My arm is numb and I am hanging upside down, trapped between flesh and steel. Above me, blood and petrol drip from the floor. Beneath me, on the chessboard ceiling, I can see a pair of nail scissors, a severed arm, two dead men and an open overnight bag. The white queen is broken, I am a killer and no one is breathing inside the car. Not even me. That is why I will die soon. Close my eyes and give up. Giving up is wonderful. I don't want to wait any longer now. Hence the hurry to tell this story, this variant, this story about the angle of the bodies relative to one another.

■ ■ ■ ■

PART ONE:
FIRST INTERVIEW

■ ■ ■ ■

1
CANDIDATE

The candidate was terrified.

He was dressed in Gunnar Øye attire: grey Ermenegildo Zegna suit, hand-sewn Borelli shirt and burgundy tie with sperm-cell pattern, I guessed Cerrutti 1881. However, I was certain about the shoes: hand-sewn Ferragamo. I once had a pair myself.

The papers in front of me revealed that the candidate came armed with excellent credentials from NHH — the Norwegian School of Economics and Business Administration, in Bergen — a spell in Stortinget for the Conservative Party and a four-year success story as the managing director of a medium-sized manufacturing company.

Nevertheless, Jeremias Lander was terrified. His upper lip glistened with sweat.

He raised the glass of water my secretary had placed on the low table between us.

'I'd like . . .' I said with a smile. Not the open, unconditional smile that invites a

11

complete stranger to come in from the cold, not the *frivolous* one. But the courteous, semi-warm smile that, according to the literature, signals the interviewer's professionalism, objectivity and analytical approach. Indeed, it is this lack of emotional commitment that causes the candidate to trust his interviewer's integrity. And as a result the candidate will in turn — according to the aforementioned literature — provide more sober, objective information, as he has been made to feel that any pretence would be seen through, any exaggeration exposed and ploys punished. I don't put on this smile because of the literature, though. I don't give a damn about the literature; it is chock-a-block with various degrees of authoritative bullshit, and the only thing I need is Inbau, Reid and Buckley's nine-step interrogation model. No, I put on this smile because I really *am* professional, objective and analytical. I am a headhunter. It is not that difficult, but I am king of the heap.

'I'd like,' I repeated, 'I'd like you to tell me a little about your life, outside of work, that is.'

'Is there any?' His laughter was a tone and a half higher than it should have been. On top of that, when you deliver a so-called 'dry' joke at a job interview it is unwise both to laugh at it yourself and to watch your interlocutor to see whether it has hit home.

'I would certainly hope so,' I said, and his laughter morphed into a clearing of the throat. 'I believe the management of this enterprise attaches great importance to their new chief executive leading a balanced life. They're seeking someone who will stay with them for a number of years, a long-distance-runner type who knows how to pace himself. Not someone who is burnt out after four years.'

Jeremias Lander nodded while swallowing another mouthful of water.

He was approximately fourteen centimetres taller than me and three years older. Thirty-eight then. A bit young for the job. And he knew; that was why he had dyed the hair around his temples an almost imperceptible grey. I had seen this before. I had seen everything before. I had seen applicants afflicted with sweaty palms arrive with chalk in their right-hand jacket pocket so as to give me the driest and whitest handshake imaginable. Lander's throat issued an involuntary clucking sound. I noted down on the interview feedback sheet: *Motivated. Solution-orientated.*

'I see you live in Oslo,' I said.

He nodded. 'Skøyen.'

'And married to . . .' I flicked through his papers, assuming the irritated expression that makes candidates think I am expecting them to take the initiative.

'Camilla. We've been married for ten years. Two children. School age.'

'And how would you characterise your marriage?' I asked without looking up. I gave him two drawn-out seconds and continued before he had collected himself enough to answer. 'Do you think you will still be married in six years' time after spending two-thirds of your waking life at work?'

I peered up. The confusion on his face was as expected. I had been inconsistent. Balanced life. Need for commitment. That didn't add up. Four seconds passed before he answered. Which is at least one too many. 'I would certainly hope so,' he said.

Secure, practised smile. But not practised enough. Not for me. He had used my own words against me, and I would have registered that as a plus if there had been some intentional irony. In this case, unfortunately, it had merely been the unconscious aping of words used by someone considered superior in status. *Poor self-image,* I jotted down. And he 'hoped', he didn't know,

14

didn't give voice to anything visionary, was not a crystal-ball reader, didn't show that he was up to speed with the minimum requirement of every manager: that they must appear to be clairvoyant. *Not an improviser. Not a chaos-pilot.*

'Does she work?'

'Yes. In a law office in the city centre.'

'Nine to four every day?'

'Yes.'

'And who stays at home if either of the children is ill?'

'She does. But fortunately it's very rare for Niclas and Anders to —'

'So you don't have a housekeeper or anyone at home during the day?'

He hesitated in the way that candidates do when they are unsure which answer puts them in the best light. All the same, they lie disappointingly seldom. Jeremias Lander shook his head.

'You look like you keep yourself fit, Lander.'

'Yes, I train regularly.'

No hesitation this time. Everyone knows that businesses want top executives who won't fall victim to a heart attack at the first hurdle.

'Running and cross-country skiing perhaps?'

'Right. The whole family loves the outdoor life. And we have a mountain cabin on Norefjell.'

'Uh-huh. Dog, too?'

He shook his head.

'No? Allergic to them?'

Energetic shaking of the head. I wrote: *Lacks sense of humour?*

Then I leaned back in the chair and steepled my fingertips. An exaggerated, arrogant gesture, of course. What can I say? That's the way I am. 'How much would you say your reputation was worth, Lander? And how have you insured it?'

He furrowed his already sweaty brow as he struggled to give the matter some thought. Two seconds later, resigned, he said: 'What do you mean?'

I sighed as if it ought to be obvious. Cast my eyes around the room as if searching for a pedagogical allegory I had not used before. And, as always, found it on the wall.

'Are you interested in art, Lander?'

'A bit. My wife is, at any rate.'

'Mine, too. Can you see the picture I have over there?' I pointed to *Sara Gets Undressed,* painted on vinyl, over two metres in height, a woman in a green skirt with her arms crossed, about to pull a red sweater over her head. 'A present from my wife. The artist's name is Julian Opie and the picture's worth a quarter of a million kroner. Do you possess any art in that price range?'

'As a matter of fact I do.'

'Congratulations. Can you see how much it's worth?'

'When you know, you can.'

'Yes, when you know, you can. The picture hanging there consists of a few lines, the woman's head is a circle, a zero without a face, and the coloring is plain and lacks texture. In addition, it was done on a computer and millions of copies can be printed out at the mere press of a key.'

'Goodness me.'

'The only — and I do mean the only — thing that makes this picture worth a quarter of a million is the artist's reputation. The buzz that he is good, the market's faith in the fact that he is a genius. It's difficult to put your finger on what constitutes genius, impossible to know for sure. It's like that with top directors, too, Lander.'

'I understand. Reputation. It's about the confidence the director exudes.'

I jot down: *Not an idiot.*

'Exactly,' I continued. 'Everything is about reputation. Not just the director's salary, but also the company's value on the stock exchange. What is, in fact, the work of art

17

you own and how much is it valued at?'

'It's a lithograph by Edvard Munch. *The Brooch.* I don't know what it's worth, but . . .'

With a flourish of my hand I impatiently urged him on.

'The last time it was up for auction the price bid was about 350,000 kroner,' he said.

'And what have you done to insure this valuable item against theft?'

'The house has a good alarm system,' he said. 'Tripolis. Everyone in the neighbourhood uses them.'

'Tripolis systems are good, though expensive. I use them myself,' I said. 'About eight grand a year. How much have you invested to protect your personal reputation?'

'What do you mean?'

'Twenty thousand? Ten thousand? Less?'

He shrugged.

'Not a cent,' I said. 'You have a CV and a career here which are worth ten times the lithograph you mentioned. A year. Nevertheless, you have no one to guard it, no custodian. Because you think it's unnecessary. You think your success with the company you head up speaks for itself. Right?'

Lander didn't answer.

'Well,' I said, leaning forward and lowering my voice as though about to impart a secret, 'that's not the way it works. Success is like Opie's pictures, a few lines plus a few zeros, no face. Pictures are nothing, reputation is everything. And that is what we can offer.'

'Reputation?'

'You're sitting in front of me as one of six good applicants for a director's job. I don't think you'll get it. Because you lack the reputation for this kind of post.'

His mouth dropped as if in protest. The protest never materialised. I thrust myself against the high back of the chair, which gave a screech.

'My God, man, you *applied* for this job! What you should have done was to set up a straw man to tip us off and then pretend you knew nothing about it when we contacted you. A top man has to be headhunted, not arrive ready-killed and all carved up.'

I saw that had the desired effect. He was rattled. This was not the usual interview format, this was not Cuté, Disc or any of the other stupid, useless questionnaires hatched up by a motley collection of, to varying extents, tone-deaf psychologists and human resource experts who themselves had nothing to offer. I lowered my voice again.

'I hope your wife won't be too disappointed when you tell her the news this afternoon. That you missed out on the dream job. That, career-wise, you'll be on standby once again this year. Just like last year . . .'

He jerked back in his chair. Bullseye. Naturally. For this was Roger Brown in action, the most radiant star in the recruitment sky right now.

'Last . . . last year?'

'Yes, isn't that right? You applied for the top job at Denja's. Mayonnaise and liver paste, is that you?'

'I understood that sort of thing was confidential,' Jeremias Lander said meekly.

'So it is. But my job is to map out resources. And that's what I do. Using all the methods at my disposal. It's stupid to apply for jobs you won't get, especially in your position, Lander.'

'My position?'

'Your qualifications, your track record, the tests and my personal impression all tell me you have what it takes. All you're missing is reputation. And the fundamental pillar in constructing a reputation is exclusivity. Applying for jobs at random undermines exclusivity. You're an executive who does not seek challenges but *the* challenge. The one job. And that's what you will be offered. On a silver platter.'

'Will I?' he said with another attempt at the intrepid, wry smile. It no longer worked.

'I would like you in our stable. You must not apply for any more jobs. If other recruitment agencies contact you with tempting offers you must not take them. Stick with us. Be exclusive. Let us build up your reputation. And look after it. Let us be for your reputation what Tripolis is for your house. Within two years you'll be going home to your wife with news of a better job than the one we're talking about now. And that's a promise.'

Jeremias Lander stroked his carefully shaven chin with his thumb and forefinger. 'Hmm. This interview has moved in a different direction from the one I had anticipated.'

The defeat had made him calmer. I leaned forward. Opened my arms. Held up my palms. Sought his eyes. Research has proved that seventy-eight per cent of first impressions at interviews are based on body language and a mere eight per cent on what you actually say. The rest is about clothes, odours from armpits and mouth, what you have hanging on the walls. My body language was fantastic. And right now it was expressing openness and trust. Finally, I invited him in from the cold.

'Listen, Lander. The chairman of the board of directors and the finance director are coming here tomorrow to meet one of the candidates. I'd like them to meet you, too. Would twelve o'clock be convenient?'

'Fine.' He had answered without checking any form of calendar. I liked him better already.

'I want you to listen to what they have to say and thereafter you can politely account for why you are no longer interested, explain that this is not the challenge you were seeking and wish them well.'

Jeremias Lander tilted his head. 'Backing out like that, won't it be seen as frivolous?'

'It will be seen as ambitious,' I said. 'You will be regarded as someone who knows his own worth. A person whose services are exclusive. And that's the starting point for the story we refer to as . . .' I gave a flourish of the hand.

He smiled. 'Reputation?'

'Reputation. Do we have an agreement?'

'Within two years?'

'I'll guarantee it.'

'And how can you guarantee it?'

I noted: *Quick to regain the offensive.*

'Because I'm going to recommend you for one of the posts I'm talking about.'

'So? It's not you who makes the decisions.'

I half closed my eyes. It was an expression my wife Diana said reminded her of a sluggish lion, a satiated lord and master. I liked that.

'My recommendation is my client's decision, Lander.'

'What do you mean?'

'In the same way that you will never again apply for a job you are not confident of getting, I have never made a recommendation a client has not followed.'

'Really? Never?'

'Not that anyone can remember. Unless I am one hundred per cent sure the client will go along with my recommendation, I don't recommend anyone and prefer the job to go to one of the competitors. Even though I may have three brilliant candidates and am ninety per cent sure.'

'Why's that?'

I smiled. 'The answer begins with *R*. My entire career is based on it.'

Lander laughed and shook his head. 'They said you were tough, Brown. Now I know what they mean.'

I smiled again and rose to my feet. 'And

now I suggest you go home and tell your beautiful wife that you're going to refuse this job because you've decided to aim higher. My guess is you can look forward to a pleasant evening.'

'Why are you doing this for me, Brown?'

'Because the commission your employer will pay us is a third of your first year's gross salary. Did you know that Rembrandt used to go to auctions to raise the bidding for his own pictures? Why would I sell you for two million a year when, after a little reputation building, we can sell you for five? All we are asking is that you stick with us. Do we have a deal?' I proffered my hand.

He grabbed it with gusto. 'I have a feeling this has been a profitable conversation, Brown.'

'Agreed,' I said, reminding myself to give him a couple of tips on handshaking technique before he met the client.

Ferdinand slipped into my office as soon as Jeremias Lander had departed.

'Argh,' he said, cutting a grimace and wafting his hand. 'Eau de camouflage.'

I nodded while opening the window to let in some fresh air. What Ferdinand meant was that the applicant had slapped on too much aftershave to hide the nervous sweats that pervade interview rooms in this branch of work.

'But at least it was Clive Christian,' I said. 'Bought by his wife, like the suit, the shoes, the shirt and the tie. And it was her idea to dye his temples grey.'

'How do you know?' Ferdinand took a seat in the chair Lander had been sitting in, but jumped up again with an expression of revulsion as he felt the clammy body heat that still clung to the upholstery.

'He went as white as a sheet when I pressed the wife button,' I answered. 'I mentioned how disappointed she would be when he told her the job wouldn't be his.'

'The wife button! Where do you get this stuff from, Roger?' Ferdinand had settled into one of the other chairs, his feet on a pretty good copy of a Noguchi coffee table. He had taken an orange and was peeling it, releasing an almost invisible spray which covered his newly ironed shirt. Ferdinand was unbelievably slapdash for a homosexual. And unbelievably homosexual for a head-hunter.

'Inbau, Reid and Buckley,' I said.

'You've mentioned that method before,' Ferdinand said. 'But what exactly is it? Is it better than Cuté?'

I laughed. 'It's the FBI's nine-step interrogation model. It's a machine gun in the world of pea-shooters, an instrument that would blast a hole through a haystack, that doesn't take prisoners, but gives quick, tangible results.'

'And what results are they, Roger?'

I knew what Ferdinand was fishing for, and that was fine by me. He wanted to find out what gave me the edge, what made me the best and him — for the time being — less than the best. And I gave him what he sought. For those were the rules, knowledge was to be shared. And because he would never be better than me. He'd always turn up with shirts reeking of citrus, forever wondering whether someone had a model, a method or a secret that was better than his.

'Submission,' I answered. 'Confession. Truth. It's based on very simple principles.'

'Such as?'

'Such as beginning by questioning the suspect about his family.'

'Pah,' Ferdinand said. 'I do that as well. It makes them feel secure if they can talk about something familiar, something close to them. Plus it opens them up.'

'Precisely. But it also allows you to probe their weak points. Their Achilles heel. Which you will be able to use later on in the

26

interrogation.'

'Hey, what terminology!'

'Later on in the interrogation when you have to discuss what rankles, what happened, the murder he is suspected of having committed, what makes him feel lonely and abandoned by everyone and what makes him want to hide, you make sure you have a roll of kitchen towel on the table, positioned just out of the suspect's reach.'

'Why?'

'Because the interrogation has come to its natural crescendo and the time has come for you to press the emotion button. You ask him what his children will think when they find out that their dad is a murderer. And then, when the tears well up in his eyes, you pass him the roll. You have to be the person who understands, who wants to help, in whom he can confide about all the bad things. About that silly, silly murder that just happened, as if of its own accord.'

'Murder? What the hell are you on about? We recruit people, don't we? We're not trying to convict them of murder.'

'I am,' I said, taking my jacket from the office chair. 'And that's why I'm the best headhunter in Oslo. By the way, I've put you down for the interview with Lander and the client tomorrow at twelve.'

27

'Me?'

I went out of the door and down the corridor with Ferdinand skipping after me as we passed the other twenty-five offices that constituted Alfa, a medium-sized recruitment company that had survived for fifteen years and brought in between fifteen and twenty million kroner per annum, which, after a far too modest bonus had been paid out to the best of us, was pocketed by the owner in Stockholm.

'Piece of cake. All the details are in the file. OK?'

'OK,' said Ferdinand. 'On one condition.'

'Condition? I'm doing you a favour.'

'The private view your wife is having at the gallery this evening . . .'

'What about it?'

'Can I go?'

'Are you invited?'

'That's the point. Am I?'

'Doubt it.'

Ferdinand came to an abrupt halt and was gone from my field of vision. I continued, knowing that he was standing there with his arms down by his sides, watching me and musing that once again he would not be able to raise a toast in champagne with Oslo's jet-setters, queens of the night, celebrities and the wealthy, that he would not

28

partake in the modicum of glamour that surrounded Diana's private views, nor come into contact with potential candidates for a job, bed or other sinful intercourse. Poor fellow.

'Roger?' It was the girl behind the reception desk. 'Two calls. One —'

'Not now, Oda,' I said without stopping. 'I'll be away for three-quarters of an hour. Don't take any messages.'

'But —'

'They'll ring back if it's important.'

Nice-looking girl, but she still had a bit to learn, Oda did. Or was it Ida?

2
SERVICE INDUSTRY

The tangy saline taste of exhaust fumes in the autumn air evoked associations of sea, oil extraction and gross national product. Dazzling sunlight slanted on the glass of the office buildings, casting sharp, rectangular shadows over what had once been an industrial estate. Now it was a kind of urban quarter with overpriced shops, overpriced apartments and overpriced offices for overpriced consultants. I could see three fitness centres from where I stood, all of them fully booked from morning till evening. A young guy in a Corneliani suit and geek-chic glasses greeted me deferentially as we passed and I reciprocated with a gracious nod. I had no idea who he was, could only assume he would have to be from another recruitment agency. Edward W. Kelley perhaps? No one else but a headhunter would greet another headhunter with deference. Or to be precise: no one else greets me; they don't know who I am. Firstly, I have a limited social circle when not with my wife, Diana. Secondly, I work for a company which — in common with Kelley's — belongs to an elite, one which avoids the media spotlight, one which you believe you have never heard of until you qualify for one of the country's top jobs, whereupon you receive a call from us and the name rings a bell: Alfa, where have you heard that before? Was it at a group management meeting in connection with the appointment of a new regional director? So you have heard of us after all. But you know nothing. For discretion is our greatest virtue. The only one we have. Of course, the majority of our work from beginning to end is lies, of the most contemptible kind, such as when you hear me rounding off the second interview with my standard mantra: 'You're the man I want for this job. A job for which I not only think but know you are perfect. And that means the job is perfect for you. Believe me.'

Well, OK, don't believe me.

Yes, I reckoned it was Kelley. Or Amrop. With that suit he was definitely not from one of the large, uncool, un-exclusive agencies like Manpower or Adecco. Nor was he from one of the micro, cool ones like Hopeland, otherwise I would have known him.

Although he could have been from one of the large, medium-cool ones like Mercuri Urval or Delphi, of course, or the small, uncool anonymous ones that recruit middle management and only on rare occasions are given the opportunity to compete with us, the big boys. And then lose and go back to scouting for shop managers and financial directors. And greet the likes of me with respect in the hope that one day we will remember them and offer them a job.

There is no official ranking list for headhunters, no status research as in the broker industry, nor are there award ceremonies for the gurus of the year, as in TV and advertising. But we know. We know who the king of the heap is, who the challengers are, who is heading for a fall. Triumphs take place in silence, funerals in deadly silence. But the guy who just greeted me knew I was Roger Brown, the headhunter who has never nominated a candidate for a job he did not get, who if necessary manipulates, forces, levers and rams the candidate in, who has clients who trust his judgement implicitly, who without a moment's hesitation place their company's fate in his — and only his — hands. To put it another way, it was not Oslo Port Authority who appointed their new traffic director last year, it was not Avis who appointed their Scandinavian director and it was quite definitely not the local authority who appointed the director of the power station in Sirdal. It was me.

I decided to make a mental note of the guy. *Good suit. Knows how to show respect to the right people.*

I rang Ove from a telephone box next to the Narvesen kiosk while checking my mobile phone. Eight messages. I deleted them.

'We have a candidate,' I said when Ove answered. 'Jeremias Lander, Monolittveien.'

'Shall I check if we have him?'

'No, I know you've got him. He's been selected for a second interview tomorrow. Twelve till two. Twelve hundred hours. Give me one hour. Got that?"

'Yep. Anything else?'

'Keys. Sushi&Coffee in twenty minutes?'

'Thirty.'

I strolled down the cobbled street towards Sushi&Coffee. The reason they have chosen a road surface that makes more noise, pollutes more and in addition costs more than normal tarmac is presumably because of the need for an idyll, the desire for something traditional, lasting and authentic. More authentic than this anyway, this mock-up of a neighbourhood where once things were created by the sweat of workers' brows, where products were crafted with a fiery hiss and the ring of hammer blows. Echoed now by the drone of the espresso machine and the clanging of iron against iron in the fitness centre. For this is the service industry's triumph over the industrial worker, the triumph of design over the housing shortage, the triumph of fiction over reality. And I like it.

I peered at the diamond earrings that had caught my eye in the jeweller's window opposite Sushi&Coffee. They would grace Diana's ears to perfection. And they would spell disaster for my finances. I rejected the idea, crossed the street and entered the doorway to the place that nominally prepares sushi, but in fact just serves dead fish. However, there was nothing you could say against their coffee. Inside, it was half full. Slim platinum blondes fresh from training, still in their workout gear, because it would not occur to them to shower at a fitness centre in full view of others. Strange in a way, since they had spent a fortune on these bodies, which celebrated the triumph of fiction. They belonged to the service sector, to be more precise, the serving staff who tended to their wealthy husbands' needs. Had these women been lacking in intelligence, that would be one thing, but they had studied law, information technology and art history as a part of their beauty treatment, they had let Norwegian taxpayers finance years at university just so that they could end up as overqualified, stay-at-home playthings and sit here exchanging confidences about how to keep their sugar daddies suitably happy, suitably jealous and suitably on their toes. Until they finally chained him down with children. And, of course, after children everything is changed, the balance of power has been turned upside down, the man castrated and held in check. Children . . .

'Double cortado,' I said, perching on one of the bar stools.

I watched the women in the mirror with satisfaction. I was a lucky man. Diana was so different from these smart, empty-brained parasites. She had everything I lacked. A caring nature. Empathy. Loyalty. Height. To sum up, she was a beautiful soul in a beautiful body. Her beauty, though, was not of the perfect kind, her proportions were too special for that. Diana had been drawn in manga-style, like those doll-like Japanese cartoon figures. She had a small face with a tiny, narrow mouth, a small nose and large eyes filled with wonderment, which had a tendency to bulge when she was tired. But in my view it was precisely these deviations from the norm that made her beauty stand out, made it striking. So what had made her choose me? A chauffeur's son, a slightly above-average student of economics with slightly below-average prospects and well under medium height. Fifty years ago one metre sixty-eight would not have elicited the term 'short', at least not in most parts of Europe. And any anthropometric history would tell you that only a hundred years ago one sixty-eight was indeed the average height in Norway. However, events had taken an unfortunate turn for me.

That she had chosen me in a moment of insanity was one thing, but it was quite another, and beyond my understanding, how a woman like Diana — who could have had absolutely anyone she wanted — should wake up every morning and want me for another day. What sort of mysterious blindness was it that made her incapable of seeing my contemptibility, my treacherous nature, my weakness when I encountered adversity, my mindless wickedness when I encountered mindless wickedness? Didn't she want to see? Or was it just guile and skill on my part that had allowed the real me to end up in this love-blessed blind spot.

And then of course there was the child that I had so far denied her. What power was it I had over this angel in human form? According to Diana, the very first time we met I had bewitched her with my contradictory mixture of arrogance and self-deprecating irony. It had been during a Scandinavian student evening in London, and my first impression of Diana had been that she was just like the women sitting here: a blonde Nordic beauty from Oslo studying art history in an international metropolis, who did the odd modelling job, was against war and poverty and enjoyed partying and all things fun. It had taken three hours and half a dozen pints of Guinness before I realised that I had been wrong. First of all, she was genuinely interested in art, almost to the point of being a nerd. Secondly, she was able to articulate her frustration at being part of a system that waged war against people who did not want to be part of Western capitalism. It was Diana who had explained to me that industrialised countries' exploitation of the Third World minus Third World aid made, and had always made, a plus. Thirdly, she had a sense of humour, my sense of humour, a prerequisite for guys like me to get women taller than one metre seventy. And fourthly — and this

37

is without doubt what did it for me — she was poor at languages and good at logical thought. She spoke clumsy English, to put it mildly, and with a smile she had told me that it had never even occurred to her to have a go at French or Spanish. Then I had asked whether she had a masculine brain and liked maths. She had just shrugged, but I had persisted and told her about job interview tests at Microsoft where candidates were presented with a particular logic problem.

'The point is as much to see how the candidate deals with the challenge as whether or not they can solve it.'

'Come on then,' she said.

'Prime numbers —'

'Hang on! What are prime numbers again?'

'Numbers that cannot be divided by numbers other than themselves and one.'

'Oh yes.' She still hadn't got that distant look women often get when numbers are introduced into the conversation, and I continued.

'Prime numbers are often two consecutive odd numbers. Like eleven and thirteen. Twenty-nine and thirty-one. Are you with me?'

'I'm with you.'

'Are there any examples of three consecutive odd numbers being prime numbers?'

'Of course not,' she said, raising her glass of beer to her mouth.

'Oh? Why not?'

'Do you think I'm stupid? In a sequence of five consecutive numbers one of the odd numbers has to be divisible by three. Go on.'

'Go on?'

'Yes, what's the logic problem?' She had taken a large gulp of beer and looked at me with genuinely expectant curiosity. At Microsoft, candidates are given three minutes to come up with the proof she had given me in three seconds. On average, five out of every hundred could do that. And I think that was when I fell in love with her. At least I remember jotting down on my serviette: *Hired.*

And I had known that I would have to make her fall in love with me while we were sitting there; as soon as I stood up the spell would be broken. So I had talked. And talked. I had talked myself up to one metre eighty-five. I can do the talking bit. But she had interrupted me when I was in full flow.

'Do you like football?'

'Do . . . do *you?*' I asked, amazed.

'QPR are playing Arsenal in the league

cup tomorrow. Interested?'

'Certainly am,' I said. And of course I meant in her. I couldn't give a toss about football.

She had worn a blue-and-white-striped scarf and screamed herself hoarse in London's autumn mist at Loftus Road as her poor little team, Queens Park Rangers, were being thumped by their big brother, Arsenal. Fascinated, I had studied her impassioned face and derived no more from the match than the fact that Arsenal wore attractive red-and-white tops while QPR had diagonal blue stripes on a white background, making the players look like lollipops in motion.

At half-time I had asked why she had not chosen a big winning team like Arsenal instead of comical small fry like QPR.

'Because they need me,' she had answered. Seriously. *They need me.* I intuited a wisdom I could not fathom in her words. Then she had laughed that gurgling laugh of hers and drained the plastic beaker of beer. 'They're like helpless babies. Look at them. They're so *sweet.*'

'In baby outfits,' I said. 'So, suffer the little children to come unto me, is that your life's motto?'

'Erm,' she had answered, angling her head and looking down at me with a broad beam,

40

'it might become that.'

And we had laughed. Loud, liberating laughter.

I don't remember the outcome of the match. Or, rather, I do: a kiss outside a strict girls' brick boarding house in Shepherd's Bush. And a lonely, sleepless night of wild dreams.

Ten days later I was looking down into her face in the flickering gleam of a candle stuffed into a wine bottle on her bedside table. We made love for the first time, and her eyes were closed, the vein in her forehead stood out and her expression varied between fury and pain as her hip bones thrashed against mine. The same passion as when she had watched QPR being sent out of the league cup. Afterwards she said she loved my hair. This was a refrain I had heard throughout my life, yet I seemed to be hearing it for the first time.

Six months were to pass before I told her that because my father worked in the diplomatic service it didn't necessarily mean he was a diplomat.

'Chauffeur,' she had repeated, pulling down my face and kissing it. 'Does that mean he can borrow the ambassador's limousine to drive us from the church?'

I had not answered, but that spring we

got married with more circumstance than pomp at St Patrick's Church in Hammersmith. The absence of pomp was down to my talking Diana into a wedding without friends and family. Without Dad. Just us, pure and innocent. Diana provided the circumstance; she shone like two suns and a moon. Chance would have it that QPR were promoted that same afternoon, and the taxi crawled back home to her bedsit in Shepherd's Bush through a jubilant procession of lollipop-colored flags and banners. Joy and merriment everywhere. Not until we had moved back to Oslo did Diana mention children for the first time.

I looked at my watch. Ove ought to be here by now. I raised my eyes to the mirror over the counter and met those of one of the blondes. Our eyes held for just as long as it takes to misunderstand whether we wanted to or not. Porn-attractive, good surgical work. I didn't want to. So my eyes drifted away. In fact, that was precisely the way my only shameful affair had started; with eyes holding on for a little too long. The first act had taken place in the gallery. The second here at Sushi&Coffee. The third act in a small flat in Eilert Sundts gate. But now Lotte was a thing of the past for me, and it would never, ever happen again. My gaze wandered round the room and stopped.

Ove was sitting at the table by the front door.

To all outward signs, reading *Dagens Næringsliv,* a financial paper. An amusing idea in itself. Ove Kjikerud was not only totally bored by the movements of stocks and shares and most of what was happening in so-called society, he could barely read. Or write. I can still picture his application for the security boss job: it had contained so many spelling mistakes that I had burst out laughing.

I slid off the stool and walked over to his table. He had folded up *Dagens Næringsliv* and I nodded towards the newspaper. He gave a fleeting smile to indicate that he had finished with it. I took the paper without a word and went back to my place at the counter. One minute later I heard the front door close and when I peered at the mirror again, Ove Kjikerud had gone. I flicked through to the shares pages, discreetly wrapped my hand around the key that had been left there and slipped it into my jacket pocket.

When I returned to the office there were six text messages waiting for me on my mobile phone. I deleted five without reading them and opened the one from Diana.

Don't forget the private view tonight, darling. You're my lucky mascot.

She had added a smiley with sunglasses, one of the sophistications of the Prada telephone I had given her on her thirty-second birthday this summer. 'This is what I wanted most!' she had said, opening the present. But we both knew what she wanted most. And which I was not going to give her. Nonetheless she had lied and kissed me. What more can you ask of a woman?

3
PRIVATE VIEW

One metre sixty-eight. I don't need a brain-dead psychologist to tell me that compensation is a factor, that small physical stature is a great motivator. A surprisingly large number of the world's great works of art have been created by small men. We have conquered empires, thought the smartest thoughts, laid the most beautiful female stars of the screen: in short we have always been on the lookout for the biggest platform shoes. Many an idiot has made the discovery that some blind people are good musicians and that some autistic people can work out square roots in their heads, and this has led them to conclude that all handicaps are a blessing in disguise. Firstly, that is nonsense. Secondly, I am, despite everything, not a dwarf, just marginally under average height. Thirdly, over seventy per cent of all people in the highest management positions are of above-average height in their respective countries. Height also has a positive correlation with intelligence, income and popularity surveys. When I nominate someone for a top job in business, height is one of my most important criteria. Height instills respect, trust and authority. Tall people are visible, they can't hide, they are masters, all nastiness air-blasted away, they have to stand up and be counted. Short people move around in the sediment, they have a hidden plan, an agenda which revolves around the fact that they are short.

Of course, this is rubbish, but when I propose a candidate for a job I don't do it because the person in question is the best but because he is the one the client will employ. I provide them with a head that is good enough, placed on the body they want. They are not qualified to judge the first; they can see the second with their own eyes. Like the stinking rich so-called art connoisseurs at Diana's exhibitions, they are not qualified to give an opinion about the portrait, but they are capable of reading the artist's signature. The world is full of people who pay serious money for bad pictures by good artists. And mediocre heads on tall bodies.

I steered my new Volvo S80 round the bends, climbing up towards our new, beautiful and somewhat too expensive home on Voksenkollen. I bought it because Diana had this pained expression on her face when we were being shown round. The vein on her forehead that tended to expand when we made love had turned blue and was quivering above her almond-shaped eyes. She had raised her right hand and drawn short strands of fine, straw-colored hair behind her right ear as if to hear better, to listen carefully to be sure her eyes had not deceived her; that this was the house for which she had been searching. And there was no need for her to say a word; I knew it was. Even as the gleam in her eyes died when the estate agent told us that they already had an offer of one and a half million over the asking price, I knew I had to buy it for her. Because this was the only offering I could make to compensate for talking her out of having the child she wanted. I no longer quite remember the arguments I had used in favour of abortion, just that none of them had been the truth. Which was that even though we were two people with 320 exorbitant square metres, there was no room for a child. That is, no room for a child and me. For I knew Diana. She was, in contrast to me, perversely monogamous. I would have hated the child from

47

day one. So instead I had given her a new start, a home, and a gallery.

I swung into the drive. The garage door had sensed the car a long time ago and opened automatically. The Volvo glided into the chilly darkness and the engine breathed its last as the door slid to behind me. I went out through the side door of the garage and along the flagstone path leading up to the house. It was a magnificent construction, vintage 1937, designed by Ove Bang, the functionalist who considered cost to be less important than aesthetics and was thus one of Diana's soulmates.

I often thought that we could sell up, move into something a bit smaller, a bit more normal, a bit more practical even. But every time I came home and it was like now, with the low afternoon sun causing the contours to stand out clearly, the play of light and shade, the autumnal forest behind, glowing like red gold, I knew it was impossible. That I couldn't stop. Quite simply because I loved her and could therefore do nothing else. And with that came the rest: the house, the financial drain of a gallery, the costly and unnecessary demonstrations of my love and the lifestyle we could not afford. All to alleviate her longing.

I unlocked the house, kicked off my shoes

and deactivated the alarm within the twenty seconds I had before a bell would go off at Tripolis. Diana and I had discussed the code for a long time before reaching an agreement. She had wanted it to be DA-MIEN after her favourite artist, Damien Hirst, but I knew that was the name she had given our aborted child, and thus I insisted on a random collection of letters and numbers that could not be guessed. And she had given in. As always, when I stood up to her, tough on tough. Or tough on soft. For Diana was soft. Not weak, but soft and flexible. Like clay where even the slightest pressure leaves a mark. The strange thing was that the more she gave in, the bigger and stronger she became. And the weaker I became. Until she towered above me like a gigantic angel, a firmament of guilt, debts and bad conscience. And however hard I grafted, however many heads I brought home, however much of Stockholm's central office bonus pot I raked in, it was not enough to bring me absolution.

I walked upstairs to the living room and kitchen, took off my tie, opened the Sub-Zero fridge and helped myself to a bottle of San Miguel. Not the usual Especial but 1516, the extra mild beer that Diana preferred because it was brewed according to purity laws. From the living-room window I looked down on the garden, the garage and the neighbours. Oslo, the fjord, Skagerrak, Germany, the world. And discovered I had already finished the beer.

I fetched another and went down to the ground floor to change for the private view.

Passing the Forbidden Room I noticed the door was ajar. I pushed it open and at once saw that she had laid fresh flowers by the tiny stone figure standing on the low, altar-like table beneath the window. The table was the only furniture in the room and the stone figure looked like a child monk with a contented Buddha smile. Beside the flowers were a pair of small children's shoes and a yellow rattle.

I went in, took a swig of beer, crouched down and ran my fingers over the figure's smooth bare head. It was a *mizuko jizo,* a figure that according to Japanese tradition protected aborted children, or *mizuko* — meaning a water child. I had brought the figure home after an unsuccessful headhunt in Tokyo. It was the first months after the abortion while Diana was still shattered, and I had thought it might be of some comfort. The salesman's English had been too poor for me to understand all the details, but the Japanese idea appears to be that when the foetus dies the child's soul returns to its original fluid state — it becomes a water child. Which — if you mix in a bit of Japanese-style Buddhism — is waiting to be reborn. In the meantime you carry out what is known as *mizuko kuyo,* ceremonies and simple sacrifices to protect the unborn child's soul and, at the same time, the parents against the water child's revenge. I never told Diana about the last part. To begin with, I had been happy, and she had seemed to find comfort in the stone figure. But as her *jizo* gradually became an obsession and she wanted it in the bedroom, I had to put my foot down. And I said that from then on she should not pray or make sacrifices to the figure. Although on that particular point I had never been tough. For I knew that I could lose Diana. And that would be unforgivable.

I went into my study, switched on my PC, searched on the Net until I found a high-resolution picture of Edvard Munch's *The Brooch,* also known as *Eva Mudocci.* Three hundred and fifty thousand on the legal market. Hardly more than two hundred on mine. Fifty per cent to the fence, then twenty per cent to Kjikerud. Eighty thousand to me. That was the usual split; hardly worth the trouble and definitely not the risk.

The picture was in black and white. 58 ×
45 cm. Just right for a piece of A2 paper.
Eighty thousand. Too little to pay for the
next quarterly instalment of the mortgage.
And nowhere near enough to cover the
previous year's deficit on the gallery that I
had promised the accountant to pay during
November. For some reason the intervals
between decent pictures turning up were
getting longer and longer, too. The last one,
Model in High Heels, by Søren Onsager, had
been more than three months ago, and even
that had barely brought in sixty thousand.
Something would have to happen soon.
QPR would have to score a flukey goal, a
mishit cross that — deserved or otherwise
— would send them to Wembley. That sort
of thing happened, I had heard. I sighed
and sent *Eva Mudocci* to the printer.

Champagne was the order of the evening,
so I rang for a taxi. After getting in, I just
said the name of the gallery, as usual — it
was a kind of test of our marketing skills —
but, also as usual, the driver just looked at
me in the mirror, bewildered.

'Erling Skjalgssons gate,' I sighed.

Diana and I had discussed the location
long before she had chosen the rooms. I
had been keen to make sure it lay on the

Skillebekk–Frogner axis since that is where you find the clients with the means to pay and other galleries of a certain *niveau.* To be located outside the cluster can mean an early death for a new gallery. Diana's ideal had been the Serpentine Gallery in Hyde Park in London, and she had been determined that the gallery should not face onto one of the busy thoroughfares, like Bygdøy allé or Gamle Drammensvei, but should be situated in a quiet street where there was room for contemplation. Furthermore, a set-back location emphasised exclusivity, signalled that it was for initiates, connoisseurs.

I had expressed agreement, thinking that perhaps the rent would not have to be ruinous after all.

Until she had added that in that case she would be able to spend money on extra square metres for a salon where there could be receptions after private views. In fact, she had already looked at a vacant site in Erling Skjalgssons gate, which was perfect, the best of the best. I was the one who had come up with the name: Galleri E. E for Erling Skjalgssons gate. It was, moreover, the same formulation as the best run gallery in town, Galleri K, and hopefully showed that we were targeting the affluent, the quality-conscious and the cool.

I had not argued that the pronunciation in Norwegian made it sound like *the* gallery. Diana didn't like that kind of cheap gimmick.

The lease had been signed, the extensive decoration work was under way and our financial ruin secured.

When the taxi pulled up outside the gallery I noticed more Jaguars and Lexuses parked up and down the pavement than usual. A good omen, although of course it could have been because of a reception in one of the surrounding embassies or that Celina Midelfart was having a party in her GDR fortress.

Bass-dominated eighties ambient music poured out through the speaker system at a pleasantly low volume as I entered the rooms. It would be followed by the Goldberg Variations. I had burned the CD for Diana.

It was already half full despite it being only half past eight. A good sign — usually Galleri E clientele didn't appear before half past nine. Diana had explained to me that packed private views were seen as vulgar; half-full ones accentuated the exclusivity. My experience was now, however, that the more people there were, the more pictures would be sold. I nodded to the left and right without anyone reciprocating and headed for the mobile bar. Diana's permanent bartender, Nick, passed me a glass of champagne.

'Expensive?' I asked, tasting the bitter bubbles.

'Six hundred,' Nick said.

'Better sell a few pictures,' I said. 'Who's the artist?'

'Atle Nørum.'

'I know his name, Nick, just not what he looks like.'

'Over there.' Nick angled his big ebony-black head to the right. 'Next to your wife.'

I noted that the artist was a hunk of a man with a beard but that was all. Because she was there.

A pair of white leather trousers clung to long, slim legs, making her seem even taller than she was. Her hair hung down on either side of her fringe, which had been cut straight, and this perpendicular frame heightened the impression of Japanese comic-strip art. Under the spot lighting, the loose silk blouse shone almost bluish-white on her narrow, muscular shoulders and breasts, which in profile resembled two perfectly formed waves. My God, she would really have set off the diamond earrings!

Reluctantly, my gaze left her and swept around the rest of the room. Those invited stood making polite conversation in front of the pictures. They were the usual suspects. Rich, successful financiers (suit with tie) and celebrities of the right sort (suit with designer T-shirt), the ones who had actually achieved something. The women (designer clothes) were actresses, writers or politicians. And then there was, of course, the flock of young, so-called promising and allegedly poor, rebellious artists (jeans with holes, T-shirts with slogans) whom in my own mind I termed QPR. When, at the beginning, I had wrinkled my nose up at these elements on the guest list, Diana had argued that we needed 'some spice', some life, something a bit more dangerous than art patrons, calculating investors and those who came just to have their public images massaged. Fair enough, but I knew that the scum were here because they had asked Diana nicely for an invitation. And even though Diana knew that they were here angling for buyers of their own works, it was well documented that Diana could never say no if she was asked for a favour. I noticed several people — mostly men — occasionally casting furtive glances in Diana's direction. Be my guest. She was finer than anyone they would ever get. This was not just an assumption, but an unshakeable logical fact as she was the finest of the finest. And she was mine. Just how unshakeable was something with which I tried not to torment myself. For the time being I found peace of mind thinking that she seemed to be permanently blind.

I counted how many men there were wearing ties. As a rule, they were the ones who bought. The current square-metre price for Nørum's works lay at around fifty thousand. With fifty-five per cent commission to the gallery you didn't need many sales before this would become a lucrative evening. To put it another way: it had better be; Nørums were few and far between.

People were streaming in through the doors now, and I had to move out of the way to let them get to the tray of champagne glasses.

I ambled towards my wife and Nørum to tell him what a grovelling admirer I was. An exaggeration, of course, but not a bare-faced lie; the guy was good, no doubt about that. But as I was going to stretch out my hand, the artist was collared by a sputum-spouting man he obviously knew and dragged off to a giggling woman in apparent dire need of the toilet.

'Looks good,' I said, standing next to Diana.

'Hi, darling.' She smiled down at me, then motioned to the twin girls that they should do another round with the finger food. Sushi was out, but I had suggested the new Algerian catering service, French-inspired North African, very hot. In all senses. But I could see that she had ordered the food from Bagatelle again. It was good, too, my goodness. And three times as expensive.

'Good news, my love,' she said, slipping a hand into mine. 'Do you remember the job for that firm in Horten you told me about?'

'Pathfinder. What about it?'

'I've found the perfect candidate.'

I observed her with mild surprise. As a headhunter, from time to time naturally I used Diana's customer portfolio and circle of acquaintances, which counted many business honchos among its number, without any pangs of conscience; after all, it was me who was financing this drain on the budget. What was unusual was that Diana had herself come up with a specific candidate for a specific job.

Diana took the underside of my arm, leaned closer and whispered: 'His name is Clas Greve. Dutch father, Norwegian mother. Or the other way round. Whatever.

He stopped working three months ago and has just moved to Norway to do up a house he's inherited. He was the CEO of one of Europe's biggest GPS technology companies in Rotterdam. He was a co-owner until they were bought up by the Americans this spring.'

'Rotterdam,' I said, sipping some champagne. 'What's the company's name?'

'HOTE.'

I almost choked on the champagne. 'HOTE? Are you sure?'

'Pretty sure.'

'Have you got the guy's number?'

'No.'

I groaned. HOTE. Pathfinder had named HOTE their model company in Europe. Just as Pathfinder was now, HOTE had been a small high-tech business specialising in delivering GPS technology to the defence industry in Europe. An ex-CEO from there would be absolutely ideal. And it was urgent. All recruitment agencies say that they only take assignments where they have exclusive rights because it is a prerequisite for serious, systematic work. But if the carrot is big and orange enough, when the gross annual salary begins to approach seven figures, everyone modifies their principles. And the top job with Pathfinder was extremely big, extremely orange and extremely competitive. The assignment had been given to three agencies: Alfa, ISCO and Korn/Ferry International. Three of the best. That was why this was not solely about money. Whenever we work on a no win, no fee basis, we first get a one-off fee to cover costs and then a fee if the candidate we present fulfils the needs we have agreed with the client. For us to get the real payout, however, the client has to appoint the person we recommend. OK by me, but what this was really, *really* about was simple: winning. Being king of the heap. Platform shoes.

I leaned over to Diana. 'Listen, sweetie, this is important. Have you any idea at all how I can get hold of him?'

She chuckled. 'You're so nice when something catches your interest, darling.'

'Do you know where . . . ?'

'Of course.'

'Where, where?'

'He's standing over there.' She pointed.

In front of one of Nørum's expressive paintings — a bleeding man in a bondage hood — stood a slim, erect figure in a suit. The spotlight reflected on his shiny, bronzed skull. He had hard, knotted blood vessels in his temples. The suit was tailor-made. Savile Row, I assumed. Shirt without a tie.

'Shall I bring him over, darling?'

I nodded and watched her. Prepared myself. Noted his gracious bow when Diana approached and pointed. They came towards me. I smiled, but not too broadly, stretched out my hand slightly before he arrived, but not too prematurely. My whole body turned to him, my eyes on his. Seventy-eight per cent.

'Roger Brown, pleased to meet you.' I pronounced both names in the English way.

'Clas Greve. The pleasure is all mine.'

Apart from the un-Norwegian formal greeting, his Norwegian was nigh on perfect. His hand was warm, dry, the handshake firm without overdoing it, the recommended duration of three seconds. His eyes were calm, curious, alert; the smile friendly without being forced. My only complaint was that he was not as tall as I had hoped. Just under one metre eighty, a bit disappointing considering that Dutch men are the anthropometric world champions with an average height of 183.4 centimetres.

A guitar chord sounded. To be precise, a G11sus4, the opening chord of the Beatles 'A Hard Day's Night' from the album of the same name, 1964. I knew that because it was me who had put it on the Prada phone and set it as the ringtone before giving it to Diana. She raised the attractively slim object to her ear, nodded to us in apology and distanced herself.

'I understand you have just moved here, herr Greve?' I could hear myself sounding like an old radio play, using the Norwegian formal terms 'De' and 'herr', but during the introductory sales pitch it is important to adapt and assume low status. The metamorphosis would come soon enough.

'I inherited my grandmother's apartment in Oscars gate. It's stood empty for a couple of years and needs redecorating.'

'I see.'

I raised both eyebrows with a smile, curious, but not insistent. Just enough. If he was able to follow the social code, he would now reply with a little more information.

'Yes,' said Greve. 'It's a pleasant break after so many years' hard graft.'

I saw no reason not to go straight to the point. 'At HOTE, from what I understand.'

He sent me a look of mild surprise. 'Do you know the company?'

'The recruitment agency I work for has its competitor, Pathfinder, on its books. Have you heard of them?'

'Bits and pieces. Main office in Horten, if I'm not much mistaken. Small but competent, isn't that right?'

'They must have grown quite a lot in the months you've been out of circulation.'

'Things move quickly in the GPS industry,' Greve said, twirling the champagne glass in his hand. 'Everyone thinks expansion. The motto is: Expand or die.'

'So I understand. Perhaps that was why HOTE was bought up?'

Greve's smile produced a fine network of creases in the tanned skin around the pale blue eyes. 'The fastest way to grow is, as you know, to be bought up. Experts reckon that those not among the top five GPS companies in two years' time are finished.'

'Doesn't sound like you agree?'

'I think that innovation and flexibility are the most important survival criteria. And that, as long as there is sufficient funding, a small unit that can adapt quickly is more important than size. So I have to confess that, even though I became a rich man through the sale of HOTE, I was against selling and resigned straight afterwards. I'm obviously not quite in sync with current thinking . . .' Again this flashing smile that softened the hard but well-cared-for exterior. 'But perhaps that is just the guerrilla warrior in me. What do you think?'

He used the informal form of 'you'. A good sign.

'I only know that Pathfinder is looking for a new boss,' I said, signalling to Nick that he should bring us more champagne. 'Someone who can resist the overtures from foreign companies.'

'Uh-uh?'

'And to me it sounds like you could be a very promising applicant for them. Interested?'

Greve laughed. It was an engaging laugh. 'My apologies, Roger. I have an apartment to do up.'

Christian name.

'I didn't think you would be interested in the job, Clas. Just in talking about it.'

'You haven't seen the apartment, Roger. It's old. And big. Yesterday I found a new room behind the kitchen.'

I looked at him. It wasn't only down to Savile Row that the suit fitted him so well; he was in good shape. No, not in good shape; excellent shape was the expression. There were no bulging muscles here, just the sinewy strength that reveals itself with discretion, in the blood vessels in the neck, in the posture, in the low resting heart rate, in the blue oxygen capillaries on the back of his hands. Nevertheless, you had a sense of the muscular strength that lay beneath the suit material. Stamina, I thought. Unrelenting stamina. I had already made up my mind; I wanted this head.

'Do you like art, Clas?' I asked, passing him one of the glasses Nick had brought.

'Yes. And no. I like art that shows something. But most of what I see claims a beauty or a truth that isn't there. It may have been in the artist's mind, but the communicative talent is absent. If I don't see beauty or truth, it isn't there, simple as that. An artist who maintains that he has been misunderstood is almost always a bad artist who, I'm afraid to say, has been understood.'

'We're on the same wavelength there,' I said, lifting my glass.

'I forgive a lack of talent in most people, I suppose because I have been dealt so little myself,' Greve said, barely moistening his thin lips with the champagne. 'But not in artists. We, the untalented, make a living by the sweat of our brow and pay them to play on our behalf. Fair enough, that's the way it is. But then they have to play bloody well.'

I had already seen enough and knew that test results and in-depth interviews would only confirm what I knew. This was the man. Even if ISCO or Mercuri Urval had been given two years, they would not have found such a perfect candidate as this one.

'Do you know what, Clas? We're going to

have to have a chat. You see, Diana has insisted on it.' I passed him my business card. There were no addresses, fax numbers or websites, just my name, my mobile phone number and Alfa in tiny letters in one corner.

'As I said —' Greve began, examining my card.

'Listen,' I interrupted. 'No one who values their health refuses Diana. I don't know what we will talk about, probably about art. Or the future. Or decorating a house. I happen to know a couple of Oslo's best and most reasonably priced craftsmen. But talk we will. What about three o'clock tomorrow?'

Greve smiled at me for a while. Then he stroked his chin with a narrow hand. 'I thought the original idea of a business card was that it should equip the receiver with enough information to pay a call?'

I rummaged for my Conklin pen, wrote down the office address on the back of the card and watched it disappear into Greve's jacket pocket.

'Look forward to talking to you, Roger, but now I have to get off home and psych myself up to remonstrate with the carpenters in Polish. Say goodbye to your charming wife.' Greve made a stiff, almost military bow, turned on his heel and went to the door.

Diana sidled up to me as I watched him leave. 'How did it go, darling?'

'Fantastic specimen. Just look at how he walks. Feline. Perfect.'

'Does that mean . . . ?'

'He even made out that he wasn't interested in the job. My God, I want that head on my wall, stuffed and with bared teeth.'

She clapped her hands with glee like a little girl. 'So I was of some help? I was really of some help?'

I stretched up and put my arms around her shoulders. The rooms were vulgarly, wonderfully packed. 'You are hereby a certified headhunter, my little blossom. How are sales?'

'We're not selling this evening. Didn't I say that?'

I hoped for a second that I had misheard. 'It's just . . . an exhibition?'

'Atle didn't want to let go of any of his pictures.' She smiled as though in apology. 'I understand him. I suppose you wouldn't want to lose something that was so beautiful?'

I closed my eyes and swallowed. Thought those soft thoughts.

'Do you think that was stupid, Roger?' I

heard Diana's disconcerted voice say and myself answer: 'Not at all.'

Then I felt her lips against my cheek. 'You're so kind, my love. And we can do the selling later anyway. This projects our image and makes us exclusive. You said yourself how important that is.'

I forced a smile. 'Of course, darling. Exclusive is good.'

She brightened up. 'And do you know what? I've ordered a DJ for the reception! The guy in Blå who plays seventies soul you always said was the best in town . . .' She clapped her hands and my smile felt as though it was detaching itself from my face, falling and smashing on the floor. But in the reflection on her raised champagne glass it was still in place. John Lennon's G11sus4 chord rang out again and she fumbled for her phone in her trouser pocket. I studied her as she twittered away to someone enquiring about whether they could come.

'Of course you can, Mia! Not at all, bring the baby with you. You can change her in my office. Of course we want children's screams, it'll liven things up! But you have to let me hold her, do you promise?'

My God, how I loved the woman.

My eyes scanned over the gathering once again. And stopped at a small pale face. It could have been her. Lotte. The same melancholy eyes that I had seen right here for the first time. It wasn't her. All that was finished. But the image of Lotte pursued me like a stray dog for the rest of the evening.

4
EXPROPRIATION

'You're late,' Ferdinand said as I entered the office. 'And hung-over.'

'Feet off the table,' I said, walking round the desk, switching on the computer and closing the blinds. The light was less invasive and I removed my sunglasses.

'Does that mean that the private view was a success?' Ferdinand nagged in that pitch that cuts straight to the brain's pain centre.

'There was dancing on the tables,' I said, looking at my watch. Half past nine.

'Why are the best parties always the ones you didn't go to?' Ferdinand sighed. 'Anyone well known there?'

'Anyone you know, you mean?'

'Any celebs, you idiot.' A flick through the air with a crack of the wrist. I had stopped getting annoyed at his insistence on looking like something off the stage.

'Some,' I said.

'Ari Behn?'

'No. You still have to meet Lander and the client here at twelve today, don't you?'

'Yes, indeed. Was Hank von Helvete there? Vendela Kirsebom?'

'Come on, out, I have to work.'

Ferdinand put on an offended expression, but did as I said. When the door slammed behind him, I was already googling Clas Greve. A few minutes later I knew that he had been the boss and co-owner of HOTE for six years until it was bought out, that he had a marriage with a Belgian model behind him and that he was the Dutch military pentathlon champion in 1985. In fact, I was surprised that there was not more there. Fine, by five we would have been through a soft version of Inbau, Reid and Buckley, and then I would know everything I needed.

Before that I had a job to do. A tiny expropriation. I leaned back and closed my eyes. I loved the tension during the act, but I hated the waiting period. Even now my heart was beating faster than normal. The thought entered my mind that I wished it had been for something that made my heart beat even faster. Eighty thousand. It is less than it sounds. Worth less in my pockets than Ove Kjikerud's share in his. Sometimes I envied him his simple life, a life on his own. That was the first thing I had checked when I interviewed him for the head of security job, that he didn't have too many ears around him. How had I known that he was my man? Firstly, there was this conspicuous defensive-aggressive attitude of his. Next, he had parried my questions in a way that suggested he knew the interview technique. Hence, when checking his background, I was almost amazed not to find his name on the state offender registry. So I had rung a female contact we have on our unofficial payroll. She has a job that allows her access to SANSAK, the restoration of rights archive which lists all those who have been held on remand and released and whose names — despite the name of the archive — are never deleted. And she was able to tell me that I had not made a mistake after all: Ove Kjikerud had been interviewed by the police so many times that he knew the nine-step model inside out. However, Kjikerud had never been charged with anything, which told me that the man was no idiot, just very dyslexic.

Kjikerud was of relatively short stature and had, like me, thick, dark hair. I had persuaded him to have a haircut before starting as head of security, had explained to him that no one has confidence in a guy who looks like a roadie for a washed-up hard-rock band. But there was nothing I could do about his teeth, which were discolored from chewing Swedish snus. Or his face, an oblong oar blade with a protruding jaw that could on occasion make me feel that the snus-stained set of teeth was going to jump out in the air and snap, a bit like that wonderful creature in the *Alien* films. But that, of course, would have been too much to ask of a person with Kjikerud's limited ambitions. He was lazy. But keen to get rich. And so the clash between Ove Kjikerud's desires and personal attributes continued; he was a criminal and an arms collector with violent tendencies, but he actually wanted to live a life of peace and quiet. He wanted, nay, almost begged for friends, but people seemed to sense that something was not right with him, and kept their distance. And he was a devout, incurable romantic who now sought love with prostitutes. At present he was hopelessly in love with a hard-working Russian whore by the name of Natasha whom he refused to cheat on despite the fact that she — as far as I could establish — had absolutely no interest in him. Ove Kjikerud was an unattached floating mine, a person without an anchor, a will or any driving force, someone who let themselves drift on the current towards inevitable disaster. Someone who could only be saved by another person throwing a line around him and giving his life direction and meaning. A person like me. Someone who could appoint a sociable, diligent young man with a clean record as head of security. The rest would be simple.

I switched off the computer and left.

'Back in an hour, Ida.'

Walking downstairs, I felt it had sounded wrong. It was definitely Oda.

At twelve o'clock I drove into the car park in front of a Rimi supermarket that according to my satnav was precisely three hundred metres from Lander's address. The GPS was a gift from Pathfinder, a sort of consolation prize in case we didn't win the competition to appoint their boss, I assume. They had also given me a speedy introduction into what a GPS — or Global Positioning System — actually was and explained how a network of twenty-four satellites in orbit around the earth with the aid of radio signals and atomic clocks could locate you and your GPS sender wherever you were on the planet, down to a radius of three metres. If the signal was picked up by four satellites or more, it could even tell you the elevation, in other words whether you were sitting on the ground or were up in a tree. The whole system had — like the Internet — been developed by the US Defense Department to guide Tomahawk rockets, Pavlov bombs and other fallout-fruit one might want to drop on the right person. Pathfinder had also more than hinted that they had developed transmitters that had access to land-based GPS stations no one knew about, a network that functioned in all weathers, transmitters that could penetrate thick house walls. The chairman of Pathfinder had also told me that to get GPS to work you had to factor in that one second on earth is not one second for a satellite at top speed in space, that time is distorted, that one ages more slowly out there. Satellites actually proved Einstein's theory of relativity.

My Volvo slipped into a line of cars all in the same price bracket and I turned off the ignition. No one would remember the car. I took the black portfolio and walked up the hill to Lander's house. My jacket was in my car and I had put on a blue boiler suit without any markings or logos. The cap concealed my hair, and no one would be surprised by sunglasses as it was still one of those radiant autumn days with which Oslo is so blessed. Nevertheless I cast my eyes down on meeting one of the Filipina girls who push prams for the ruling classes in this suburb. But the short street where Lander lived was otherwise deserted. The sun flashed against the panoramic windows. I checked the Breitling Airwolf watch that Diana had given me for my thirty-fifth birthday. Six minutes past twelve. It was six minutes since the alarm in Jeremias Lander's house had been deactivated. It had happened quietly on a computer in the security company's operations room, via a technical back door that ensured that the outage would not be registered on the data log of shutdowns and power cuts. The day I employed the security chief of Tripolis had indeed been manna from heaven.

I went up to the front door and listened to the birds chirping and the setters barking in the distance. In the interview Lander had said he didn't have a housekeeper, a wife or grown-up children in the house during the day or any dogs. But you could never be one hundred per cent sure. I generally worked on a ninety-nine and a half per cent basis, and the uncertainty of the half a per cent was compensated for by the supply of adrenalin: I observed, listened and sensed better.

I took out the key I had been given by

Ove at Sushi&Coffee, the spare key that all customers have to deposit with Tripolis in case of burglary, fire or a systems failure while they are away. It slid into the lock and turned with a well-lubricated click.

Then I was inside. The discreet alarm on the wall slept with extinguished plastic eyes. I put on the gloves and taped them to the sleeves of my overall so that no loose body hairs should fall onto the floor. Pulled the bathing cap from under my hat down over my ears. The important thing was not to leave any DNA evidence. Ove had once asked me if it wouldn't be just as well to shave my head.

I had given up trying to explain to him that after Diana my hair was the last thing with which I was willing to part.

I had plenty of time but still hurried down the hall. On the wall above the staircase hung portraits of what must have been Lander's children. I am at a complete loss to understand what it is that makes grown people spend money on whoring artists' embarrassing lachrymose versions of their beloved offspring. Do they *like* to see their guests blush? The living room was lavishly furnished but humdrum. Apart from Pesche's fire-engine-red chair, which looked like a buxom woman with her legs apart who had just given birth to a baby: the big square pouffe you can rest your feet on. Doubt if it was Jeremias Lander's idea.

Above the chair hung the picture, *Eva Mudocci,* the British violinist Munch had met at around the turn of the previous century and whom he had sketched straight onto stone when doing her portrait. I had seen other copies of the print before, but it wasn't until now, in this light, that I could see who Eva Mudocci resembled. Lotte. Lotte Madsen. The face in the picture had the same pallor and melancholy in her eyes as the woman I had so emphatically deleted from my memory.

I took the picture off the wall and placed it on the table face down. Used a Stanley knife to cut. The lithograph was printed on beige paper and the frame was modern, so there were no pins or tacks that had to be removed. In short, the simplest of jobs.

Without warning the silence was broken. An alarm. An insistent pulsation fluctuating in frequency from under a thousand hertz to eight thousand, a sound that cuts through the air and background noise so effectively that you can hear it several hundred metres away. I froze. It lasted only a few seconds, then the alarm in the street stopped. The car owner must have been careless.

I continued working. Opened the portfolio, laid the lithograph inside and took out the A2 sheet of Miss Mudocci that I had printed off at home. Within four minutes it was framed, in place and hanging on the wall. I angled my head and inspected it. It could be weeks before the victims of our scam discovered the most ridiculously obvious of fakes. In the spring I had replaced an oil painting, Knut Rose's *Horse with Small Rider,* with a picture I had scanned from an art book and blown up. Four weeks passed before the theft was reported. Miss Mudocci would probably be given away by the whiteness of the paper, but it might take some time. And by then it would be impossible to pinpoint the time of the theft, and the house would have been cleaned enough times to remove all traces of DNA. Because I knew they would look for DNA. Last year, after Kjikerud and I had performed four burglaries in under four months, Inspector Brede Sperre — that blond, media-horny idiot — appeared in *Aftenposten* maintaining that a gang of professional art thieves was on the prowl. And that even though the values involved were not the highest, the Robberies Unit — in order to nip this turn of events in the bud — were using investigative methods normally reserved for murder and the big drug busts. All citizens of Oslo could rest assured on that account, Sperre had said, letting his boyish locks flutter in the wind and looking into the camera lens with steely grey eyes as the photographer snapped away. Of course he had not told the truth: that this priority was being pushed on them by the residents of these areas, the affluent people with political influence and the will to protect theirs and their kind. And I had to admit that I gave a start when Diana, earlier that autumn, had told me that the dashing policeman in the papers had been into the gallery, wanting to know whether anyone had been grilling her about her clients and who had which works of art in their homes. Apparently the art thieves were well informed about what was hanging where. When Diana had queried the reason for my furrowed brow, I had given her the wry smile and replied that I didn't much like having a rival closer than two metres to her. To my surprise, Diana had blushed before laughing.

I marched smartly back to the front door, removed the bathing cap and the gloves with care, wiped the door handle on both sides before letting myself out. The street lay just as morning-still and crisply autumn-dry in the unbroken sunshine.

On my way to the car I checked my watch. Fourteen minutes past twelve. It was a record. My pulse was fast but regulated. In forty-six minutes Ove would activate the alarm in the operations room. And at roughly the same time I guessed that Jeremias Lander would be getting to his feet in one of our interview rooms and shaking the chairman's hand with a final apology before leaving our offices and placing himself out of my control. But in my stable of candidates, of course. Ferdinand would — as I had instructed him — have to explain to the client it was a shame that this hadn't worked out, but that if they were going to angle for applicants as good as Lander, they ought to consider jacking up the salary by twenty per cent. A third of more is, as we all know, more.

And this was just the start. In two hours and forty-six minutes I would be going on a big game hunt. A Greve hunt. I was underpaid, so what? Fuck Stockholm and fuck Brede Sperre; I was king of the heap.

I whistled. The leaves crackled beneath my shoes.

5
CONFESSION

It has been said that when the American police investigators Inbau, Reid and Buckley published *Criminal Interrogation and Confessions* in 1962, they laid the foundations for what have since become the prevailing interview techniques in the Western world. The truth is, of course, that the techniques prevailed long before then, that Inbau, Reid and Buckley's nine-step model merely summarised the FBI's hundred-year experience of extracting confessions from suspects. The method has shown itself to be enormously effective, on both the guilty and the innocent. After DNA technology made it possible for old cases to be re-examined, hundreds of people were found to have been wrongly imprisoned in the USA alone. Around a quarter of these wrongful convictions were based on confessions extracted by the nine-step model. That says everything about what a fantastic tool it is.

My goal is to induce the candidate to admit he is bluffing, that he is unsuitable for the job. If he can get through the nine steps without confessing this, there is reason to assume that the candidate himself really believes he has the necessary qualifications. And those are the candidates I am looking for. I persist in saying 'he' as the nine-step model is most usefully applied to men. My not inconsiderable experience is that women seldom apply for jobs they are not qualified — and they prefer to be overqualified — to do. And even then it is the easiest task in the world to make her break down and confess she hasn't got what is required. False confessions are not uncommon with men, too, of course, but that's fine. After all, they don't land in prison, they only miss out on a management job that requires calm under pressure.

I have absolutely no scruples about using Inbau, Reid and Buckley. It is a scalpel in a world of healing, herbs and psychobabble.

Step one is a direct confrontation and many do not get any further than this point. You make it crystal clear to the candidate that you know everything and that you are sitting on evidence that proves the person in question does not have the requisite abilities.

'I may have been somewhat hasty in expressing an interest in your application, Greve,' I said, leaning back in my chair. 'I've been doing a bit of research, and it turns out that the HOTE shareholders consider that you failed as a CEO. That you were weak, you lacked the killer instinct and it was your fault the company was bought up. Being bought up is precisely what Pathfinder fears, so I'm sure you understand that it will be difficult to view you as a serious candidate. But . . .' With a smile, I raised my cup of coffee. 'Let's enjoy the coffee and talk about other things instead. How's the decorating going?'

Clas Greve sat on the other side of the fake Noguchi table with an erect back, his eyes boring into mine. He laughed.

'Three and a half million,' he said. 'Plus share options, naturally.'

'I beg your pardon.'

'If the board of directors at Pathfinder is afraid the shares might motivate me to sex up the business for potential buyers, you can reassure them that we'll put in a clause about the shares becoming invalid in the case of a buyout. No parachutes. In that way the board and I have the same incentive. To build a strong company, a company that will eat rather than be eaten. The value of shares is calculated according to the Black–Scholes pricing model and added to the fixed salary after your third has been worked out.'

I put on the best smile I had. 'I'm afraid you're taking some things for granted, Greve. There are several points here. Don't forget you're a foreigner, and Norwegian companies prefer to have their own to —'

'You were literally salivating all over me yesterday at your wife's gallery, Roger. And you were right to. After your proposition I did some research into you and into Pathfinder. I became immediately aware that even though I am a Dutch citizen, you will have difficulty finding a more appropriate candidate than me. The problem then was that I wasn't interested. But one can do a lot of thinking in twelve hours. And in that time, for example, one might conclude that the pleasures of house renovation may be restricted over the long term.'

Clas Greve folded his suntanned hands in front of him.

'It's time I got back in the saddle. Pathfinder is perhaps not the sexiest company I could have chosen, but it has potential, and a person with vision and the board on his side could build it up into something really interesting. However, it is by no means certain that the board and I share the same vision, so your job is, I suppose, to bring us together as soon as possible in order that we might see whether there is any point continuing.'

'Listen, Greve —'

'I am in no doubt that your methods work on many people, Roger, but with me you can give the show a miss. And go back to calling me Clas. After all, this is supposed to be just a cosy chat, isn't it?'

He lifted his coffee cup as if he were going to make a toast. I grabbed the opportunity for a timeout and lifted my own.

'You seem a bit stressed, Roger. Are there competitors for this commission of yours?'

My laryngeal reflex has a tendency to kick in when I am caught unawares. I had to swallow quickly so as not to cough up coffee over *Sara Gets Undressed*.

'I understand all too well that you have to go for it, Roger,' Greve smiled, leaning closer.

I could smell the heat of his body and a faint aroma which reminded me of cedar trees, Russian leather and citrus. Cartier's Declaration? Or something in that price range.

'I'm not at all offended, Roger. You're a pro, and I am, too. Naturally, you just want to do a good job for the client, that's what they're paying you for, after all. And the more interesting the candidate, the more important it is to give the person in question a thorough going-over. The claim that HOTE shareholders were not happy is not a stupid one. I would have tried something like that if I'd been you.'

I couldn't believe my ears. He had thrown step one right back in my face by stating that we should give the show a miss; my ploy had been blown. And now he was running step two, what Inbau, Reid and Buckley call 'sympathising with the suspect by normalising actions'. And the most incredible thing was that even though I knew exactly what Greve was doing, it did build up, this feeling I had read so much about: the suspect's desire to throw in his cards. I almost felt like laughing out loud.

'I don't quite understand what you mean now, Clas.' Although I was trying to appear relaxed, I could hear that my voice had a metallic timbre and my thoughts were wading through syrup. I was unable to mobilise a counter-attack before the next question came.

'Money is not actually my motivation, Roger. But if you like, we can try to increase the salary. A third of more . . .'

. . . is more. He had taken over the interview completely now and gone straight from step two to step seven: Present the alternative. In this case, give the suspect an alternative motivation for confessing. The execution was perfect. Of course he could have brought my family into play, said something about how proud my deceased parents or my wife would be if they heard how I had pushed up the salary, our commission, my bonus. But Clas Greve knew that would be going too far, of course he knew that. I had quite simply met my match.

'OK, Clas,' I heard myself say. 'I give in. It is just as you say.'

Greve leaned back in his chair again. He had won, and now he was letting his breath out and smiling. Not with a sense of triumph, just happy that it was over. *Used to winning,* I noted down on the sheet I already knew I would throw away afterwards.

The strangest part about it was that it didn't feel like a defeat, but a relief. Yes, I felt nothing less than invigorated.

'Nevertheless, the client requires concrete information,' I said. 'Would you mind if we went on?'

Clas Greve closed his eyes, placed the tips of his fingers against each other and shook his head.

'Fine,' I said. 'Then I would like you to tell me about your life.'

I made notes as Clas Greve told his story. He had grown up as the youngest of three. In Rotterdam. It was a rough seaport, but his family were among the privileged, his father had a top job with Philips. Clas and his two sisters had learned Norwegian during the long summers with their grandparents in a chalet in Son, on the Oslo fjord. He had had a strained relationship with his father, who considered the youngest child spoilt and lacking in discipline.

'He was right,' Greve smiled. 'I was used to achieving good results at school and on the sports track without doing any work. By the time I was around sixteen everything bored me, and I began to visit "shady areas". They're not hard to find in Rotterdam. I had no friends there and didn't make any new ones, either. But I did have money. So, systematically, I began to try out everything that was forbidden: alcohol, hash, prostitution, minor break-ins and, bit by bit, harder drugs. At home my father believed I had taken up boxing and that was why I returned with a bloated face, a runny nose and bloodshot eyes. I was spending more and more time in these places where people let me stay and above all left me in peace. I don't know if I cared for this new life of mine. Those around me saw me as a weirdo, a lonely sixteen-year-old they couldn't make out. And it was precisely this reaction that I liked. Gradually my lifestyle began to show in my school results, but I didn't care. Eventually my father woke up. And perhaps I thought I finally had what I had always wanted: his attention. He spoke to me in calm, serious tones; I yelled back. Sometimes I could see he was on the point of losing control. I loved it. He sent me to my grandparents in Oslo where I did my last two years of school. How did you get on with your father, Roger?'

I jotted down three words with 'self'. *Self-assured. Self-deprecating.* And *Self-aware.*

'We didn't speak much,' I said. 'We were quite different.'

'Were? So he's dead?'

'My parents died in a road accident.'

'What did he do?'

'Diplomatic corps. The British Embassy. He met my mother in Oslo.'

Greve tilted his head and studied me. 'Do you miss him?'

'No. Is your father alive?'

'Doubt it.'

'Doubt it?'

Clas Greve took a deep breath and pressed his palms together. 'He went missing when I was eighteen. He didn't come home for dinner. At work they said he had left at six as usual. My mother rang the police. They immediately went into action as this was a time when left-wing terrorist groups were kidnapping rich business people in Europe. There hadn't been any accidents on the motorway; no one by the name of Bernhard Greve had been taken to hospital. He wasn't on any passenger lists and the car had not been registered anywhere. He was never found.'

'What do you believe happened?'

'I don't believe anything. He may have driven to Germany, stayed at a motel under a false name, unable to shoot himself. So instead he could have pushed on in the middle of the night, come across a black lake in some forest and driven in. Or maybe he was kidnapped in the car park outside Philips, two men with pistols on the back seat. Put up a fight, got a bullet through his head. The car with Dad in it was then driven to a breaker's yard the same night, crushed into a metal pancake and cut up into tiny bits. Or perhaps he's sitting somewhere with umbrella-adorned cocktail in one hand and call girl in the other.'

I tried to detect a reaction in Greve's face, in his voice. Nothing. Either he had considered the thought too often, or else he was just a stony-hearted bastard. I didn't know which I preferred.

'You're eighteen years old and living in Oslo,' I said. 'Your father's gone missing. You're a young man with problems. What do you do?'

'I finished school with top grades and applied to join the Dutch Royal Marines.'

'Commandos. The macho elite stuff, eh?'

'Definitely.'

'The sort where one in a hundred get in.'

'That kind of thing. I was selected to take part in the preliminary tests where they spend a month systematically trying to break you down. And afterwards — if you survive — four years building you up.'

'Sounds like something I've seen in films.'

'Believe me, Roger, you won't have seen this in a film.'

I looked at him. I believed him.

'Later I joined the counter-terrorism unit BBE in Dorn. I was there for eight years. Got to see the whole world. Suriname, the Dutch West Indies, Indonesia, Afghanistan. Winter exercises in Harstad and Voss. I was taken prisoner and tortured during an anti-drug campaign in Suriname.'

'Sounds exotic. But you kept your mouth shut?'

Clas Greve smiled. 'Shut? I chatted away like an old fishwife. Cocaine barons don't play at interrogation.'

I leaned forward. 'Really? What did they do?'

Greve observed me thoughtfully with a raised eyebrow before answering. 'I don't think you really want to know, Roger.'

I was a little disappointed, but nodded and sat back.

'So your comrades were picked off or something like that?'

'No. When they attacked the positions I had given away, of course everything had been moved on. I spent two months in a cellar living on rotten fruit and water infested with mosquito eggs. When the BBE carried me out I weighed forty-five kilos.'

I looked at him. Tried to imagine how they had tortured him. How he had taken it. And what the forty-five-kilo variant of Clas Greve had looked like. Different, of course. But not that much, not really.

'Hardly surprising you stopped,' I said.

'That wasn't why. The eight years in the BBE were the best in my life, Roger. First of all, it is in fact the stuff you've seen in films. The comradeship and the loyalty. But

93

in addition there was what I learned, what came to be my craft.'

'Which is?'

'Finding people. In the BBE there was something called TRACK. A unit which specialised in tracking down people in all possible situations and places in the world. They were the ones who found me in the cellar. So I applied to the unit, was accepted, and there I learned everything. From ancient Indian tracking skills to interrogation methods and the most modern electronic tracking devices in existence. That was how I got to know HOTE. They had made a transmitter the size of a shirt button. The idea was to attach it to someone and then follow all his movements via a receiver, the kind you saw in spy films way back in the sixties, but which no one had actually managed to operate satisfactorily. Even HOTE's shirt button turned out to be useless; it couldn't take body sweat, temperatures below minus ten, and the signals only penetrated the thinnest of house walls. But the HOTE boss liked me. He had no sons of his own . . .'

'And you had no father.'

Greve sent me an indulgent smile.

'Go on,' I said.

'After eight years in the military I started

Engineering Studies in The Hague, paid for by HOTE. During my first year at HOTE we had made a tracking device which would function under extreme conditions. After five years I was number two in the command chain. After eight I took over as boss, and the rest you know.'

I leaned back in my chair and sipped my coffee. We were already there. We had a winner. I had even written it. *Hired*. Perhaps that was why I hesitated to go on, perhaps there was something inside me that said enough was enough. Or perhaps it was something else.

'You look as if you would like to know more,' Greve said.

I replied with an evasion. 'You haven't talked about your marriage.'

'I've talked about the important things,' said Greve. 'Would you like to hear about my marriage?'

I shook my head. And decided to wind things up. But then fate intervened. In the form of Clas Greve himself.

'Nice picture you've got,' he said, turning to the wall behind him. 'Is that an Opie?'

'*Sara Gets Undressed*,' I said. 'A present from Diana. Do you collect art?'

'I've made a small start.'

Something inside me still said no, but it

was too late; I had already asked: 'What's the best thing you've got?'

'An oil painting. I found it in a hidden room behind the kitchen. No one in the family knew my grandmother had it.'

'Interesting,' I said, feeling my heart give a curious jump. Must have been from the tension earlier in the day. 'What's the painting?'

He studied me for a long time. A tiny smile stole onto his mouth. He formed his lips to answer, and I had a strange premonition. A premonition that made my stomach recoil like a boxer's abdominal muscles do when they see a blow coming. But his lips changed shape. And all the premonitions in the world could not have prepared me for his reply.

'*The Calydonian Boar Hunt.*'

'*The . . .*' In two seconds my mouth had gone as dry as dust. *'The Boar Hunt?'*

'Do you know anything about it?'

'If you mean the picture by . . . by . . .'

'Peter Paul Rubens,' Greve completed.

I concentrated on one thing only. Keeping the mask. But something was flashing in front of me, like a scoreboard in the London fog in Loftus Road: QPR had just lobbed the ball into the top corner. Life had been

turned upside down. We were on our way to
Wembley.

■ ■ ■ ■ ■

PART TWO:
CLOSING IN

■ ■ ■ ■ ■

6
RUBENS

'Peter Paul Rubens.'

For a moment it was as if all movement, all sound in the room had been frozen. *The Calydonian Boar Hunt* by Peter Paul Rubens. The sensible assumption would of course be that this was a reproduction, a famous, fantastically good forgery that in itself might be worth a million or two. However, there was something in his voice, something about the stress, something about this person, Clas Greve, that left me in no doubt. It was the original, the bloody hunting motif of Greek mythology, the fantasy animal pierced by Meleager's spear, the painting that had been lost since the Germans plundered the gallery in Rubens's home town of Antwerp in 1941 and which until the end of the war people had believed and hoped was in some Berlin bunker. I am no great art connoisseur, but for natural reasons I sometimes had occasion to go onto the Net and check the lists of missing and sought-after art. And this painting had headed the top ten for the last sixty years, eventually more as a curiosity since it was thought that it had been burned up together with half of the German capital. My tongue endeavoured to gather moisture from my palate.

'You just *found* a painting by Peter Paul Rubens in a hidden room behind the kitchen in your deceased grandmother's apartment?'

Greve nodded with a grin. 'This sort of thing can happen, I have heard. Now, it's not his best or his best-known painting, but it must be worth something.'

I nodded without speaking. Fifty million? A hundred? At least. Another of Rubens's rediscovered paintings, The Massacre of the Innocents, had gone for fifty million at an auction just a few years ago. Pounds sterling. Over half a billion kroner. I needed water.

'By the way, it wasn't a complete bolt out of the blue that she had hidden art,' Greve said. 'You see, my grandmother was very beautiful when she was young, and like almost all of Oslo high society she fraternised with the top German officers during the Occupation. Especially with one of them, a colonel who was interested in art, and who she often told me about when I lived here. She said he'd given her some paintings to hide for him until the war was over. Unfortunately he was executed by members of the Resistance in the last days of the hostilities, people who, ironically enough, had drunk his champagne when times had been better for the Germans. In fact, I didn't believe most of my grandmother's stories. Right up until the Polish builders found this door behind the shelving in the maid's room inside the kitchen.'

'Fantastic,' I whispered involuntarily.

'Isn't it? I haven't checked if it is the original yet, but . . .'

But it is, I thought. German colonels didn't collect reproductions.

'Your builders didn't see the picture?' I asked.

'Yes, they did. But I doubt they knew what it was.'

'Don't say that. Is there an alarm in the flat?'

'I hear what you're saying. And the answer is yes. All the flats in the block use the same security company. And none of the builders has a key since they only work between eight and four in accordance with the house rules. And when they're there, I'm generally with them.'

'I think you should continue to do that.

Do you know which company the block uses?'

'Trio something or other. In fact, I was thinking of asking your wife if she knows anyone who can help me to determine whether it's an original Rubens or not. You're the first person I've spoken to about this. I hope you won't mention it to anyone.'

'Of course not. I'll ask her and ring you back.'

'Thank you, I'd appreciate that. For the time being, I only know that if it is genuine, it's not one of his best-known pictures.'

I flashed a fleeting smile. 'Such a shame. But back to the job. I like to strike while the iron is hot. Which day could you meet Pathfinder?'

'Any day you wish.'

'Good.' My mind whirled as I looked down at my diary. Builders there from eight to four. 'It suits Pathfinder best if they can come into Oslo after working hours. Horten's a good hour's drive away, so if we find a day this week at about six, would that be all right?' I said it as lightly as I could, but my off-key tone grated.

'Fine,' said Greve, who didn't seem to have picked up anything. 'As long as it's not tomorrow, that is,' he added, getting to his feet.

'That would be too short notice for them, anyway,' I said. 'I'll ring the number you gave me.'

I escorted him out to reception. 'Could you order a taxi, please, Da?' I tried to read from Oda's or Ida's face whether she was comfortable with the abbreviation but was interrupted by Greve.

'Thank you. I have my own car here. Regards to your wife, and I'll wait to hear from you.'

He proffered his hand, and I shook it with a broad smile. 'I'll try to ring you tonight, because you're busy tomorrow, aren't you?'

'Yes.'

I don't know why I didn't stop there. The rhythm of the conversation, the sense that an exchange was over told me that it was here I should say the closing 'Goodbye'. Perhaps it was a gut feeling, a premonition; perhaps a terror that had already implanted itself in me, which made me extra careful.

'Yeah, decoration is a pretty all-engrossing activity,' I said.

'It's not that,' he said. 'I'm catching the early-morning plane to Rotterdam tomorrow. To get the dog. He's been stuck in quarantine. I won't be back until late evening.'

'Oh yes,' I said, releasing his hand so that

he wouldn't notice how I had stiffened. 'What breed of dog is it?'

'Niether terrier. Tracker dog. But as aggressive as a fighting dog. Good to have in the house when you have pictures like this up on the walls, don't you think?'

'Indeed,' I said. 'Indeed it is.'

A dog. I hated dogs.

'I see,' I heard Ove Kjikerud say at the other end of the line. 'Clas Greve, Oscars gate 25. I've got the key here. Handover at Sushi&Coffee in an hour. The alarm is deactivated at seventeen hundred hours tomorrow. I'll have to find a pretext for working in the afternoon. Why such short notice by the way?'

'Because after tomorrow there'll be a dog in the flat.'

'OK. But why not during working hours, as usual?'

The young man in the Corneliani suit and geek-chic glasses came along the pavement towards the public telephone box. I turned my back on him to avoid a greeting and pressed my mouth closer to the receiver.

'I want to be one hundred per cent sure that there are no builders there. So you ring Gothenburg this minute and ask them to get hold of a decent Rubens reproduction.

There are lots, but say that we must have a good one. And they must have it ready for you when you come with the Munch print tonight. It's short notice, but it's important that I have it for tomorrow, do you understand?'

'OK, OK.'

'And then you tell Gothenburg that you'll be back with the original tomorrow night. Do you remember the name of the picture?'

'Yes, *The Catalonian Boar Hunt*. Rubens.'

'Close enough. You're absolutely sure we can rely on this fence?'

'Jesus, Roger. For the hundredth time, yes!'

'I'm just asking!'

'Listen to me now. The guy knows that if he pulls a fast one at any time, he'll be out of the game for life. No one punishes thieving harder than thieves.'

'Great.'

'Just one thing: I'll have to put off the second Gothenburg trip by a day.'

That was no problem, we had done it before; the Rubens would be safe inside the ceiling, but I could feel the hairs on my neck rising anyway.

'Why's that?'

'I've got a visitor tomorrow evening. A dame.'

'You'll have to postpone it.'

'Sorry, can't.'

'Can't?'

'It's Natasha.'

I could hardly believe my ears. 'The Russian harlot?'

'Don't call her that.'

'Isn't that what she is?'

'I don't call your wife a Barbie doll, do I?'

'Are you comparing my wife with a tart?'

'I said I *didn't* call your wife a Barbie doll.'

'All the better for you. Diana is a hundred per cent natural.'

'You're lying.'

'Not at all.'

'OK, I'm impressed. But I won't be going tomorrow night all the same. I've been on Natasha's waiting list for three weeks, and I want to film the session. Get it on tape.'

'Film it? You're taking the piss.'

'I have to have something to look at before the next time. God knows when that'll be.'

I laughed out loud. 'You're crazy.'

'Why do you say that?'

'You're in love with a whore, Ove! No real man can love a whore.'

'What do you know about that?'

I groaned. 'And what are you going to say to your beloved when you pull out a bloody camera?'

'She'll know nothing about it.'

'Hidden camera in the wardrobe?'

'Wardrobe? My house has total surveillance, man.'

Nothing Ove Kjikerud told me about himself could surprise me any longer. He had told me that when he wasn't working, he mostly watched TV in his little place high up in Tonsenhagen, on the edge of a forest. And he liked to shoot at the screen if there was something he really didn't care for. He had boasted about his Austrian Glock pistols, or 'dames' as he called them, because they didn't have a hammer that stood up before ejaculation. Ove used blank cartridges to shoot at the TV, but once he had forgotten he had loaded a round of live ammunition and had shot a brand-new Pioneer plasma screen costing thirty thousand to smithereens. When he wasn't shooting at the TV he took potshots through the window at an owl's nesting box he himself had rigged up on a tree trunk behind the house. And one evening, sitting in front of the TV, he had heard something crashing through the trees, so he opened the window, took aim with a Remington rifle and fired. The bullet had hit the animal in the middle of the forehead, and Ove had had to empty the freezer, which was stuffed with Grandiosa pizzas. For the next six months it had been elk steaks, elk burgers, elk stew, elk meatballs and elk chops until he could stand it no longer and had emptied the freezer again and restocked it with Grandiosa. I found all these stories totally credible. But this one . . .

'Total surveillance?'

'There are certain fringe benefits to working at Tripolis, aren't there?'

'And you can activate the cameras without her noticing?'

'Yep. I fetch her, we go into the flat, and if I don't enter the password within fifteen seconds the cameras begin to work at Tripolis.'

'And the alarm begins to howl in your flat?'

'Nope. Silent alarm.'

Of course I was aware of the concept. The alarm just went off at Tripolis. The idea was not to frighten off the burglars while Tripolis rang the police, who were on the spot within fifteen minutes. The aim was to catch the thieves red-handed before they disappeared with the loot or, if this didn't work, they could identify them on the video recordings.

'I've told the boys on duty not to turn up, right. They can just sit back and enjoy the sight on the monitors.'

'Do you mean to say the boys will be watching you and the Russ— Natasha?'

'Have to share the delights, don't I? But I have made sure the camera doesn't show the bed, that's a private area. But I'll get her to undress at the foot of the bed, in the chair beside the TV, right. She'll follow my stage directions, that's the beauty of it. Get her to sit there touching herself. Perfect camera angle. I've done a bit of work on the lights. So that I can wank off-camera, right.'

Far too much information. I coughed. 'Then you come and get the Munch tonight. And the Rubens the night after tomorrow, OK?'

'OK. Everything all right with you, Roger? You sound stressed.'

'Everything's fine,' I said, running the back of my hand across my forehead. 'Everything's absolutely fine.'

I put down the phone and went on my way. The sky was clouding over, but I hardly noticed. Because everything was OK, wasn't it? I was going to be a multi-millionaire. To buy my freedom, freedom from everything. The world and everything in it — including Diana — would be mine. The rumbles in the distance sounded like hearty laughter. Then the first raindrops fell, and the soles

of my shoes clattered cheerfully over the
cobblestones as I ran.

7

PREGNANT

It was six o'clock, it had stopped raining and in the west gold streamed into the Oslo fjord. I put the Volvo in the garage, switched off the ignition and waited. After the door had closed behind me, I put on the internal light, opened the black portfolio and took out the day's catch. *The Brooch. Eva Mudocci.*

I ran my eyes over her face. Munch must have been in love with her, he couldn't have drawn her like that otherwise. Drawn her as Lotte, caught the silent pain, the quiet ferocity. I swore under my breath, inhaled hard and hissed through my teeth. Then I pulled back the ceiling upholstery above my head. It was my own invention, designed for concealing pictures that had to be transported across national borders. I had just loosened the ceiling liner — the head liner as they say in car-speak — where it was attached to the top of the windscreen. Then I had stuck two strips of Velcro on the inside, and after a bit of careful cutting around the front ceiling light I had the perfect hidey-hole. The problem with moving large pictures, especially old, dry oil paintings is that they have to lie flat and must not be rolled up, because then there is a risk that the paint will crack and the picture will be ruined. In other words, transportation requires room and the cargo is somewhat conspicuous. But with a roof surface of approximately four square metres there was room for even the big pictures, and they were hidden from prying customs officers and their dogs, who luckily did not sniff around for paint or varnish.

I slid Eva Mudocci inside, fastened the lining with the Velcro, got out of the car and went up to the house.

Diana had stuck a note on the fridge saying that she was out with her friend Cathrine and would be home at about midnight. That was almost six hours away. I opened a San Miguel, sat down on the chair by the window and started to wait for her. Fetched another bottle and thought about something I remembered from the Johan Falkberget book Diana had read to me the time I had mumps: 'We all drink according to how thirsty we are.'

I had been lying in bed with a temperature and aching cheeks and ears and looked like a sweaty pufferfish while the doctor checked the thermometer and said 'it wasn't too bad'. And it hadn't felt too bad, either. It was only after pressure from Diana that he had mentioned ugly words like meningitis and orchitis, which he had even more reluctantly translated as an inflammation of the tissues round the brain and inflammation of the testicles, but straight away he had added that they were 'highly unlikely in this case'.

Diana read to me and laid cold compresses on my forehead. The book was *The Fourth Night Watch,* and since I had nothing else to occupy my inflammation-threatened brain with, I listened carefully. There were two particular things that caught my attention. First there was Sigismund the priest who excuses a drunk with those words 'We all drink according to how thirsty we are'. Maybe because I found comfort in such a view of humanity: If that's your nature, then it's fine.

The second was a quotation from what are known informally as 'Pontoppidan's Explanations' in which he declares that a person is capable of killing another person's soul, infecting it, dragging it down into sin in such a way that redemption is precluded. I found less comfort in that. And the thought that I might be defiling angel wings meant that I never let Diana in on all the things I was doing to acquire extra income.

She took care of me for four days and nights, and it was a source of both pleasure and annoyance. For I knew I would not have done the same for her, at least not if she had only had lousy mumps. So when I finally asked her why she had done it, I was genuinely curious. Her response was simple and straightforward.

'Because I love you.'

'It's just mumps.'

'Perhaps I won't get a chance to show it later. You're so healthy.'

It sounded like an accusation.

And, sure enough, the day afterwards I got out of bed, went for a job interview with a recruitment agency called Alfa and told them they would have to be idiots not to employ me. And I know how I was able to say that to them with such unshakeable self-assurance. Because there is nothing that makes a man grow beyond his own stature than a woman telling him she loves him. And however much she might have lied to him, there will always be a part of him that is grateful to her for this, and that will harbour some love for her.

I took one of Diana's art books, read about Rubens and the little there was about *The Calydonian Boar Hunt* and studied the picture with great care. Then I put down the book and tried to think through the following day's operation in Oscars gate step by step.

An apartment in a block meant of course a risk of bumping into neighbours on the stairs. Potential witnesses who could catch a glimpse of me. Just for a few seconds, though. They wouldn't be suspicious then, wouldn't make a note of my face as I would be wearing overalls and would let myself into an apartment that was being redecorated. So what was I frightened of?

I knew what I was frightened of.

He had read me like an open book during the interview. But how many of the pages? Could he have suspected something? No. He had recognised a method of interrogation he had used himself in the military, that was all.

I grabbed my mobile phone and called Greve's number to tell him that Diana was out and the name of a possible expert to check the picture's authenticity would have to wait until he was back from Rotterdam. Greve's answerphone voice said in English:

'Please leave a message,' and so I did. The bottle was empty. I considered a whisky, but dismissed the idea, didn't want to wake up with a hangover tomorrow. A last beer, great.

The call was about to go through when I realised what I had done. I lowered my phone and hurriedly pressed the red button. I had dialled Lotte's number, the one under the discreet L in the address book, an L which had made me tremble the few times it had appeared on the display as an incoming call. Our rule had been that I was to ring. I went into the address book, found L and pressed 'Delete'.

'Do you really want to delete?' the phone replied.

I scrutinised the alternatives. The cowardly, faithless 'no' and the mendacious 'yes'.

I pressed 'yes'. Knowing that her number was printed in my brain in a way that defied deletion. What that meant I neither knew nor wanted to know. But it would fade. Fade and disappear. It had to.

Diana returned home at five minutes to midnight.

'What have you been doing today, darling?' she asked, making for the chair, squatting on the arm and giving me a hug.

'Not much,' I said. 'I interviewed Clas Greve.'

'How did it go?'

'He's perfect, except that he's a foreigner. Pathfinder said they wanted a Norwegian as head; they've even said publicly they set great store by being Norwegian down to the last detail. So it will have to be a persuasion job.'

'But you're the world's greatest at that.' She kissed me on the forehead. 'I've heard people talking about your record.'

'Which record?'

'The man who always has his candidate appointed, I suppose.'

'Oh, that one,' I said, acting surprised.

'You'll manage this time, too.'

'How was it with Cathrine?'

Diana ran her hand through my thick hair. 'Fantastic. As usual. Or, even more fantastic than usual.'

'She's going to die of happiness one day.'

Diana pressed her face into my hair and spoke into it. 'She's just found out she's pregnant.'

'So it won't be that fantastic for a while.'

'Nonsense,' she mumbled. 'Have you been drinking?'

'A tiny bit. Shall we raise a glass to

Cathrine?'

'I'm heading for bed. I'm exhausted from all this happiness chat. Are you coming?'

Lying curled up behind her in the bed, enclosing her and feeling her spine against my chest and stomach, I suddenly realised something I knew I must have thought ever since the interview with Greve. That now I could make her pregnant. That I was finally on terra firma, on safe ground; a child could not supplant me now. With the Rubens I would at last be the lion, the master Diana talked about. The irreplaceable provider. It wasn't that Diana had had any doubts before, but I had doubted. Doubted whether I could be the guardian of the nest that Diana deserved. And that a child of all things could cure her blessed blindness. But now she could go ahead and see, see all of me. More of me, at any rate.

The sharp, cold air from the open window was giving my skin goose pimples on top of the duvet and I could feel an erection coming.

But her breathing was already deep and even.

I let go of her. She rolled onto her back, secure and defenceless like an infant.

I slipped out of bed.

The *mizuko* altar did not seem to have

been touched since yesterday. It was rare for a day to pass without her making some kind of visible change: replacing the water, putting in a new candle, new flowers.

I went up to the living room, poured myself a whisky. The parquet floor by the window was cold. The whisky was a thirty-year-old Macallan, a present from a satisfied client. They were listed on the stock exchange now. I looked down at the garage, which was bathed in moonlight. Ove was probably on his way. He would let himself into the garage and get into the car with the spare keys he held. Remove the *Eva Mudocci*, put her in the portfolio and return to his car which was parked at a reassuringly safe distance, far enough away not to be connected with our house. He would drive to the art dealer in Gothenburg, deliver the picture and be back by the early morning. But the *Eva Mudocci* was no longer interesting now, an irritating filler job that just had to be dispatched. On Ove's return from Gothenburg he would hopefully have a usable reproduction of Rubens's *Boar Hunt*, which he would put under the ceiling of the Volvo before we or the neighbours were up.

In the past Ove had used my car to go to Gothenburg. I had never spoken to the dealer, and I hoped he didn't know that anyone else apart from Ove was involved. That was how I wanted it, as few contacts as possible, as few people as possible who could point a finger at me. Criminals are caught sooner or later and so it was important to have the maximum distance between them and me. That was why I made a point of never being seen in conversation with Kjikerud publicly, and that was why I used a payphone when I called him. I didn't want any of my phone numbers to be on Kjikerud's calls log when he was arrested. The sharing out of money and the more strategic planning were done in an out-of-the-way cabin in the Elverum area. Ove rented the cabin from a hermit farmer and we always arrived in separate cars.

I had been on my way to this cabin when it had struck me just how risky it was to let Ove use my car to drive the pictures to Gothenburg. I had passed a speed trap, and there I had seen his almost thirty-year-old Mercedes, a stylish black 280SE, parked next to a police car. And I realised that Kjikerud was obviously one of those notorious drivers who are incapable of keeping to speed limits. I had drummed it into him that he should always remove the AutoPASS unit from the windscreen when he drove my Volvo to Gothenburg as any use was logged, and I was not interested in explaining to the police why I had driven up and down the E6 in the middle of the night several times a year. But when I passed Ove's Mercedes in the speed trap on the way to Elverum I realised that was the greatest risk we ran: that the police would stop fast drivers and old acquaintances of theirs like Ove Kjikerud on his way to Gothenburg and wonder what on earth he could be doing with a car belonging to the respectable, hmm, headhunter Roger Brown. And from thereon in it would be bad news all the way. Because Kjikerud versus Inbau, Reid and Buckley had only one outcome.

I thought I could make out something moving in the dark by the garage.

Tomorrow was D-Day. Dream Day. Domesday. Demob Day. If everything went to plan this would be the last coup. I wanted to be finished, free, the one who got away with it.

The town sparkled full of promise beneath us.

Lotte answered on the fifth ring. 'Roger?' Careful, gentle. As if she had been the one to wake me and not vice versa.

I hung up.

And drained the glass in one swig.

8
G11sus4

I awoke with a splitting headache.

I supported myself on my elbows and saw Diana's delicate, panty-clad backside sticking up in the air as she rummaged through her handbag and the pockets of the clothes she had been wearing the previous day.

'Looking for something?' I asked.

'Good morning, darling,' she said, but I could hear that it was not. And I agreed.

I dragged myself out of bed and into the bathroom. Saw myself in the mirror and knew the rest of the day could only get better. Had to get better. Would get better. I turned on the shower and stood under the ice-cold jets listening to Diana cursing under her breath in the bedroom.

'And it's gonna be . . .' I howled in pure defiance: 'PERFECT!'

'I'm off,' Diana called. 'I love you.'

'And I love you,' I shouted, but didn't know if she managed to catch it before the door slammed behind her.

At ten o'clock I was sitting in my office try-ing to concentrate. My head felt like a transparent, pulsating tadpole. I had regis-tered that Ferdinand had had his mouth open for several minutes and had formed it into what I assumed were words of varying interest. And even though his mouth was still open, he had stopped moving it and instead was staring at me with what I interpreted as an expectant look.

'Repeat the question,' I said.

'I said it's great I'm doing the second interview with Greve and the client, but you have to tell me a bit about Pathfinder first. I haven't been told anything, and I'm going to look a complete fool!' At this point his voice rose into the obligatory hysterical fal-setto.

I sighed. 'They make tiny, almost invisible transmitters which can be attached to people and tracked via a receiver connected to the world's most advanced GPS. Priori-tised service from satellites of which they are part-owners, etc., etc. Ground-breaking technology, ergo buy-out potential. Read the annual report. Anything else?'

'I've read it! Everything about the prod-ucts is stamped secret. And what about Clas

Greve being a foreigner? How am I going to get this obviously nationalistic client to swallow that?'

'You won't have to. I will. Don't worry yourself about it, Ferdy.'

'Ferdy?'

'Yes, I've been giving it some thought. Ferdinand is too long. Is that all right?'

He stared at me in disbelief. 'Ferdy?'

'Not with clients present, of course.' I beamed and could feel my headache lifting already. 'Have we finished, Ferdy?'

We had.

Through to lunch I chewed Paralgin and stared at the clock.

At lunch I went to the jeweller's opposite Sushi&Coffee.

'Those ones,' I said, pointing to the diamond earrings in the window.

I had funds to cover the card. For as long as they lasted. And the scarlet box's chamois surface was as soft as puppy fur.

After lunch I continued to chew Paralgin and stare at the clock.

At five on the dot I parked the car in Inkognitogata. Finding a place was easy; both the people who worked and lived here were obviously on their way home. It had just rained and my shoe soles squelched on the tarmac. The portfolio felt light. The reproduction had been of average quality and of course horrendously overpriced at fifteen thousand Swedish kroner, but that was not very important at this moment.

As far as there can be said to be a fashionable street in Oslo, Oscars gate is it. The apartment buildings are a hotchpotch of architectural styles, mostly new Renaissance. Facades with neo-Gothic patterns, planted front gardens, this was where the directors and top civil servants had their estates at the end of the nineteenth century.

A man with a poodle on a lead was coming towards me. No hunting dogs here in the centre. He looked through me. City centre.

I walked up to number 25, according to the Internet search a block with 'a Hanoverian variant of medieval-inspired architecture'. It was more interesting to read that the Spanish Embassy no longer had its premises here, hence there would hopefully be no annoying CCTV cameras. There was no one about in front of the property, which greeted me with silent black windows. The key I had been given by Ove was supposed to fit both the front and the apartment door. Anyway, it worked for the front door. I strode up the stairs. Purposeful. Not heavy, not light steps. A person who knows where he is going and has nothing to hide. I had the key ready so that I would not have to stand fumbling by the apartment door; that sort of noise travels in an old apartment building.

Second floor. No name on the door, but I knew it was here. Double door with wavy glass. I was not as calm as I had believed, for my heart was pounding inside my ribs and I missed the keyhole. Ove had once told me that the first thing that goes when you are nervous is motor coordination. He had read it in a book about one-on-one combat, how the ability to load a weapon fails you when you are faced with another gun. Nevertheless I found the keyhole at the second attempt. And the key turned, soundless, smooth and perfect. I pressed the handle and pulled the door towards me. Pushed it away from me. But it wouldn't open. I pulled again. Bloody hell! Had Greve had an extra lock put on? Would all my dreams and plans be crushed by an extra bloody lock? I pulled at the door with all my strength, I almost panicked. It came away from the frame with a loud crack and the glass in the frame quivered as the echo resounded down the staircase. I slipped inside, carefully closed the door behind me and exhaled. And the thought that had struck me the previous evening suddenly seemed stupid. Would I miss this tension to which I had become so accustomed?

As I inhaled, my nose, mouth and lungs were filled with solvents: latex paint, varnish and glue.

I stepped over the paint pots and the rolls of wallpaper in the hall. Grey protective paper on chequered oak parquet floor, wainscoting, brick dust, old windows that were clearly going to be replaced. Rooms the size of small ballrooms in a line, one after the other.

I found the half-finished kitchen behind the middle room. Strict lines, metal and wood, expensive, no doubt about that; I guessed it was a Poggenpohl. I went into the maid's room, and there was the door behind the shelves. I had already taken into account that it might be locked, but I knew that if necessary there would be tools in the apartment I could use to break it open.

It wasn't necessary. The hinges creaked a warning as the door opened.

I stepped into the dark, empty, rectangular room, took the pocket flashlight from inside my overalls and shone the pale yellow light on the walls. There were four pictures hanging in there. Three of them were unknown to me. The fourth was not.

I stood in front of it and felt the same dryness in my mouth as when Greve had mentioned the title.

'*The Calydonian Boar Hunt.*'

Light seemed to be forcing its way out of the underlying, 400-year-old layers of paint. Together with the shadows it gave the hunting scene an outline and form, what Diana had explained to me was called chiaroscuro. The picture had an almost physical impact, a magnetism that drew you in, it was like meeting a charismatic person you have only known from photos and hearsay. I was unprepared for all this beauty. I recognised the colors from earlier, better known hunting pictures of his in Diana's art books — *The Lion Hunt, The Hippopotamus and Crocodile Hunt, The Tiger Hunt.* In the book I had read yesterday it had said that this was Rubens's first hunting motif, the departure point for later masterpieces. The Calydonian boar had been sent by Artemis to murder and ravage in Calydon in revenge for humanity's neglect of the goddess. But it was Calydon's best hunter, Meleager, who killed the boar with his spear in the end. I stared at Meleager's naked muscular torso, the hate-filled expression that reminded me of someone, at the spear entering the beast's body. So dramatic and yet reverent. So naked and yet secretive. So simple. And so valuable.

I lifted the picture, carried it into the kitchen and placed it on the bench. The old frame had, as I assumed it would, a canvas stretcher attached to the back. I produced the only two tools I had brought with me and needed: an awl and wire cutters. I snapped off most of the tacks, pulled out those I would reuse, slackened the stretcher and used the awl to force out the pins. I fumbled more than I usually do; perhaps Ove had been right about motor coordination skills after all. But twenty minutes later the reproduction was finally in position in the frame and the original in the portfolio.

I hung up the picture, closed the door behind me, checked that I had not left any clues and left the kitchen with a sweaty hand round the portfolio handle.

Walking through the middle room, I cast a glance out of the window and caught a glimpse of a semi-stripped crown of a tree. I stopped. The glowing red leaves that remained made the tree look as if it were aflame in the oblique rays of sunlight that leaked out between the clouds. Rubens. The colors. They were his colors.

It was a magical moment. A moment of

triumph. A moment of metamorphosis. In such a moment you see everything so clearly that decisions which had seemed fraught with difficulty before suddenly appear as self-evident. I was going to become a father, I had planned to tell her tonight, but I knew now that this was the right moment. Now, here, at the scene of the crime, with Rubens under my arm and this beautiful, majestic tree before me. This was the moment that should be cast in bronze, the eternal memory Diana and I should share and take out on rainy days. The decision that she, unsullied, would believe was taken in a moment of lucidity and for no other reason than love for her and our child-to-be. And only I, the lion, the paterfamilias, would know the dark secret: that the zebra's throat had been savaged after an ambush, that the ground had been bloodied before the prize had been laid before them, my innocents. Yes, that's how our love should be consolidated. I took out my phone, removed one glove and selected the number of her Prada phone. I tried to formulate the sentence in my head while waiting to be connected. 'I want to give you a child, my darling.' Or: 'My darling, let me give you . . .'

John Lennon played his G11sus4 chord.

'It's been a hard day's night . . .' So true,

so true. Elated, I smiled.

But in a flash I understood.

That I could *hear* it.

That something was wrong.

I lowered my phone.

And in the distance, but clear enough, I heard the Beatles beginning to play 'A Hard Day's Night'. Her ringtone.

My feet were cemented to the grey paper on the ground.

Then they began to move in the direction of the sound, my heart like the heavy beat of kettle drums.

The sound came from behind a half-open door to the corridor on the far side of the reception rooms.

I opened the door.

It was a bedroom.

The bed in the middle of the room was made but had obviously been slept in. At the foot lay a suitcase, and beside it was a chair with some clothes draped over the back. A suit hung on a hanger in the open wardrobe. The suit Clas Greve had worn at the interview. From somewhere in the room Lennon and McCartney were singing in unison with an energy they were never to regain on subsequent records. I looked around. And knelt. Bent down. And there it was. The Prada mobile phone. Under the bed. It must have slipped out of her pocket. Presumably as he tore her trousers off. And she had not realised the phone was gone until . . . until . . .

I visualised her tempting backside this morning, the furious search through clothes and handbag.

I stood up again. Much too quickly, I suppose, for the room began to whirl around. I stuck out a hand against the wall.

The answerphone cut in, and there was her chirrupy voice.

'Hi, this is Diana. I haven't got my phone to hand . . .'

True enough.

'But you know what to do . . .'

Yes, I did. My brain had registered somewhere that I had used the ungloved hand to support myself, and that therefore I would have to remember to wipe the wall.

'Have a brilliant day!'

That might be difficult, though.

Beep.

PART THREE:
SECOND INTERVIEW

9
SECOND INTERVIEW

My father, Ian Brown, was a keen, though not a very good, chess player. He had been taught to play by his father when he was five, and he read chess manuals and studied classic games. However, he didn't teach me to play chess until I was fourteen, when my most receptive years were over. I had an aptitude for chess, though, and when I was sixteen I beat him for the first time. He smiled as though he were proud of me, but I know he hated it. He reassembled the pieces and we began a revenge match. I played with the white pieces as usual; he tried to make me believe that he was giving me an advantage. After a few moves he excused himself and went into the kitchen, where I knew he took a swig from a bottle of gin. When he returned I had swapped two pieces, but he didn't realise. Four moves later he sat gawping at my white queen opposite his black king. And he saw that the next move would be checkmate. He was so funny to look at that I couldn't restrain myself and started to laugh. And I could see from his expression that he knew what had happened. He stood up and swept all the pieces off the board. Then he hit me. My knees gave way and I fell, more out of terror than the force of the blow. He had never hit me before.

'You switched some pieces,' he hissed. 'My son does not cheat.'

I could taste blood in my mouth. The white queen lay on the floor in front of me. The crown was chipped. Hatred burned like bile through my throat and chest. I picked up the damaged queen and put it back on the board. Then the other pieces. One by one. Replaced them exactly as they had been.

'Your move, Dad.'

For that is what the player with the most cold-blooded hatred does when he has been on the point of winning and his opponent has unexpectedly hit him in the face, struck somewhere it hurts, found his terror. He doesn't lose his overview of the board but puts his terror aside and keeps to his plan. Breathes in, reconstructs, continues the game, walks away with the victory. Leaves the scene without any triumphant gestures.

I sat at the end of the table and saw Clas Greve's mouth moving. Saw his cheeks tensing and relaxing and forming words that were obviously comprehensible to Ferdinand and the two Pathfinder representatives, at any rate they were clearly satisfied, all three of them. How I hated that mouth. Hated the grey-pink gums, the solid tombstone teeth, yes, even the shape of that revolting orifice; a straight cleft between two upward-pointing corners suggesting a smile, the same incised smile with which Bjørn Borg had charmed the world. And with which Clas Greve was now seducing his future employer, Pathfinder. But most of all I hated his lips. The lips that had touched my wife's lips, my wife's skin, probably her pale red nipples and for certain her dripping wet, open vagina. I imagined I could see a blonde pubic hair in a crease in the fleshy part of his lower lip.

I had sat silently for almost half an hour while Ferdinand with imbecilic commitment had reeled off idiotic questions from the interview guide as though they were his own.

At the beginning of the interview Greve had exclusively addressed himself to me. But increasingly he realised that I was only there as an unannounced, passive monitor and that his job today was to enlighten the other three with the gospel according to Greve. He had, however, at regular intervals sent me quick questioning looks as though searching for a hint as to my role.

After a while the two representatives from Pathfinder, the company chairman and the public relations manager, had asked their questions, which naturally enough had centred around Greve's time with HOTE. And Greve had given an account of how he and HOTE had taken a leading role in the development of TRACE, a lacquer containing around a hundred transmitters per millilitre which could be applied to any object. Its advantage was that the varnish was almost invisible and just like normal varnish it adhered so firmly to the object that it was impossible to get rid of it without using a paint scraper. The disadvantage was that the transmitters were so small that their signals were too weak not to penetrate any matter denser than air that might cover the transmitters, such as water, ice, mud or the extremely thick layers of dust to which vehicles in desert wars might be subject.

On the other hand, walls, even made of thick bricks, were seldom a problem.

'Our experience was that soldiers painted with TRACE lost contact with our receivers when the dirt on them reached a certain point,' Greve said. 'We don't yet have the technology to make microscopic transmitters more powerful.'

'We do at Pathfinder,' the chairman said. He was a sparse-haired man in his fifties who kept twisting his neck at various junctures as though afraid it would stiffen, or else he had swallowed something big that he couldn't quite get down. I suspected it was an involuntary spasm caused by a muscular disease for which there was only one outcome. 'But unfortunately we don't have the TRACE technology.'

'Technologically speaking, HOTE and Pathfinder would have made the perfect married couple,' Greve said.

'Just so,' the chairman said pointedly. 'With Pathfinder as the housewife, receiving a few miserable titbits from the monthly pay packet.'

Greve chuckled. 'Quite right. Besides, HOTE's technology would be easier for Pathfinder to acquire than the other way round. That's why I believe there is only one viable route for Pathfinder. And that is to undertake the journey on its own.'

I saw the Pathfinder representatives exchange glances.

'Anyway, you have an impressive CV,

Greve,' the chairman said. 'But what we set great store by at Pathfinder is that our CEO should be a stayer . . . what do you call it in your recruitment-speak?'

'A farmer,' Ferdinand sprang to the rescue.

'A farmer, yes. A good image. In other words, someone who cultivates what is already there, who builds things up, brick by brick. Who is tough and patient. And you have a record which is erm . . . spectacular and dramatic, but it doesn't tell us if you have the stamina and doggedness that is necessary for the director we are seeking.'

Clas Greve had listened to the chairman with a serious expression and now he was nodding.

'First of all, I would like to say that I share your view of the type of director Pathfinder should be looking for. Secondly, I wouldn't have shown any interest in this challenge if I had not been that type.'

'You are that type?' the second representative from Pathfinder asked carefully, a diplomatic type I had already pigeonholed as a public relations boss before he introduced himself. I had nominated a number of them.

Clas Greve smiled. A hearty smile that not only softened the flinty face, but changed it totally. I had seen this trick of his a few times now, which was intended to show the boyish rascal he could also be. It had the same effect as the physical contact that Inbau, Reid and Buckley recommended, the intimate touch, the vote of confidence, the one that says I am laying myself bare here.

'Let me tell you a story,' Greve said, still smiling. 'It's about a matter I find hard to admit. Namely, that I am a dreadful loser. I'm the sort of person who finds it difficult to lose at heads or tails.'

Chuckles round the room.

'But I hope it will tell you something about my stamina and staying power,' he continued. 'In the BBE I was once chasing a, sad to say, pretty insignificant drug smuggler in Suriname . . .'

I could see the two Pathfinder men unconsciously leaning forward a tad. Ferdinand took care of the coffee refills while sending me a confident smile.

And Clas Greve's mouth moved. Crept forward. Devoured greedily where it had no right to be. Had she screamed? Of course she had. Diana simply couldn't hold back, such easy meat for his lusts. The first time we had made love I had been reminded of the Bernini sculpture in the Cornaro Chapel: *The Ecstasy of S. Teresa di Avila.*

Partly because of Diana's half-open mouth, the suffering, almost pain-filled facial expression, the tensed vein and the concentrated furrow in her forehead. And partly because Diana screamed, and I have always thought that Bernini's Carmelite saint is screaming as the angel pulls the arrow from her chest, ready to thrust it in again. That is what it looks like to me at any rate, in-out-in, an image of divine penetration, fucking at its most sublime, but fucking nevertheless. But not even a saint could scream like Diana. Diana's scream was a pained enjoyment, an arrow-point in the eardrum that sent shivers throughout your body. It was a lament and an enduring moan, a tone that merely rose and fell, like a model aeroplane. So piercing that after the first act of love I had woken up with a ringing in my ears, and after three weeks of lovemaking I thought I could detect the first symptoms of tinnitus; a continual torrent of water falling, or at least a brook, accompanied by a whistling sound that came and went.

I had happened to express concern about my hearing, as a joke of course, but Diana had not seen the funny side. On the contrary, she had been horrified and on the point of tears. And when we made love the next time, I had felt her soft hands around my ears, which I first perceived as a slightly unusual caress. But when they cupped around my ears forming two warm protective domes, I realised what an act of love this was. The effect was limited, from an auditory point of view — the scream still bored into the cerebral cortex — but all the greater emotionally. I am not a man given to tears, but as I came I began to sob like a baby. Probably because I knew that no one, no one else would ever love me as much as this woman.

So watching Greve now, in the certainty that she had screamed in his embrace too, I tried not to think of the question this threw up. But, just like Diana, I couldn't hold myself back: Had she covered his ears, too?

'The track led mostly through thick jungle and swampland,' Greve said. 'Eight-hour marches. Nevertheless, we were always a bit behind, always just too late. The others gave up, one by one. Fever, dysentery, snake bites or sheer, utter exhaustion. And the guy was, of course, of minor significance. The jungle devours your reasoning. I was the youngest, yet in the end I was the one who was given the command. And the machete.'

Diana and Greve. When I had parked the Volvo in the garage, after driving home from Greve's apartment, I had for a second considered rolling down the window, letting the motor run and breathing in carbon dioxide, monoxide, or whatever the fuck it is you breathe in; anyway, it is supposed to be a pleasant death.

'After following his trail for sixty-three days over three hundred and twenty kilometres of the worst terrain you can imagine, the hunting pack was reduced to me and a young stripling from Groningen who was too stupid to go mad. I contacted HQ and had a Niether terrier flown in. Do you know the breed? No? It is the best hunting dog in the world. And infinitely loyal, it attacks everything you point to, whatever the size. A friend for life. Literally. The helicopter dropped the dog, a whelp of just over a year old, in the middle of the jungle in the vast Sipaliwini district, that's where they drop cocaine, too. The drop zone turned out to be ten kilometres from where we were hiding, though. It would be a miracle if it survived for twenty-four hours in the jungle, let alone tracked us down. It took the dog just under two hours to find us.'

Greve leaned back in his chair. He was in total control now.

'I called it Sidewinder. After the heat-seeking missile, you know? I loved that dog. That's why I have a Niether terrier today. I went to collect it from Holland yesterday; in fact, it is Sidewinder's grandchild.'

Diana had been sitting in the living room watching the news when I came home after burgling Greve. There was a press conference with Inspector Brede Sperre behind a forest of microphones. He was talking about a murder. A murder that had been solved. A murder he alone had solved by the sound of it. Sperre's voice had a masculine jar to it, like a radio with interference, specks of outage, a typewriter with a worn letter you could just make out on paper. 'The perperator will appear before court to-orrow. Any other questions?' Every trace of east Oslo was gone from his language now, but according to Google he had played basketball for Ammerud for eight years. He had left Police College as the second highest performer in his year's intake. In a personal interview for a women's magazine he had refused to say whether he had a significant other, for professional reasons. Any partner would be subject to undesirable attention from the media and the criminal elements he was chasing, he said. But nothing in the pin-up photos for the same magazine — half-unbuttoned shirt, half-closed eyes, trace of a half-smile — signalled a partner.

I had stood behind Diana's chair.

'He's started in Kripos now,' she said. 'Murder and all that.'

I knew that of course, I googled Brede Sperre every week to find out what he was doing, whether he had made an announcement to the press about a clampdown on art thieves. On top of that, I made my own enquiries about Sperre whenever an occasion presented itself. Oslo is not a big town. I knew things.

'A shame for you,' I said, relieved. 'No more visits to the gallery from him.'

She had laughed and looked up at me, and I had looked down at her, smiled, and our faces were upside down in relation to each other. And for an instant I thought that the business with Greve had not happened, it had just been something I had painted in slightly too vivid colors, the way people do sometimes, trying to imagine the worst thing that can happen, if for no other reason than to feel what it is like, to see if it would be tolerable. And as if to confirm that it was just a dream, I had said I had changed my mind, she was right, we really ought to book the trip to Tokyo in December. But she had looked at me in surprise and said that she couldn't close the gallery right before Christmas, that was the peak period, wasn't it? And no one went to Tokyo in December, it was freezing cold. What about spring then? I said. I could book tickets. And she had said that was a little too much long-range planning, wasn't it, couldn't we just wait and see? Fine, I had answered and said I was going to bed, I was really tired.

And when I was downstairs, I had gone into the nursery, over to the *mizuko jizo* figure and knelt down. The altar was still untouched. Too much long-range planning. Wait and see. Then I had taken the little red box out of my pocket, run my fingertips over the smooth surface and placed it beside the little stone Buddha that kept an eye on our water child.

'Two days later we found the drug smuggler in a small village. He was being kept hidden by a very young foreign girl who, it later transpired, was his girlfriend. They usually find themselves such innocent-looking girls and then use them as couriers. Until the girl is caught by customs and gets life. Sixty-five days had passed since the hunt had started.' Clas Greve drew a deep breath. 'For my part, another sixty-five would have been fine.'

In the end it was the public relations manager who broke the ensuing silence. 'And you arrested the man?'

'Not only him. He and his girlfriend gave

us enough information to arrest twenty-three of his colleagues at a later point.'

'How . . .' the chairman started. 'How do you arrest someone like that?'

'In this case it wasn't so dramatic,' Greve said with his hands behind his head. 'Equality has come to Suriname. When we stormed the house he had laid down his weapons on the kitchen table and was helping his girlfriend with a mincer.'

The chairman burst into laughter and glanced across at the public relations manager who obediently chimed in with a jerky, though more tentative, laugh. The chorus became a three-part harmony as Ferdinand added to the merriment with his bright squeal. I studied the four shiny faces while thinking about how dearly I wished I had a hand grenade at this very moment.

After Ferdinand had rounded off the interview, I made it my job to escort Clas Greve out while the other three took a break before summing up.

I accompanied Greve to the lift doors and pressed the button.

'Convincing performance,' I said, folding my hands in front of my suit trousers and peering up at the floor indicator. 'You're a big hit with your seduction skills.'

'Seduction . . . not sure about that. I assume you don't perceive it as dishonourable to sell yourself, Roger.'

'Not at all. I would've done exactly the same if I'd been you.'

'Thank you. When will you be writing the report?'

'Tonight.'

'Good.'

The lift doors opened, we stepped in and stood waiting.

'I was just wondering,' I said. 'The person you were pursuing . . .'

'Yes?'

'It wasn't by any chance the same person who had tortured you in the cellar?'

Greve smiled. 'How did you know?'

'Pure guesswork.' The lift doors slid into place. 'And you confined yourself to arresting him?'

Greve raised an eyebrow. 'Do you find that difficult to believe?'

I shrugged. The lift began to move.

'The plan was to kill him,' Greve said.

'Did you have so much to avenge?'

'Yes.'

'And how do you answer to murder charges in the Dutch army?'

'You make sure you aren't caught. Curacit.'

'Poison? As in poison-tipped arrows?'

'That's what headhunters use in our part of the world.'

I assumed the ambiguity was deliberate.

'A solution of Curacit in a rubber ball the size of a grape with a barely detectable sharp needle. You hide it in the target's mattress. When he goes to bed the needle pricks the skin and the weight forces the poison in the rubber ball into his body.'

'But he was at home,' I said. 'And had a witness in this girl.'

'Precisely.'

'So how did you get him to snitch on his pals?'

'I offered him a deal. I got my colleague to hold him down while I fed his hand into the mincer and said we would grind it into pieces and let him watch our dog eat the minced flesh. Then he talked.'

I nodded, visualising the scene. The lift doors opened and we walked to the front entrance. I held the door open for him. 'And what about after he talked?'

'What about it?' Greve squinted up at the sky.

'Did you keep your part of the deal?'

'I . . .' Greve said, fishing out a pair of Maui Jim titanium sunglasses from his breast pocket and putting them on, 'always keep my part of the deal.'

'A measly arrest then? Was it worth two months of chasing and risking your own life?'

Greve laughed softly. 'You don't understand, Roger. Giving up a chase is never an option for types like me. I'm like my dog, a result of genes and training. Risk doesn't exist. Once fired up, I'm a heat-seeking missile that cannot be stopped, that basically seeks its own destruction. Put your first-year psychology course to the test on that.' He placed a hand on my arm, gave a thin smile and whispered: 'But keep the diagnosis to yourself.'

I stood holding the door. 'And the girl? How did you get her to talk?'

'She was fourteen years old.'

'And?'

'What do you think?'

'I don't know.'

Greve released a deep sigh. 'I don't know how you've got such an impression of me, Roger. I don't interrogate underage girls. I took her with me to Paramaribo, bought a ticket with my soldier's wage and put her on the first plane home to her parents before the Surinamese police got their hooks into her.'

My eyes followed him as he strode over to

a silver-grey Lexus GS 430 in the car park.

The autumn weather was stunningly beautiful. It had rained on my wedding day.

10
HEART CONDITION

I pressed Lotte Madsen's doorbell for the third time. In fact, her name was not on the bell, but I had rung at enough doors in Eilert Sundts gate to know that it was hers.

Darkness and the temperature had fallen early and fast. I was shivering in my shoes. She had hesitated for a long time when I rang her from work after lunch to ask whether I could visit her at around eight. And when, at length, she had, with a monosyllable, granted me an audience, I knew she must have broken a vow she had made to herself: not to have anything more to do with this man who had left her so emphatically.

The lock buzzed and I tore at the door as if frightened it was the only chance I would get. I went upstairs; I didn't want to risk ending up in the lift with some nosy neighbour who had time on their hands to gawp, take note and draw conclusions.

Lotte had opened the door a crack and I glimpsed her pale face.

I stepped inside and closed the door behind me.

'Here I am again.'

She didn't answer. She usually didn't.

'How are you?' I asked.

Lotte Madsen shrugged. She looked just the way she had the first time I saw her: a timid whelp, small and scruffy with fearful, brown puppy eyes. Greasy hair hung lifelessly down on both sides of her face, her posture was stooped, and shapeless, colorless clothes gave the impression that she was a woman who spent more time concealing rather than drawing attention to her body. Which she had no reason to do; Lotte was slim, shapely and had smooth, perfect skin. But she radiated the kind of submissiveness I imagine you find in those women who are always being beaten up, always being left, never getting the deal they deserve. That may have been what aroused something that I had hitherto never guessed I possessed: a protective instinct. As well as the less platonic feelings that were the springboard for our short-term relationship. Or affair. Affair. Relationship is present tense, affair past.

The first time I saw Lotte Madsen was at

one of Diana's private views in the summer. Lotte had stood at the other end of the room, fixed her gaze on me and reacted a little too late. Catching women in the act like this is always flattering, but when I saw that her gaze was not going to return to me, I ambled over to the picture she was studying and introduced myself. Mostly out of curiosity, of course, since I have always been — considering my nature — sensationally faithful to Diana. Malicious tongues might claim that my fidelity was based more on risk analysis than love. That I knew Diana played in a higher league than I did, attraction-wise, and that consequently I was not in a position to take such risks unless I was willing to play in lower divisions for the rest of my days.

Maybe. But Lotte Madsen was in my division.

She looked like a freaky artist, and I automatically assumed that was what she was, or possibly the lover of one. There was no other way of explaining how a pair of limp, brown cord jeans and a boring, tight grey sweater could have gained admission to the private view. But it turned out she was a buyer. Not with her own money, naturally, but for a company in Denmark needing to fit out its new rooms in Odense.

She was a freelance translator from Norwegian and Spanish: brochures, articles, user manuals, films and the odd specialist book. The firm was one of her more regular customers. She spoke softly and with a tentative little smile as if she didn't understand why anyone would waste their time talking to her. I was immediately taken with Lotte. Yes, I think taken is the right word. She was sweet. And small. One fifty-nine. I didn't need to ask, I have a good eye for heights. By the time I left that evening, I had her phone number to send her photographs of other pictures by the exhibiting artist. At that point I probably thought my intentions were honest.

The next time we met was over a cappuccino at Sushi&Coffee. I had explained to her that I would rather show her printouts of the pictures than email them because screens — just like me — can lie.

After quickly flicking through the pictures, I told her I was unhappy in my marriage, but I was sticking it out because I felt obliged to do so because of my wife's boundless love for me. It's the world's oldest cliché in the married-man-picking-up-unmarried-woman or vice versa scenario, but I had an inkling she hadn't heard it before. I hadn't either for that matter, but I

158

had definitely heard *of* it and presumed it worked.

She had checked her watch and said she had to go, and I had asked if I could pop round one evening to show her another artist I considered a much better investment for her customer in Odense. She had hesitantly agreed.

I had taken along some poor pictures from the gallery and a bottle of good red wine from the cellar. She had appeared resigned to her fate from the moment she had opened the door to me that warm summer evening.

I had told her amusing stories about my blunders, the kind that seem to put you in a bad light, but actually show that you have enough self-confidence and success to be able to afford self-deprecation. She said she was an only child, had travelled round the world with her parents when she was young and that her father was the chief engineer for an international waterworks company. She didn't belong to any particular country; Norway was as good as anywhere. That was it. For someone who spoke several different languages she said very little. Translator, I had thought. She preferred other people's stories to her own.

She had asked me about my wife. Your wife, she said, even though she must have known Diana's name as she had been invited to the private view. In that sense she certainly made it easier for me. And for herself.

I had told her that my marriage had received a buffeting when 'my wife' became pregnant and I didn't want to have the baby. And, according to her, had persuaded her to have an abortion.

'Did you?' Lotte had asked.

'I suppose so.'

I had seen something change in Lotte's expression and asked what it was.

'My parents persuaded me to have an abortion. Because I was a teenager and the child would not have a father. I still hate them for that. Them and myself.'

I had gulped. Gulped and explained. 'Our foetus had Down's syndrome. Eighty-five per cent of all parents who go through this experience opt for abortion.'

I had instantly regretted saying that. What had I been thinking? That Down's syndrome would make my not wanting to have a child with my own wife more understandable?

'There is a great probability that your wife would have lost the child anyway,' Lotte had said. 'Down's syndrome often goes hand in hand with a heart condition.'

Heart condition, I had thought, and

inwardly thanked her for being a team player, for making things simple for me once again. For us. An hour later we had taken off all our clothes and I was celebrating a victory that for a person more accustomed to conquests certainly would have appeared cheap but which put me on cloud nine for days. Weeks. To be more precise, three and a half. I had a lover, nothing less. Whom I left after twenty-four days.

As I looked at her now, in front of me in the hall, it seemed quite unreal.

Hamsun wrote that we humans are soon sated with love. We don't want anything that is served up in excessively large portions. Are we really so banal? Apparently. But that wasn't what happened to me. What happened was that I was assailed by a bad conscience. Not because I couldn't return Lotte's love but because I loved Diana. It had been an ineluctable realisation, but the final blow came in something of a bizarre episode. It was late summer, the twenty-fourth day of sin, and we had gone to bed in Lotte's cramped two-room flat in Eilert Sundts gate. Before that we had been talking all evening — or, to be more precise, I had been talking. Describing and explaining life the way I see it. I'm good at that, in a

Paulo Coelho kind of way, that is, a way which fascinates the intellectually amenable of us and irritates the more demanding listener. Lotte's melancholic brown eyes had hung on my lips, swallowed every word, I could literally see her stepping into my world of homespun fantasy, her brain assimilating my reasoning into hers, her falling in love with my mind. As for myself, I had long fallen in love with her love, the loyal eyes, the silence and the low, almost inaudible, moaning during lovemaking that was so different from the whine of Diana's circular saw. Falling in love had put me in a state of constant wantonness for three and a half weeks. So when I finally stopped the monologue, we just looked at each other, I bent forward, placed my hand on her breast, a shiver ran through her or perhaps me — and we made a charge for the bedroom door and the 101-centimetre-wide IKEA bed with the inviting name of Brekke, or break. This evening the moaning had been louder than usual, and she had whispered something Danish in my ear that I didn't understand, since from an objective standpoint Danish is a difficult language — Danish children learn to speak later than any other children in Europe — but nonetheless I found it uncommonly erotic and increased the tempo. Usually, Lotte had been some-what against these increases in tempo, but on this evening she had grabbed my but-tocks and pulled me into her, which I interpreted as a wish for a further step-up both in thrust and frequency. I obeyed while concentrating on my father in the open cof-fin during the funeral, a method that had proved to be effective in preventing prema-ture ejaculation. Or, in this case, any ejacu-lation at all. Even though Lotte said she was on the pill, the thought of pregnancy gave me palpitations. I didn't know whether Lotte reached an orgasm when we made love; her quiet, controlled manner suggested to me that an orgasm would only manifest itself as tiny ripples on the surface, which I might simply fail to notice. And she was much too delicate a creature for me to expose her to any stress by asking. That was why I was totally unprepared for what hap-pened. I sensed I had to stop but allowed myself a final hard poke. And sensed that I had hit something deep inside. Her body stiffened as her eyes and mouth were thrust open wide. This was followed by some trembling and for one tiny insane moment I was afraid I had induced an epileptic fit. Then I felt something hot, even hotter than her vagina, enveloping my genitals, and then a tidal wave washed against my stomach, hips and balls.

I levered myself up with my arms and stared in disbelief and horror at the point where our bodies were conjoined. Her lower abdomen was contracting as if she wanted to eject me, she gave a deep groan, a kind of lowing I had never heard before, and then came the next wave. The water poured out of her, spurted out between our hips and ran down into the mattress that still had not succeeded in absorbing the first wave. My God, I thought. I have poked a hole in her. Panicking, my brain searched for causal connections. She's pregnant, I thought. And I have just poked a hole in that bag containing the foetus, and now all of the crap is soaking into the bed. My God, we're swimming in life and death, it's a water child, another water child! Well, I might have read about women's so-called wet orgasms, OK, I may have seen it in the odd porn film too, but I had considered it a trick, a sham, a male fantasy about having a partner with equal ejaculation rights. All I could think as I lay there was that this was the retribution, the gods' punishment for my persuading Diana to have an abortion: for my killing another innocent child with my reckless prick.

I struggled onto the floor, pulling the duvet off the bed with me. Lotte gave a start, but I didn't notice her huddled-up naked body, I just stared at the dark circle still spreading outwards on the sheet. Slowly I realised what had happened. Or, even more important, what by a happy chance had not happened. But the damage was done, it was too late, there was no way back.

'I have to go,' I said. 'This cannot go on.'

'What are you doing?' Lotte, barely audible, whispered from her foetal position.

'I'm terribly sorry,' I said. 'But I have to go home and beg Diana for forgiveness.'

'You won't get it though,' Lotte whispered.

I didn't hear a sound from the bedroom while rinsing the smell of her off my hands and mouth in the bathroom, and I left, closing the front door carefully behind me.

And now — three months later — I was standing in her hall again, and I knew that it was not Lotte but me who had puppy eyes this time.

'Can you forgive me?' I asked.

'Couldn't she?' Lotte asked in a monotone. But perhaps it was just Danish intonation.

'I never told her what happened.'

'Why not?'

'I don't know,' I said. 'It's very likely that

I have a heart condition.'

She sent me a long searching look. And I caught the suggestion of a smile at the back of those brown and much too melancholic eyes of hers.

'Why are you here?'

'Because I can't forget you.'

'Why are you here?' she repeated with a firmness I had not heard before.

'I just think we should —'

'Why, Roger?'

I sighed. 'I don't owe her anything any more. She has a lover.'

A long silence ensued.

She jutted out her bottom lip a fraction. 'Has she broken your heart?'

I nodded.

'And now you want me to put it together for you again?'

I hadn't heard this woman of few words express herself in such a light, effortless fashion before.

'You can't, Lotte.'

'No, I suppose not. Do you know who her lover is?'

'Just a guy who's applied for a job with us he won't get, let me put it like that. Can we talk about something else?'

'Just talk?'

'You decide.'

'Yes, I will. Just talk. And that's your department.'

'Yep. I brought a bottle of wine.'

She gave an imperceptible nod of the head. Then she turned, and I followed.

I talked us through the wine and fell asleep on the sofa. When I awoke, I was lying with my head in her lap and she was stroking my hair.

'Do you know what the first thing I noticed about you was?' she asked when she spotted that I was awake again.

'My hair,' I said.

'Have I told you before?'

'No,' I said, looking at my watch. Half past nine. It was time to go home. Well, the ruins of a home. I dreaded it.

'May I come back?' I asked.

I saw her hesitate.

'I need you,' I said.

I knew this argument didn't carry much weight. It was borrowed from a woman who chose QPR because the club had made her feel wanted. But it was the only argument I had.

'I don't know,' she said. 'I'll have to think about it.'

Diana was sitting in the living room reading a large book when I went in. Van Morrison was singing '. . . *someone like you makes it all worth while'*, and she didn't hear me until I was standing in front of her and reading the title on the front cover out loud.

'*A Child is Born?*'

She gave a start, but brightened up and hurriedly put the book back on the shelf behind her.

'You're late, darling. Have you been doing something nice or just working?'

'Both,' I said, walking over to the living-room window. The garage was bathed in white moonlight, but Ove wasn't due to collect the painting for several hours. 'I've been answering a few phone calls and thinking a bit about which candidate to nominate for Pathfinder.'

She clapped her hands with enthusiasm. 'So exciting. It's going to be the one I helped you with, that . . . oh, what's his name again?'

'Greve.'

'Clas Greve! I'm becoming so forgetful. I hope he buys a really expensive painting from me when he finds out. I deserve that, don't I?'

She gave a bright laugh, stretched out her slim legs which had been tucked beneath her and yawned. It was like a claw tightening round my heart and squeezing it like a water balloon, and I had to turn quickly back to the window so that she wouldn't see the pain in my face. The woman I had believed devoid of all deception was not only successfully maintaining the mask, she was playing the role like a professional. I swallowed and waited until I was sure I had my voice under control.

'Greve is not the right person,' I said, scrutinising her reflection in the window. 'I'm going to select someone else.'

Semi-professional. She didn't tackle this one quite so well. I saw her chin drop.

'You're joking, darling. He's perfect! You said so yourself . . .'

'I was mistaken.'

'Mistaken?' To my great satisfaction I could hear a low screech in her voice. 'What in the name of God do you mean?'

'Greve is a foreigner. He's under one eighty. And he suffers from serious personality disorders.'

'Under one eighty! My God, Roger, you're under one seventy. You're the one with the personality disorder!'

That hurt. Not the bit about the personality disorders, she might have been right about that, of course. I strained to keep my voice calm.

'Why the passion, Diana? I had hopes for

Clas Greve too, but people disappointing us and not living up to expectations is something that goes on all the time.'

'But . . . but you're wrong. Can't you see that? He's a real man!'

I turned to her with an attempt at a condescending smile. 'Listen, Diana, I'm one of the best at what I do. And that is judging and selecting people. I may make mistakes in my private life . . .'

I saw a tiny twitch in her face.

'But never in my work. Never.'

She was silent.

'I'm exhausted,' I said. 'I didn't sleep much last night. Goodnight.'

Lying in bed, I heard her footsteps above. Restless, to and fro. I didn't hear any voices, but I knew she tended to pace the floor when she was on the phone. It struck me that this was a feature of the generations that had grown up without cordless communication, that we moved about while talking on the telephone as though still fascinated that it was possible. I had read somewhere that modern man spends six times as many hours communicating as our forefathers. So we communicate more, but do we communicate any better? Why, for example, had I not confronted Diana with the fact that I knew she and Greve had made love in his apartment? Was it because I knew she would not be able to communicate why, that I would be left to my own assumptions and conjecture? She might have told me it was a chance meeting, for example, a one-off, but I would have known it was not. No woman tries to manipulate her husband into giving a well-paid job to a man because she has had casual sex with him.

There were other reasons for keeping my mouth shut, though. For as long as I pretended not to know about Diana and Greve, no one could accuse me of being too partial to assess his application, and instead of having to leave Alfa's appointment to Ferdinand, I could enjoy my pathetic little revenge in peace and quiet. Then there was the matter of explaining to Diana how I had come to have suspicions. After all, revealing to Diana that I was a thief and regularly broke into other people's homes was out of the question.

I tossed and turned in bed, listening to her stiletto heels banging down their monotonous, incomprehensible Morse signals to me. I wanted to sleep. I wanted to dream. I wanted to escape. And wake up having forgotten everything. For that was of course the most important reason for not saying anything to her. As long as things remained unsaid, there was still a chance that we could forget. That we could sleep and dream in such a way that when we awoke it had disappeared, become something abstract, scenes from something that only took place in our heads, on the same level as those treacherous thoughts and fantasies that are the daily infidelity in every — even the most all-consuming — loving relationship.

It occurred to me that if she was talking on a mobile phone now, she must have bought a new one. And that the sight of the new one would be irrefutable, concrete, commonplace evidence that what had happened was not just a dream.

When at last she entered the bedroom and undressed, I pretended I was asleep. But in a pale strip of moonlight that crept in between the curtains, I managed to catch a glimpse of her switching off the phone before slipping it into her trouser pocket. And that it was the same one. A black Prada. So I might have been dreaming. I felt sleep catch hold of me and begin to drag me down. Or perhaps he had bought one just like it. The drift downwards came to a halt. Or perhaps she had found her phone and they had met again. I rose upwards, broke the surface and knew that I was not going to sleep tonight.

At midnight I was still awake and through the open window I thought I heard a faint noise from the garage which might have been Ove, come to collect the Rubens. Even though I tried, I did not hear him leaving. Perhaps I had gone to sleep after all. I dreamed about a world under the sea. Happy, smiling people, silent women and children with speech bubbles rumbling and rising out of their mouths. Nothing pointing towards the nightmare that was awaiting me at the other end of my sleep.

11
CURACIT

I got up at eight o'clock and ate breakfast on my own. For someone sleeping the sleep of the guilty Diana slept extremely well. I had only had a couple of hours myself. At a quarter to nine I went down to the garage and unlocked it. From an open window nearby I recognised the tones of Turbonegro, not by the music, but by the English pronunciation. The light came on automatically and shone on my Volvo S80 waiting majestically but subserviently for its master. I grabbed the door handle and immediately recoiled. Someone was sitting in the driver's seat! After the first fright had passed I saw that it was Ove Kjikerud's oar-blade face. Night work over the last few days had clearly taken its toll for he was sitting there with closed eyes and a half-open mouth. And he was obviously fast asleep because when I opened the door he still didn't react.

I used the voice from the three-month

sergeants' course I had gone on, against my father's wishes: 'Good morning, Kjikerud!'

He didn't stir an eyelid. I inhaled to blow a reveille when I noticed that the ceiling liner was open and the edge of the Rubens was sticking out. A sudden chill, as when a fluffy spring cloud sails past the sun, made me shudder. And instead of making more noise, I grabbed his shoulder and shook him lightly. Still no reaction.

I shook harder. His head frolicked to and fro on his shoulders, without any resistance.

I placed my first finger and thumb against where I thought the main artery ran, but it was impossible to determine whether the pulse I felt came from him or my wildly racing heart. But he was cold. Too cold, wasn't he? With trembling fingers I opened his eyelids. And that settled the matter. Involuntarily, I backed away when I saw the lifeless black pupils staring at me.

I have always thought of myself as the kind of person who can think clearly in critical situations, someone who won't panic. Of course, that could be because there have never really been any situations in my life that were critical enough for me to panic. Apart from the time when Diana became pregnant, of course, and on that occasion I hadn't found it difficult to panic. So perhaps

175

I was a panicky type after all. In any case, at this moment decidedly irrational thoughts entered my head. Like the car needing a wash. That Kjikerud's shirt — with a Dior label sewn on — had presumably been bought on one of his holidays in Thailand. And that Turbonegro were actually what everyone thought they were not, that is, a decent band. But I knew what was happening, that I was about to lose my grip, and I clenched my eyes shut and blasted the thoughts out of my head. Then I opened my eyes again and had to concede that a tiny little bit of hope had managed to sneak in. But no, the realities were the same, the body of Ove Kjikerud was still sitting there.

The first conclusion I drew was simple: Ove Kjikerud had to go. If anyone found him here, all would be revealed. Resolutely, I pushed Kjikerud forward against the steering wheel, leaned over his back, grabbed him round the chest and dragged him out. He was heavy and his arms were pulled upwards as though he was trying to wriggle out of my grasp. I lifted him up again and took a new hold, but the same thing happened; his hands swung up in my face and a finger got caught in the corner of my mouth. I felt a bitten-down nail scrape against my tongue and in horror I spat, but the taste of bitter nicotine remained. I dropped him onto the garage floor and opened the car trunk, but when I tried to pull him up, only his jacket and fake Dior shirt followed; he remained firmly on the cement floor. I cursed, grabbed the inside of his trouser belt with one hand, jerked him up and shoved him head first into the 480-litre trunk. His head hit the floor with a soft thud. I slammed the trunk lid and rubbed my hands together, the way one often does after a manual job well done.

Then I went back to the driver's side. There were no traces of blood on the seat, which was covered with one of those wooden-ball mats, the type that taxi drivers use the whole world over. What the hell had caused Ove's death? Heart failure? Brain haemorrhage? Overdose of some substance or other? I realised that an amateur diagnosis was wasted time now, got in and, strange to say, noted that the wooden balls had retained body heat. The mat was the only thing of value I had inherited from my father, who had used it because of piles, and I did too as a precaution against the affliction in case it was hereditary. A sudden pain in one buttock made me jerk forward and hit my knee against the wheel. I eased myself out of the car. The pain had already gone, but something had undoubtedly stung me. I bent over the seat and stared, but could not see anything unusual in the dim compartment lighting. Could it have been a wasp? Not this late in the autumn. Something flashed between the rows of wooden balls. I bent closer. A thin, almost invisible, metal point protruded. Sometimes the brain reasons too fast for comprehension to keep abreast. That is the only explanation I have for the vague premonition that made my heart race even before I had raised the mat and caught sight of the object.

Sure enough, it was the same size as a grape. And made of rubber, just as Greve had elucidated. Not completely round; the base was flat, apparently so that the tip of the needle always pointed straight up. I held the rubber ball against my ear and shook it, but could hear nothing. Fortunately for me the entire contents had been pressed into Ove Kjikerud when he sat down on the rubber ball. I rubbed my buttock and checked for any effects. I was a bit dizzy, but who wouldn't have been after shifting the body of a colleague and being stabbed in the arse by a bloody Curacit needle, a murder weapon that had, in all likelihood, been meant for me? I could feel myself getting the giggles; now and then fear has that effect on me. I closed my eyes and breathed in. Deep. Concentrated. The laughter disappeared; anger took its place. It was fucking unbelievable. Or was it? Wasn't it exactly what one should expect, that a violent psychopath like Clas Greve would get rid of any husband? I kicked the tire hard. Once, twice. A grey mark appeared on the tip of my John Lobb shoe.

But how had Greve gained access to the car? How the hell had . . . ?

The garage door opened and the answer walked in.

12
NATASHA

Diana stared at me from the garage door. She had obviously got dressed in a hurry and her hair was sticking out in all directions. Her voice was a barely audible whisper.

'What's happened?'

I stared at her with the same question shooting through my brain. And felt my already broken heart being crumbled into even smaller bits from the answer I received.

Diana. My Diana. It couldn't have been anyone else. She had put the poison under the seat mat. She and Greve had colluded.

'I saw this needle sticking up from the seat as I was about to sit down,' I said, holding out the rubber ball.

She approached me, the murder weapon carefully held in her hand. Tellingly careful.

'You *saw* this needle?' she said without managing to hide the scepticism in her voice.

'I have sharp eyes,' I said, although I don't think she picked up on, or could be bothered with, the bitter double meaning.

'Lucky you didn't sit on it then,' she said, examining the small object. 'What is it actually?'

Yes, she certainly was a professional.

'I don't know,' I said airily. 'What did you want here?'

She looked at me, her mouth dropped open and for a second I was staring into a void.

'I . . .'

'Yes, darling?'

'I was lying in bed and I heard you go down to the garage, but the car didn't start up and drive off. Naturally enough, I wondered if something had happened. And in a sense I was right.'

'Well, nothing really happened. It's just a little needle, darling.'

'Needles like that can be dangerous, my love!'

'Can they?'

'Didn't you know? HIV, rabies, all sorts of viruses and infections.'

She came closer, I recognised the movements, the way her eyes softened, the lips pouted; she was going to hug me. But the embrace was interrupted, something had stopped her, something in my eyes perhaps.

'Oh dear,' she said, looking down at the rubber ball and putting it on the workbench I would never, ever use. Then she took one quick pace towards me, put her arms around me, stooped a little to reduce the height difference, laid her chin on the side of my neck and ran her left hand through my hair.

'I'm a bit worried about you, you know, my love.'

It was like being embraced by a stranger. Everything was different with her now, even her smell. Or was it his? It was revolting. Her hand went back and forth in a slow massaging movement as if she were shampooing me, as if her enthusiasm for my hair was reaching new heights at precisely this moment. I felt like hitting her, hitting her with a flat hand. Flat so that I could feel the contact, the smack of skin on skin, feel the pain and the shock.

Instead I closed my eyes and let her do it, let her massage me, soften me, please me. I may be a very sick man.

'I have to go to work,' I said when she didn't seem to want to stop. 'I have to have the nomination tied up by twelve o'clock.'

But she wouldn't let go, and in the end I had to release myself from her embrace. I saw a glint in the corner of her eye.

'What is it?' I asked.

But she wouldn't answer, just shook her head.

'Diana . . .'

'Have a good day,' she whispered with a little quiver to her voice. 'I love you.'

Then she was out of the door.

I wanted to run after her, but stood still. Comforting your own murderer, where was the sense in that? Where was the sense in anything? So I got into the car, exhaled deeply and looked at myself in the rear-view mirror.

'Survive, Roger,' I whispered. 'Pull yourself together and survive.'

Then I shoved the Rubens back under the lining, closed it up, started the car, heard the garage door go up behind me, reversed out and drove slowly round the bends down towards Oslo.

Ove's car was parked by the pavement four hundred metres away. Good, it could stay there for weeks without anyone reacting, until the snow and the snow ploughs came. I was more concerned that in my car I had a corpse to dispose of. I considered the problem. Paradoxically enough, it was now that my precautions when dealing with Kjikerud would receive their full reward. Once I had dumped the body somewhere, no one would be able to establish a link between the two of us. But where?

The first solution that came to mind was the waste incineration plant at Grønmo. Before I did anything else I would have to find something to wrap the body in, then I could drive right up to the plant, open the trunk and manoeuvre the body onto the ramp and from there down into the crackling sea of flames. There was a risk that other waste-disposers would be standing around me, not least staff, monitoring the incinerator. What about burning it myself in some far-flung spot? Apparently human bodies burn pretty badly. I had read that in India they reckon it takes ten hours to burn an average funeral pyre. What about driving back to the garage after Diana had left for the gallery and finally using the workbench and compass saw that my father-in-law without any apparent irony had given me as a Christmas present? Hack the body up into suitably sized chunks, wrap them in plastic together with a rock or two and then sink the packs in some of the hundreds of woodland lakes around Oslo?

I banged my fist against my forehead several times. What the hell was I thinking of? Hack the body up, why? First of all: hadn't I seen enough episodes of *CSI* to know that that was asking to be found out? A drop of blood here, marks from the teeth of father-in-law's saw there and I would be up shit creek. Secondly: why make any effort to hide the body? Why not just find a relatively deserted bridge and hoist Kjikerud's earthly remains over the parapet? The body would perhaps float to the surface and be found, but so what? There was nothing that could link me to the murder, I didn't know any Ove Kjikerud, and I couldn't even spell the word 'Curacit'.

The choice fell on Lake Maridal. It was only a ten-minute drive from town; no one would be around on a midweek morning. I rang Ida-Oda and said I would be late in today.

I drove for half an hour and had passed a few million cubic metres of forest and two hill billy settlements lying at such a shockingly short distance from Norway's capital. But there, on a gravel byroad was the bridge I was after. I stopped the car and waited for five minutes. No people, cars or houses were in seeing or hearing range, just the odd chilling bird cry. A raven? Something black, anyway. As black as the mysterious still water only a metre beneath the low wooden bridge. Perfect.

I got out and opened the trunk. Ove was

lying as I had left him, face down, his arms by his sides and his hips at an angle with his backside sticking up. I took a last glance around to make sure I was alone. Then I acted. With speed and efficiency.

The splash as the body hit the water was surprisingly restrained, more like a squelch, as if the lake had decided to be my fellow conspirator in this dark deed. I leaned against the railing and stared down at the silent, closed lake. I considered what to do next. And while I was doing that Ove Kjikerud seemed to be rising up to meet me; a pale green face with wide eyes that wanted to surface, a ghost with mud in its mouth and seagrass in its hair. I was thinking that I needed a whisky to steady my nerves when the face broke the surface of the lake and continued to rise towards me.

I screamed. And the corpse screamed, a rattling noise that seemed to drain the air around me of oxygen.

Then it was gone again, swallowed up by the black lake.

I stared down into the dark. Had it happened? Of course it had bloody happened, the echo was still rolling round the treetops.

I swung myself over the railing. Held my breath, waited for my body to be enclosed by ice-cold water. A shock ran through me from my heels to my head. And I discovered that I was standing with the water just over my waist, and that there was something moving under one foot. I stuck my hand down in the muddy water, grabbed hold of what I at first thought was seagrass until I felt the scalp beneath and pulled. Ove Kjikerud's face reappeared, he blinked water off his eyelashes, and again it was there, the deep rattle of a man who was drawing air for all he was worth.

It was too much. And for a moment I just wanted to let go of him and run away.

But I couldn't do that, could I?

In any event I started to drag him towards the bank by the end of the bridge. Ove's consciousness took another timeout and I had to fight to keep his head above water. Several times I almost lost my balance on the soft, slippery bed that shifted under my now ruined John Lobb shoes. But after a few minutes I had managed to haul both of us onto the bank and then into the car.

I rested my head against the wheel and breathed out.

The sodding bird cackled in derision as the wheels spun in the direction of the wooden bridge and we drove away.

As I have said, I had never been to Ove's

home, but I had his address. I opened the glove compartment, took out the black GPS and tapped in the street name and number, narrowly avoiding an oncoming car. The GPS calculated, reasoned and reduced the driving distance. Analytically and without any emotional involvement. Even the woman's gentle, controlled voice guiding me sounded unaffected by the circumstances. I had to be like that now, I told myself. Act correctly, like a machine, don't make stupid mistakes.

Half an hour later I was at the address. It was a quiet, narrow street. Kjikerud's small, old place lay at the far end, with a green wall of dark spruce forest in the background. I came to a halt in front of the steps, cast an eye over the house and established yet again that hideous architecture is not a modern invention.

Ove sat in the seat beside me, as hideous as sin as well, ashen and so wet that his clothes gurgled while I was searching his pockets and finally found a set of keys.

I shook some life into him and he stared at me through bleary eyes.

'Can you walk?' I asked.

He eyed me as though I were an alien. His jaw jutted forward even further than normal and made him look like a cross between the stone figures on Easter Island and Bruce Springsteen.

I walked round the car, dragged him out and leaned him up against the wall. Unlocked the door with the first key I tried on the ring, thinking that my luck might finally be on the turn, and pulled him inside.

I was on my way into the house when I remembered. The alarm. I definitely did not want security men from Tripolis swarming around here now, nor live camera surveillance of me with a half-dead Ove Kjikerud.

'What's the password?' I shouted into Ove's ear.

He lurched and almost slipped out of my grasp.

'Ove! Password?'

'Eh?'

'I have to deactivate the alarm before it goes off.'

'Natasha . . .' he mumbled with closed eyes.

'Ove! Pull yourself together!'

'Natasha . . .'

'The password!' I slapped him hard, and instantly he opened his eyes wide.

'That's what I'm telling you, you bastard. NATASHA!'

I let go of him, heard him topple to the floor as I dashed to the front of the house. I found the alarm box hidden behind the door; I had gradually understood how Tripolis operatives like to set them up. A little red light was flashing, showing the countdown to the tripping of the alarm. I tapped in the name of the Russian whore. And realised as I was about to press the final 'a' that Ove was dyslexic. Christ knows how he spelt her name! But my fifteen seconds were soon up and it was too late to ask him. I pressed the 'a' and shut my eyes, braced myself. Waited. No sound came. I opened my eyes again. The red light had stopped flashing. I breathed out, refrained from thinking about the margin of seconds I had had.

When I turned round, Ove was gone. I followed the wet footprints into a sitting room. It obviously served as a room for relaxing, working, eating and sleeping. At any rate, there was a double bed under a window at one end, a wall-mounted plasma TV at the other and in between a coffee table on top of which was a cardboard box containing the remains of a pizza. Against the longer wall there was a vice bench with a sawn-off shotgun he was clearly modifying. Ove had crawled up into the bed where he now lay groaning. With pain, I assumed. I haven't the foggiest idea what Curacit does to a human body, but I doubt anything good.

'How are you?' I asked, moving closer. I kicked something that rolled across the worn parquet floor, looked down and saw that the area around the bed was littered with empty cartridges.

'I'm dying,' he moaned. 'What happened?'

'You sat on a syringe loaded with Curacit when you got into the car.'

'CURACIT?!' He raised his head and glared at me. 'You mean the poison Curacit? I've got fucking Curacit in my body?'

'Yes, but obviously not enough.'

'Not enough?'

'To kill you. He must have messed up the dosage.'

'He? Who?'

'Clas Greve.'

Ove's head slumped back on the pillow. 'Shit! Don't tell me you've fucked up! Have you given us away, Brown?'

'Not at all,' I said, pulling a chair to the foot of the bed. 'The needle on the car seat was about . . . another matter.'

'Apart from us screwing the guy? What the hell would that be?'

'I'd rather not talk about it. But it was me he was after.'

Ove howled. 'Curacit! I have to go to

191

hospital, Brown. I'm dying! Why the hell did you bring me here? Phone for an ambulance!' He nodded to something on the bedside table that I had at first taken to be just a plastic model of two naked women in the so-called 69 position, but now I realised it was also a telephone.

I swallowed. 'You can't go to hospital, Ove.'

'Can't? I have to! I'm dying, you idiot! Dying!'

'Listen to me. When they discover you've got Curacit in you, they'll ring the police *tout de suite.* Curacit is not a medicine you get on prescription. We're talking about the most deadly poison in the world here, on a level with prussic acid and anthrax. You'll end up being interrogated by Kripos.'

'So what? I'll keep my mouth shut.'

'And how will you explain this, eh?'

'I'll find something.'

I shook my head. 'You don't have a chance, Ove. Not when they get going on Inbau, Reid and Buckley.'

'Eh?'

'You'll break down. You've got to stay here, do you understand? You're better already, anyway.'

'What the fuck do you know about that, Brown? You're a doctor, are you? No, you're a bloody headhunter and my lungs are burning up right now. My spleen is ruptured and in an hour my kidneys will give up the ghost. I have to get to a fucking hospital NOW!'

He had half sat up in bed, but I jumped up and pushed him back down.

'Listen, I'll go and find some milk in the fridge. Milk neutralises poison. They wouldn't be able to do anything different for you at the hospital.'

'Apart from pouring milk down me?'

He tried to sit up again, but I shoved him back roughly, and suddenly the breath seemed to go out of him. His pupils slid up into his skull, his mouth hung half open and his head lay on the pillow. I bent over his face and confirmed that he was exhaling stinking tobacco breath over me. Then I went round the house looking for whatever might help him with the pain.

All I could find was ammunition. And lots of it. The medicine cupboard, adorned with the officially prescribed red cross, was full of boxes that according to the label contained cartridges with bullets of nine-millimetre calibre. In the kitchen drawers there were more ammo boxes, some marked 'blanks', what we on the sergeants' course called red farts: bulletless shells. These must have been the ones Ove used to fire at the TV programs he didn't like. Sick man. I opened the fridge and there — on the same shelf as a carton of Tine semi-skimmed milk — was a shiny silver pistol. I took it out. The stock was freezing cold. The make — Glock 17 — was engraved in the steel. I weighed the weapon in my hand. There was clearly no safety catch, nonetheless there was a bullet in the chamber. In other words the gun could be grabbed and fired in one movement, for example if you were in the kitchen and received an unexpected, unwanted visitor. I peered up at the CCTV cameras on the ceiling. I realised that Ove Kjikerud was a lot more paranoid than I had imagined, that perhaps we were talking about a diagnosis here.

I took the pistol along with the carton of milk. If nothing else, I could use the weapon to keep him in check if he became unruly again.

I rounded the corner into the sitting room and found him perched up in bed. The faint had just been an act. In his hand he was holding a plastic woman, bent over and licking.

'You have to send an ambulance,' he said into the receiver loud and clear, staring at me with defiance in his eyes. He seemed to think he could allow himself that since in the other hand he was holding a weapon I recognised from films. I thought the hood, gang warfare, black-on-black crime. In short: an Uzi. A machine gun that is so small and handy, so ugly and deadly that it isn't even funny. And it was pointing at me.

'No!' I yelled. 'Don't do it, Ove! They'll just ring the pol—'

He fired.

It sounded like popcorn in a saucepan. I had time to think that, time to think that this was the music I would die to. I felt something against my stomach and looked down. Saw the jet of blood spurting from my side hit the milk carton I was holding in my hand. White blood? I realised it was the other way round, that the hole was in the milk carton. Automatically and with a kind of despair, I raised the gun, somewhat surprised that I still could, and fired. The sound kick-started my fury: at least the bang was more potent than the bloody Uzi's. And the Israeli homo pistol also went quiet then. I lowered the gun, in time to see Ove staring at me with a frown on his forehead. And there, right above the frown, was a small, elegant, black hole. Then his head fell back and hit the pillow with a soft thud. My fury was gone. I blinked and blinked, it was like having a rolling TV image on my retina. Something told me that Ove Kjikerud was not going to make any more comebacks.

13
METHANE

I drove along the E6 with my foot jammed down on the accelerator, the rain hammering against the windscreen and the wipers desperately sweeping to and fro in Kjikerud's Mercedes 280SE. It was a quarter past one, five hours since I had got up, and I had already managed to survive my wife's attempt on my life unscathed, dump the body of my partner in a lake, rescue said body, then alive and kicking, just to see my alive and kicking partner try to shoot me. Whereupon, with a flukey shot, I had seen to it that he became a corpse once again and I a murderer. And I was only halfway to Elverum.

The driving rain was bouncing off the tarmac like milk being frothed, and automatically I hunched over the wheel so as not to miss the sign for the turn-off. For the place I was going to now did not have an address I could tap into the Pathfinder GPS.

The only thing I had done before leaving Kjikerud's house was to put on some dry clothes I found in a wardrobe, grab his car keys and remove the cash and credit card from his wallet. I left him lying on the bed as he was. If the alarm went off, the bed was the only spot in the house that was not covered by a camera. I also took the Glock with me as it seemed sensible not to leave the murder weapon at the crime scene. And the bunch of keys with the key to his house and to our regular meeting place, the cabin outside Elverum. It was a place for contemplation, planning and visions. And it was a place where nobody would come looking for me, as no one knew that I knew that this place existed. Not only that, it was the only place I could go, unless I wanted to get Lotte involved in this business. And this business, what the hell was all this business actually? Well, at this very moment it involved being hunted down by a crazy Dutchman whose very profession it was to hunt people down. And before long there would be the police, too, provided they were just a little bit smarter than I supposed. If I were to have any chance, I would have to make it difficult for them. I would have to change my car, for example, as there is little that makes it easier to identify a person than a seven-figure registration number. After hearing the beep from the alarm, which was automatically activated when I let myself out of Ove's house, I drove back towards my own. I was aware that Greve might be waiting for me there, so I parked in a side street some way off. I put my wet clothes in the trunk, took the Rubens from inside the roof lining and put it in my portfolio, locked the car and walked off. Ove's car was still where I had seen it earlier. I got in, placed the portfolio on the seat next to me and headed for Elverum.

There was the turn-off. It came out of nowhere, and I had to concentrate on braking without losing control. Poor visibility, aquaplaning, it was easy to drive a car into a hedge, and I didn't need the cops or whiplash right now.

Then I was in the country. Wisps of mist hung over the farms and the undulating fields on either side of the road that gradually became narrower and narrower and more winding. I was caught in the spray from the tires of a truck advertising Sigdal Kitchens, and it was a relief when the next turn-off came and I had the road to myself. The holes in the tarmac became bigger and more frequent, and the farms smaller and fewer. A third turn-off. Gravel road. A fourth. Fucking wilderness. Rain-heavy, low-hanging branches scraped against the car like a blind man's fingers identifying a stranger. Twenty minutes more driving at a snail's pace and I was there. That was how long it had been since I'd last seen a house.

I pulled the hood on Ove's sweater over my head and jogged into the rain, past the barn with the strangely tilting extension. According to Ove, this was because Sindre Aa, the grumpy recluse of a farmer who lived here, was such a cheapskate that he hadn't laid any foundations for the annexe, which over the course of years had sunk into the clay, centimetre by centimetre. I had never spoken to the bloody farmer myself, Ove had taken care of that side of things, but I had seen him from a distance a couple of times and recognised the lean, bent figure standing on the steps of the farmhouse. God knows how he could have heard the car approaching in this rain. A fat cat was rubbing itself against his legs.

'Hello!' I shouted well before I arrived at the steps.

No answer.

'Hello, Aa!' I repeated. Still no answer.

I stopped by the foot of the steps and waited in the rain. The cat padded down the steps towards me. And there was me thinking cats hated rain. It had almond-shaped eyes, just like Diana, and pressed itself against me as though I were an old friend. Or maybe as though I were a total stranger. The farmer lowered his rifle. Ove had told me Aa used a telescopic sight on the old rifle to see who was dropping by since he was too stingy to buy himself proper binoculars. But for the same reason he had never indulged in ammunition either, so it was probably quite safe. I assumed the rifle routine also had the intended effect on the number of visitors. Aa spat over the railing.

'When's that Kjikerud comin', Brown?' His voice creaked like an unlubricated door and 'Kjikerud' was spat out as if it were a form of exorcism. How he had got hold of my name I had no idea, but it certainly wasn't from Ove.

'He's coming later,' I said. 'Can I park my car in the barn?'

Aa spat again. 'It ain't cheap. And that ain't your car, it's Kjikerud's. How's he gettin' here?'

I took a deep breath. 'On skis. How much is it?'

'Five hundred a day.'

'Five . . . hundred?'

He grinned. 'You can leave it on the road

for nothin'.'

I pulled out three of Ove's two-hundred notes, went up the steps to where Aa was waiting with a bony outstretched hand. He stuffed the money into a bulging wallet and spat again.

'You can give me the change later,' I said.

He didn't answer, just slammed the door hard behind him as he went in.

I reversed into the barn, and in the dark I almost skewered the car on the line of sharp steel prongs on a silage loader. Fortunately, the loader, which was attached to the back of Sindre Aa's blue Massey Ferguson tractor, was in the raised position. So instead of piercing the rear fender or puncturing the tires, the lower edge scraped the trunk lid and warned me just in time to avoid getting ten steel prongs through the rear window.

I parked beside the tractor, took the portfolio and ran across to the cabin. Luckily, the spruce forest was so dense that not much rain seeped through, and after letting myself into the simple log cabin, my hair was still surprisingly dry. I was going to light the fire but rejected the idea. Having taken the precaution of hiding the car, I didn't think it was a good idea to send up smoke signals to say the cabin was occupied.

It was only now that I noticed how hungry I was.

I hung Ove's denim jacket over a chair in the kitchen, went through the cupboards and at length found a solitary can of stew from the last time Ove and I had been here. There was neither cutlery nor a can-opener in the drawers, but I managed to bang a hole in the metal lid with the barrel of the Glock. I sat down and used my fingers to shovel down the greasy, salty contents.

Then I stared out of the window at the rain falling on the forest and the tiny yard between the cabin and the outside toilet. I went into the bedroom, put the Rubens portfolio under the mattress and lay down on the lower bunk to think. I didn't get to do much thinking. It must have been all the adrenalin I had produced that day because all of a sudden I opened my eyes and realised I had been asleep. I checked my watch. Four o'clock in the afternoon. I fished out my mobile and saw there were eight missed calls. Four from Diana who probably wanted to play the concerned wife and, with Greve listening over her shoulder, would ask where on earth I was. Three from Ferdinand who was probably waiting to hear about the nomination or at least instructions on what they should do now with the Pathfinder job. And one I didn't recognise immediately because I had deleted her from my address book. But not from my memory or heart. And while examining the number, it struck me that I — a person who in the course of his more than thirty years on this planet had assembled enough student friends, ex-girlfriends, colleagues and business connections for a network that filled two megabytes in Outlook — had one single acquaintance I could trust. A woman I had known, strictly speaking, for only three weeks. Well, shagged for three weeks. A brown-eyed Dane who dressed like a scarecrow, answered in monosyllables and had a name consisting of five letters. I don't know which of us this was more tragic for.

I rang directory enquiries and asked for a number abroad. Most switchboards close down at four in Norway, most likely because the majority of the receptionists have gone home, to a sick partner according to statistics, in the country with the shortest working hours in the world, the biggest health budget and the highest proportion of sick leave. The HOTE switchboard answered as if it were the most natural thing in the world. I didn't have a name or a department, but took a risk.

'Can you put me through to the new guy, please?'

'New guy, sir?'

'You know, head of technical division.'

'Felsenbrink is hardly new, sir.'

'To me he is. So, is Felsenbrink in?'

Four seconds later I was talking to a Dutchman who was not only at work but sounded both fresh and polite despite it being one minute after four.

'I'm Roger Brown from Alfa Recruiting.' True. 'Mr Clas Greve has given us your name as a reference.' False.

'Right,' said the man, not sounding in the least bit surprised. 'Clas Greve is the best manager I've ever worked with.'

'So you . . .' I started.

'Yes, sir, my most sincere recommendations. He's the perfect man for Pathfinder. Or any other company for that matter.'

I hesitated. Then changed my mind. 'Thank you, Mr Fenselbrink.'

'Felsenbrink. Any time.'

I put the phone in my trouser pocket. I didn't know why, but something told me that I had just committed a blunder.

Outside, the rain was relentless and for lack of anything better to do, I took out the Rubens painting and studied it in the light from the kitchen window. The furious face of the hunter, Meleager, as he speared the beast. And discovered who he had reminded me of when I first saw the picture: Clas Greve. A thought struck me. A coincidence, of course, but Diana had once told me that the name Diana was the Roman name of the goddess of hunters and childbirth, known as Artemis in Greek. And it was Artemis who had sent out Meleager, wasn't it? I yawned and made up my own role in the painting until I realised I had been mixing things up. It was the other way round; Artemis had sent out the beast. I rubbed my eyes; I was still tired.

At that moment I noticed that something had happened, there was a change, but I had been so absorbed by the painting that it had slipped my attention. I looked out of the window. It was the sound. It had stopped raining.

I put the picture back in the portfolio and decided to find a hiding place. I had to leave the cabin to do some shopping and a few other things, and I definitely didn't trust that snake in the grass, Sindre Aa.

I looked around and my gaze was drawn to outside the window, to the toilet. The ceiling consisted of loose boards. Walking across the yard, I could feel I should have put on a jacket.

The toilet was a shed with just the basic requirements: four walls with cracks between the upright boards to give natural ventilation, and a wooden box in which had been sawn a circular hole, covered with a square, roughly hewn lid. I removed three toilet roll tubes and a magazine featuring a photo of Rune Rudberg with pinhole pupils from the lid and clambered up onto it. Stretched up to the boards lying loose across the beams, wishing for the nine millionth time that I was a few centimetres taller. But in the end I managed to loosen a board, shove the portfolio up under the roof and replace the board. And while standing there, straddling the toilet, I froze as I stared out through a gap between the planks.

It was deafeningly quiet outside now, just occasional drips from weighed-down branches. Nevertheless, I hadn't heard a sound, not a single twig breaking, not a squelchy footstep on the muddy path. Or as much as a whimper from the dog standing by his master at the edge of the forest. Had I been sitting in the cabin, I would not have seen them; from the window they would have been in a blind spot. The dog looked like a collection of muscles, jaws and teeth packed into the bodywork of a boxer, just smaller and more compact. Let me repeat: I hate dogs. Clas Greve was wearing a camouflage-patterned cape and a green army hat. He didn't have a weapon in his hands; what he had under his cape I could only guess at. It struck me that this was the perfect place for Greve. Deserted, no witnesses, hiding a body would be child's play.

Master and mastiff set off as one, as though obeying an inaudible command.

My heart pounded with terror, yet I could not help but stare with fascination at how fast and how completely soundless their progress from the edge of the wood was, up to and alongside the cabin wall and then — without any hesitation — in through the door, which they left wide open.

I knew I had only a few seconds before Greve discovered that the cabin was empty, before he found the jacket over the back of the chair telling him I was close by. And . . . shit! . . . saw the Glock, which was lying on the worktop beside the empty can of stew. My brain was working overtime and could only reach this one conclusion — that I had nothing: no weapon, no means of retreat, no plan, no time. If I ran for it, it would be ten seconds tops before I had twenty kilos of Niether terrier at my heels and nine millimetres of lead in my skull. In short, things were going down the drain. Then my brain suggested panicking. But instead it did something I would never have believed. It simply stopped and took a step back. Back to 'going down the drain'.

An idea. A desperate and revolting idea in all ways. But nonetheless an idea which had one big thing going for it: it was the only one I had.

I grabbed one of the toilet roll tubes and put it in my mouth. Felt how tightly I could close my mouth around it. Then I lifted the toilet seat. The stench rose up to meet me. It was one and a half metres down to the tank with a viscous mixture of excrement, urine, toilet paper and rainwater running down the insides of the walls. It took at least two men to carry the tank to the pit in the forest and was a nightmare of a job. Literally. Ove and I had only been up to doing it once, and the three following nights I had dreamed about shit slopping around. And Aa had obviously shunned it too: the one-and-a-half-metre-deep tank was full to the brim. Which, as it happened, suited me fine. Not even a Niether terrier would be able to smell anything but muck.

I balanced the toilet lid on the top of my head, put my hands on either side of the hole and gingerly lowered myself.

It was an unreal feeling to sink into crap,

to feel the light pressure of men's shit against my body as I drilled my way down. The toilet seat stayed put as my head passed the edge of the hole. My sense of smell had perhaps already become overburdened, it had definitely gone on holiday, and I just registered an increased activity in my tear ducts. The top, the most fluid layer in the tank, was freezing cold, but lower down it was in fact quite warm, maybe because of the various chemical processes going on. Hadn't I read something about methane gases developing in cesspits of this kind? And that you could die if you inhaled too much? Now I had firm ground under my feet and crouched. Tears were streaming down my cheeks and my nose was running. I leaned back, made sure that the tube was pointing straight upwards, closed my eyes and tried to relax so that I could control my retching reflexes. Then I carefully hunkered down. My ears were full of shit and silence. I forced myself to breathe through the cardboard tube. It worked. No need to go any deeper now. Of course it would have been a really symbolic way to die with my mouth and ears filled, drowning in Ove's and my own faeces, but I felt no desire to die an ironic death. I wanted to live.

I seemed to hear the door opening from a

long way away.

Here we go.

I felt the vibrations of heavy footsteps. Stamping. And then it went quiet. The padding of feet. The dog. The toilet lid was opened. I knew that right now Greve was staring down at me. Inside me. He was looking down the opening of a toilet roll tube that led directly to my innards. I breathed as quietly as I could. The cardboard of the tube had gone wet and soft; I knew it would soon wrinkle, leak and crumple.

I heard a bump. What was that?

The next sound was unmistakable. A sudden explosion that progressed into a hissing, lamenting bowel tone and eventually faded. It was rounded off with a groan of well-being.

Oh hell, I thought.

And sure enough. A few seconds later I heard the splash and felt a new weight on my upturned face. For a moment death appeared to be an acceptable alternative, but not for long. Actually it was a paradox: I had never had less to live for and yet I had never wished for life more.

A longer groan now, he was obviously applying pressure. He mustn't land in the opening of the tube! I felt panic mounting,

I didn't seem to be getting enough air through the toilet roll. Another splash.

I was dizzy and my thigh muscles were already aching from maintaining a crouched position. I straightened up a tiny bit. My face broke the surface. I blinked and blinked. I was staring at Clas Greve's hairy white backside. And against his skin was the outline of a substantial, well, more than substantial, indeed an impressive dick. And since not even fear of death can expel penis envy in a man, I thought of Diana. And there and then I knew that if Greve didn't kill me first, I would kill him. Greve raised himself, light seeped in through the hole and I saw that there was something wrong, something was missing. I closed my eyes and dragged myself under again. The dizziness was almost overpowering. Was I dying of methane poisoning?

It was quiet for some time. Was it all over? I was in mid-inhalation when I realised that all of a sudden there was nothing there, that I was sucking at nothing. The air supply was blocked. Primary instincts took over and I was beginning to suffocate. I had to get up! My face broke the surface as I heard a thud. I blinked and blinked. Above, all was dark. Then I heard heavy footsteps, the door opening, padding feet and the door closing.

I spat out the toilet roll tube and saw what had happened. There was something white lying across the opening: the toilet paper Greve had wiped himself with.

I hauled myself up out of the tank and peered through the gaps between the boards in time to see Greve sending the dog into the forest while he went back into the cabin. The dog was heading towards the top of the mountain. I watched until it was swallowed up by the forest. And at that moment — perhaps because for a minute I allowed relief, the hope of salvation to flicker into life — an involuntary sob escaped my throat. No, I thought. Don't hope. Don't feel. No emotional involvement. Analytical. Come on, Brown. Think. Prime numbers. Overview of the chessboard. OK. How did Greve find me? How the hell could he know? Diana had never even heard of this place. Who had he been talking to? No answer. Right. What were my options? I had to get away, and I had two advantages: night was beginning to fall, and, covered from top to toe in shit, my smell was camouflaged. But I had a headache and the dizziness was getting worse, and I couldn't wait until it was pitch black.

I slid down the outside of the tank and my feet landed on the slope at the back of the outhouse. I squatted down and assessed the distance to the forest. From there I could make it to the barn and effect my escape by car. I had the car keys in my pocket, didn't I? I rummaged. In my left-hand pocket I had a few banknotes, Ove's credit card and my own and Ove's house keys. Right hand. I heaved a sigh of relief as my fingers met the car keys under the mobile phone.

The mobile phone.

Of course.

Mobile phones are located by base stations. To an area, it is true, not a specific place, but if one of Telenor's base stations had registered my phone out here, there wouldn't have been many options; Sindre Aa's house is the only one within the radius of a kilometre. Naturally that would mean Greve had a contact in Telenor's operations department, but nothing surprised me any more. It had begun to dawn on me what had happened. And Felsenbrink, who had sounded as if he had been waiting for a call from me, had confirmed my suspicions. This was not about a love triangle with me, my wife and a randy Dutchman. If I was right, I was in more trouble than I could ever have imagined.

14
MASSEY FERGUSON

I cautiously poked my head around the side of the outhouse and looked towards the cabin. The windowpanes were black and gave nothing away. So he hadn't switched on the light. OK. I couldn't stay here. I waited until a breath of wind rustled through the trees, then I ran. Seven seconds later I had reached the edge of the forest and was hidden behind the trees. But the seven seconds had almost knocked me out, my lungs ached, my head throbbed, and I was as dizzy as the first and only time my father had taken me to an amusement park. It was my ninth birthday, this was the present, and Dad and I had been the only visitors apart from three half-drunk teenagers sharing a Coke bottle with clear liquid in it. In his furious, broken Norwegian Dad had haggled down the price of the sole attraction that was open: a hellish machine, the point of which apparently was to sling you round and round until you spewed up cotton candy and your parents consoled you by buying popcorn and fizzy drinks. I had refused to risk my life on the rickety machinery, but my father had insisted and fastened the belts that were supposed to protect me. And now, a quarter of a century later, I was back at the same filthy, surrealist amusement park where everything stank of urine and rubbish and I was frightened and gagging the whole time.

A stream gurgled beside me. I pulled out my mobile phone and dropped it in. Trace me now, you bloody urban Red Indian. Then, on the soft forest floor, I jogged in the direction of the farm. Night had fallen between the pine trees, but there was no other vegetation, so it was easy to find the way. After no more than a couple of minutes I saw the outside light on the farmhouse. I ran down a bit further, so that the barn was between me and the farmhouse before I left the forest. There was every reason to believe that Aa would demand an explanation if he saw me in this state, and a call to the local police station would be the next step.

I crept towards the barn door and slipped the bolt. Pushed the door open and entered. My head. My lungs. I blinked in the darkness, could hardly make out the car and the tractor. What was it actually that methane gas did to you? Did you go blind? Methane. Methanol. There was a connection some-where.

Behind me, panting and the soft, barely perceptible sound of paws. Then the sound was gone. I already knew what it was but didn't have time to turn. It had jumped. Everything was quiet, even my heart had stopped beating. The next moment I fell forward. I don't know whether a Niether terrier would be able to jump up and sink its teeth into the neck of an average-sized basketball player, but I am not — I may have mentioned this before — exactly a basketball player. So I was knocked forward as the pain exploded in my brain. Claws lacerated my back and I heard the noise of flesh giving way with a groan, bones crunch-ing. My bones. I tried to grab the animal, but my limbs wouldn't obey, it was as if the jaws locked round my neck had blocked all the communication from my brain. Com-mands were simply not getting through. I lay on my stomach unable even to spit out the sawdust filling my mouth. Pressure on the main artery. My brain was being drained of oxygen. My field of vision was narrow-ing. Soon I would lose consciousness. So this is how I was to die, between the jaws of a fat, ugly lump of a dog. It was depressing, to put it mildly. Yes, it was enough to make you see red. My head began to burn, an ice-cold heat filled my body, seeped through to the tips of my fingers. A joyful curse and a sudden quiver of life-giving strength that presaged death.

I stood up with the dog dangling from my neck and down my back like a living fur stole. Staggering around, I swung my arms, but was still unable to get a hold of it. I knew this outburst of energy was my body's last desperate chance and that soon I would be out for the count. My field of vision had now shrunk to the beginning of a James Bond film, when they play the intro — or, in my case, the outro — and everything is black except for a little round hole in which you see a guy in a dinner jacket aiming at you with a pistol. And through the hole I could see a blue Massey Ferguson tractor. And a last thought reached my brain: I hate dogs.

Swaying, I turned my back to the tractor, let the weight of the dog tip me off the balls of my feet onto my heels, and I stepped back hard. I fell. The sharp steel prongs on the rear loader met us. And I knew from the sound of tearing dog fur that I would not be leaving this world on my own. My field of vision closed and the world went black.

I must have been out for some time.

I lay on the floor staring into the open mouth of a dog. Its body appeared to be hovering in mid-air, bent into what looked like a foetal position. Two steel prongs were sticking into its back. I got to my feet, the barn spun round and I had to take a couple of steps to the side to gain balance. I put a hand on my neck and felt a fresh stream of blood from where the dog's teeth had punctured my skin. And realised I was bordering on madness because instead of getting in the car, I was just standing and staring in fascination. I had created a work of art. *Speared Calydonian Dog.* It was truly beautiful. Especially the mouth still open in death. Maybe the shock had locked its jaws or maybe this breed of dog died in this way. Whatever the reason, I enjoyed the furious yet gawping expression it wore, as though in addition to having lived a foreshortened dog life, it had had to endure this final insult, this humiliating death. I wanted to spit at it, but my mouth was too dry.

Instead I rooted around in my pocket for the car keys and tottered over to Ove's Mercedes, unlocked it and turned the key in the ignition. No response. I tried again and pressed the accelerator. Dead as a dodo. I peered through the windscreen. Groaned. Then I got out and whipped up the hood. It was so dark now that I could barely make out the slashed leads that were sticking up. I had no idea what purpose they served, just that they were probably vital for the little miracle that makes cars go. Sod that bloody half-breed, Greve! I hoped he was still sitting in the cabin waiting for me to return. But he must have started to wonder what had happened to his animal. Take it easy, Brown. OK, the only way I could get away from here now was on Sindre Aa's tractor. Too slow. Greve would soon be after me again. So I would have to find the car he came in — the silver-grey Lexus must be somewhere down the road — and put it out of action just as he had the Mercedes.

I walked at a brisk pace to the farmhouse, half expecting Aa to come out onto the steps — I could see the front door was ajar — but he didn't. I knocked and then nudged the door open. In the porch I saw the rifle with the telescopic sights leaning against the wall beside a pair of filthy rubber boots.

'Aa?'

Aa, pronounced 'oh', didn't sound like a name, but as if I was asking him to continue the story he was telling. Which, in a way, was true. So I entered the house persistently repeating the idiotic monosyllable. I thought I caught a movement and turned. Any blood I had left froze to ice. A black monster on two legs had stopped at the same moment as me and was now staring back with enlarged white eyes shining out of all the black. I raised my right hand. It raised its left. I raised my left hand, it raised its right. It was a mirror. I let out a sigh of relief. The crap had dried and covered all of me: shoes, body, face, hair. I kept going. Pushed open the sitting-room door.

He was recumbent in a rocking chair wearing a grin on his face. The fat cat was lying in his lap and peered at me with its sluttish almond-shaped Diana-eyes. It rose and jumped down. Its paws landed softly on the floor and it slunk over to me with swaying hips before coming to an abrupt halt. Well, I didn't smell of roses or lavender. But after a brief hesitation it continued to pad towards me with a deep, inviting purr. Adaptable animals, cats, they know when they need a new provider. The previous one was dead, you see.

Sindre Aa's grin was caused by a blood-rimmed extension to his lips. A bluish-black tongue protruded from the slash in his cheek, and I could see the gums and teeth of his lower jaw. The grumpy farmer reminded me of a good, old-fashioned Pac-Man the way he was sitting, but the new ear-to-ear smile was unlikely to have been the cause of his death, since two corresponding blood-streaked lines formed an X across his throat. Strangulation from behind with a garrotte: thin nylon rope or steel wire. I wheezed through my nose as my brain produced a swift spontaneous reconstruction: Greve had driven past the farm, seen my car tracks turn off into the muddy yard. He may have driven on, parked some distance away, returned, peeped into the barn and confirmed that my car was there. Sindre Aa must have been standing on the steps by this time. Suspicious and cunning. He had spat and given an evasive answer to Greve's enquiry concerning me. Had Greve offered him money? Had they gone into the house? In any case, Aa must still have been on his guard because when Greve placed the garrotte over his head from behind Aa had managed to lower his chin so that it had not gone round his neck. They had struggled, the wire had slipped into his mouth and Greve had pulled, slicing Aa's cheeks. But Greve was strong, and in the end he had tightened the death-bringing wire round the neck of the desperate old codger. A silent witness, a silent murder. But why had Greve not taken the simple course of action and used a gun? After all, it was several kilometres to the nearest neighbour. Perhaps to avoid giving himself away? The obvious answer hit home: he hadn't brought a firearm with him. I cursed under my breath. For now he had one. I had served him up a new murder weapon by leaving the Glock on the work surface in the cabin. How stupid can you be!

My attention was caught by a dripping sound and the cat which had positioned itself between my legs. Its pink tongue shot in and out as it lapped up the blood falling from the edge of my shirttail and onto the floor. A stupefying tiredness had begun to creep up on me. I took three deep breaths. Had to concentrate. Keep thinking, acting, it was the only thing I could do to hold the numbing fear at arm's length. First of all, I had to find the tractor keys. I wandered aimlessly from room to room pulling out drawers. In the bedroom I found one solitary empty cartridge box. In the hall I found a scarf which I knotted around my neck, and at least that staunched the flow of blood. But no tractor keys. I glanced at my watch. Greve really must have been wondering about the dog. In the end I went back into the sitting room, bent over Aa's body and searched his pockets. There they were! They even had the words Massey Ferguson on the key ring. I was pressed for time, but I couldn't afford to be sloppy now, had to do everything right. Which meant when they found Aa, this would be a crime scene and they would look for DNA evidence. I hurried into the kitchen, wet a towel and cleaned my blood off the floors of all the rooms I had entered. Wiped possible fingerprints off all the things I had touched. Standing in the porch, ready to go, I noticed the rifle. What if some luck had finally come my way, what if there was a cartridge in the chamber after all? I grabbed the rifle and went through what I thought were loading motions, tugged and pulled and heard the bolt click, the socket or whatever the hell it's called, until at length I managed to open the chamber where a little red cloud of rust stood out in the dark. No cartridge. I heard a sound and looked up. The cat was standing on the threshold to the kitchen, staring at me with a mixture of grief and accusation: I couldn't just leave her here, could I? Cursing, I kicked out at the faithless creature, which shrank back and scurried towards the sitting room. Then I rubbed down the rifle, put it back, went outside and slammed the door shut.

The tractor started with a roar. And continued to roar as I drove out of the barn. I wasn't bothered about closing the door. Because I could hear what the tractor was roaring: 'Clas Greve! Brown's getting away! Hurry, hurry!'

I hit the accelerator. Drove the same way I had come. It was pitch black now, and the light from the tractor's headlamps danced over the bumpy road. I looked in vain for the Lexus, it had to be parked here somewhere! No, now I wasn't thinking clearly, he could have left it further up the road. I slapped my face. Blink, take a deep breath, you're not tired, not exhausted. That's the way.

Pedal down hard. A persistent, continuous roar. Where to? Away.

The light from the headlamps narrowed, the darkness was closing in. Tunnel vision again. Consciousness would soon fail me. I breathed in as deeply as I could. Oxygen to the brain. Be frightened, be alert, stay alive!

The monotonous roar of the engine was now accompanied by a higher tone.

I knew what it was and gripped the wheel tighter.

Another engine.

The lights flashed in my mirror.

The car approached from behind at a sedate pace. And why not? We were alone here in the wilds. We had all the time in the world.

My only hope was to keep him behind me so that he couldn't block the way. I positioned myself in the centre of the gravel road and sunk over the wheel so as to make myself the smallest possible target for the Glock. We came out of a bend where the road suddenly straightened and widened. And, as though well acquainted with the area, Greve had already accelerated and was alongside me. I swung the tractor to the right to force him into the ditch. But it was too late, he had slipped past, and I was on my way into the ditch. I lunged desperately at the wheel and skidded on the gravel. I was still on the road. But ahead of me a blue light flashed. Or two red ones at any rate. The brake lights on the car in front showed that he had stopped. I stopped, but sat with the engine idling. I didn't want to die here, alone in a bloody field, like a dumb sheep. My only chance now was to get him out of the car and run him over, flatten him with the ginormous rear wheels, crush him like a ginger snap beneath the huge tread.

The car door on the driver's side opened. I revved up with the tip of my toe to get a sense of how quickly the engine would respond. Not quickly. I went dizzy, and my eyes began to blur again, but I could see a figure get out and come towards me. I took aim while clinging ferociously onto consciousness. Tall, thin. Tall, thin? Greve wasn't tall and thin.

'Sindre?'

'What?' I said in English, although my father had drummed it into me that I should say 'I beg your pardon', 'Sorry, sir' or 'How can I help you, madam?' I half slumped into the seat. He had forbidden Mum to have me on her lap. Said it would make the child soft. Can you see me now, Dad? Did I become soft? Can I sit on your lap now, Dad?'

I heard a voice with wonderful Norwegian sing-song intonation hesitate in the darkness.

'Are you from the, er . . . er, reception centre for asylum seekers?'

'Reception centre for asylum seekers?' I repeated.

He had come up alongside the tractor and, still clinging to the steering wheel, I gave him a sidelong glance.

'Oh, sorry,' he said. 'You looked like a . . . erm . . . Did you fall into the muck heap?'

'I did have an accident, yes.'

'I can see that. I stopped you because I can see that's Sindre's tractor. And because there's a dog hanging from the tail end.'

So much for my concentration then. Ha ha. I had forgotten all about the sodding dog, do you hear that, Dad? Not enough blood to the brain. Too much . . .

I lost the sensation in my fingers, watched them slip off the wheel. Then I passed out.

15
VISITING TIME

I woke up and was in heaven. Everything was white and an angel with gentle eyes was looking down on me where I lay in the cloud, asking me if I knew where I was. I nodded and she said someone wanted to talk to me, but there was no hurry, he could wait. Yes, I thought, he can wait. For when he hears what I have done, he will throw me out on the spot, out of all this soft, lovely whiteness, and I will fall and fall until I am down where I belong, in the blacksmith's workshop, in the smelting room, in the eternal acid bath for my sins.

I closed my eyes and whispered that I would prefer not to be disturbed just yet.

The angel nodded sympathetically, tucked the cloud in tighter around me and disappeared to the clatter of wooden clogs. The sound of voices in the corridor reached my ears before the door closed behind her.

I touched the bandaged wound around

my throat. A few fragmented moments appeared in my memory. The tall, thin man's face above me, the back seat of a car driving at great speed down winding roads, two men in white nurses' uniforms helping me up onto a stretcher. The shower. I had been on my back having a shower! Lovely hot water, then I had drifted off again.

I felt like doing the same now, but my brain informed me that this luxury was very provisional, that the sands of time were still running, that the earth was still turning, that the course of events was inevitable. That they had just decided to wait for a while, hold their breath for a moment.

To think.

Yes, it hurt to think, it was easier to desist, to be resigned, not to rebel against the gravity of fate. It's just that the stupid, trivial course of things is so irritating that you simply lose your temper.

So you think.

There was no way it could be Greve waiting outside, but it might be the police. I looked at my watch. Eight o'clock in the morning. If the police had already found Sindre Aa's body and suspected me, it was unlikely they would send one man who would then, in addition, wait outside politely. It might be an officer who simply wanted to ask what had happened, perhaps it was because I had left the tractor in the middle of the road, perhaps . . . Perhaps I hoped it was the police. Perhaps I had had enough, perhaps all I could do now was save my skin, perhaps I should tell them everything as it was. I lay examining my feelings. And felt the laughter bubbling up inside me. Yes, an EXPLOSION!

At that moment the door opened, the sounds of the corridor reached me and a man in a white coat strode in. He was peering at something on a clipboard.

'Dog bite?' he asked, raising his head and smiling at me.

I recognised him instantly. The door slammed behind him, and we were alone.

'Sorry I couldn't wait any longer,' he whispered.

The white doctor's coat suited Clas Greve. God knows where he had got hold of it. God knows how he had found me; as far as I knew my mobile phone was at the bottom of a stream. But both God and I knew what was awaiting me. And as if to confirm my apprehensions Greve stuffed his hand in his jacket pocket and pulled out a pistol. My pistol. Or to be more accurate: Ove's pistol. Or to be painfully accurate: a Glock 17 with nine-millimetre lead bullets which fragmented on impact with human tissue, splintering up in such a way that the collective mass of lead takes with it a disproportionately large mass of flesh, muscle, bone and cerebral matter which — after passing through your body — it plasters over the wall behind you like something not dissimilar to Barnaby Furnas's paintings. The muzzle of the pistol was pointed at me. It is often alleged that your mouth goes dry in situations such as these. It does.

'Hope it's all right if I use your pistol, Roger,' said Greve. 'I didn't bring mine with me to Norway. There's so much hassle with planes and weapons nowadays. Anyway, I could hardly have anticipated —' he opened his arms — 'this. In addition, it's pretty good that the bullet can't be traced back to me, isn't it, Roger?'

I didn't answer.

'Isn't it?' he repeated.

'Why . . . ?' I started with a voice that was as hoarse as a desert wind.

Clas Greve waited with a genuinely interested facial expression for me to go on.

'Why are you doing all this?' I whispered. 'Just because of a woman you have only known five minutes?'

He furrowed his brow. 'Are you referring to Diana? Did you know that she and I —'

'Yes,' I interrupted to be spared the continuation.

He chuckled. 'Are you an idiot, Roger? Do you really think this is about her and me and you?'

I didn't answer. That *was* what I had thought. That it *wasn't* about trivial matters like life, emotions and people one loved.

'Diana was only a means to an end, Roger. I had to use her to get close to you. Since you didn't take the first bait.'

'Get close to me?'

'You, yes. We've been planning this for more than four months, ever since we knew that Pathfinder was going to look for a new CEO.'

'We?'

'Guess who.'

'HOTE?'

'And our new American owners. We were — to be quite frank — a bit on our uppers, economically speaking, when they came to us this spring. So we had to accept a couple of conditions for what perhaps looked like a buyout, but in reality was a rescue operation. One of the conditions was that we would deliver Pathfinder to them as well.'

'Deliver Pathfinder? How?'

'You know what I know, Roger. That even though, on paper, it is the shareholders and board of directors who make the decisions in a company, in practice it is the CEO who is in charge. Who in the final analysis determines whether and to whom the company is to be sold. I led HOTE by consciously feeding the board with so little information and so much uncertainty that they would choose to trust me at all times. Which, by the way, was to their benefit, regardless of what happened. The point is that every relatively competent leader with the confidence of the board will be able to manipulate and persuade a gang of semi-informed shareholders to do exactly what he wants.'

'You're exaggerating.'

'Am I? To my knowledge, you make your living from doing just that, talking round these so-called directors.'

Of course, he was right. And it confirmed the suspicion I had had after herr Felsenbrink in HOTE had recommended Greve so unreservedly for the post of CEO to HOTE's greatest rival.

'So HOTE wants to . . .' I started.

'Yes, HOTE wants to take over Pathfinder.'

'Because the Americans have made it a proviso for getting you out of a fix?'

'The money we HOTE shareholders have

received in our accounts is frozen until the buyout conditions have been fulfilled. Although nothing of what we are discussing now appears anywhere in print of course.'

I nodded slowly. 'So all that stuff about your resigning in protest against the new owners was just a masquerade to make you appear a credible candidate to take over the helm at Pathfinder?'

'Right.'

'And when you've got the job as CEO at Pathfinder your task is to force the company into American hands?'

'Not sure *force* is the right word. When Pathfinder finds out in a few months' time that their technology is no longer a secret to HOTE, they will see for themselves that they have no chance on their own and that cooperation is the best way forward.'

'Because you will have secretly leaked this technology to HOTE?'

Greve's smile was thin and as white as a tapeworm. 'It is, as I said, the perfect marriage.'

'The perfect forced marriage, you mean?'

'If you like. But with the combined technologies of HOTE and Pathfinder we will capture all the defence contracts for GPS in the western hemisphere. And a couple in the eastern into the bargain . . . It's worth a bit of manipulation, wouldn't you agree?'

'And so you had it planned that I would get you the job?'

'I'd have been a strong candidate anyway, don't you think?' Greve had taken up a position at the foot of the bed with the pistol at hip height and his back to the door. 'But we wanted to be absolutely sure. We soon found out which recruitment agencies they had contacted and did a bit of research. It turns out that you have something of a reputation, Roger Brown. If you recommend a candidate, that's it, people say. You certainly hold some kind of record. So, naturally enough, we wanted to go via you.'

'I'm honoured. But why didn't you just contact Pathfinder directly and say you were interested?'

'Come on, Roger! I'm the ex-CEO of the big bad buyout wolf. Have you forgotten? It would've caused all the alarm bells to ring if I'd gone to them. I had to be "found". For example, by a headhunter. And then persuaded. It was the only way that would seem credible for me to get into Pathfinder without malicious intentions.'

'I see. But why use Diana? Why not contact me direct?'

'Now you're playing dumb, Roger. You would've had the same suspicions if I'd put myself forward. You wouldn't have touched me with a bargepole.'

He was right that I was playing dumb. And it was right as well that he was dumb. Dumb and so proud of his brilliant, greedy plans that he couldn't resist the temptation to stand there boasting about them until someone came in through the damned door. Somebody had to come soon, I was sick for Christ's sake!

'You ascribe much too noble motives to me and my work, Clas,' I said, thinking that you don't execute people you're on first-name terms with, do you? 'I choose candidates I think will be appointed to the job, and they're not necessarily the ones I think are best for the company.'

'Really?' said Greve with a frown. 'Even a headhunter like you is not so amoral, is he?'

'You don't know much about headhunters, I guess. You should've kept Diana out of this.'

That seemed to amuse Greve. 'Should I?'

'How did you hook her?'

'Would you really like to know, Roger?' He had raised the pistol a touch. One metre. Between the eyes?

'I'm dying to know, Clas.'

'As you wish.' He lowered the pistol a fraction again. 'I dropped by her gallery a few times. Bought a number of works. At her recommendation, as time went on. Invited her out for coffee. We talked about all manner of things, about deeply personal things, the way that only strangers can. About marital problems . . .'

'You talked about our marriage?' It slipped out.

'Yes, indeed. After all, I'm divorced, so I am full of sympathy. I can understand, for example, how a beautiful, fully mature and fertile woman like Diana may not be able to accept her husband's unwillingness to give her a child. Or his persuading her to have an abortion because the baby has Down's syndrome.' Greve had a grin that was as broad as Aa's was in the rocking chair. 'Especially since I simply adore children myself.'

Blood and reason deserted my head, leaving behind one single thought: that I would kill the man standing before me. 'You . . . you told her you wanted a child?'

'No,' Greve said quietly. 'I said I wanted a child with *her*.'

I had to concentrate to control my voice: 'Diana would never leave me for a charlatan like —'

'I took her to the apartment and showed her my so-called Rubens painting.'

I was confused. 'So-called . . . ?'

'Yes, the painting is not genuine, of course, just a very good copy painted in Rubens's time. In fact, the Germans thought for a long time that it was genuine. My grandmother showed it to me when I was young and living there. Sorry for lying to you about its authenticity.'

The news should perhaps have had an effect on me, but I was already so emotionally drained that I just took it in, realising at the same time that Greve had not discovered that the painting had been switched.

'Nevertheless the copy had its uses,' Greve said. 'When Diana saw what she thought was a genuine Rubens, she must have concluded there and then that I would not only give her a child but also provide for it and her in a more than adequate way. In a nutshell, give her the life she dreams about.'

'And she . . .'

'She, of course, agreed to ensure her future husband got the CEO post that would produce the respectability that ought to follow with money.'

'You're telling me . . . that evening in the gallery . . . it was a put-up job from beginning to end?'

'Of course. Except for the fact that we didn't achieve the end as easily as we had hoped. When Diana rang me to say that you had decided not to take me . . .' He rolled his eyes in theatrical irony. 'Can you imagine the shock, Roger? The disappointment? The anger? I simply could not understand why you didn't like me. Why, Roger, why? What had I done to you?'

I gulped. He seemed so absurdly relaxed, as though he had all the time in the world to fire the bullet into my skull, heart or whichever part of my body he had designated.

'You're too small,' I said.

'I beg your pardon?'

'So you got Diana to plant the rubber ball containing Curacit in my car? She was supposed to kill me so that I wouldn't be able to write my negative report?'

Greve frowned. 'Curacit? It's interesting that you're convinced your wife would be willing to commit murder for a child and a pot of gold. And for all I know you may be right. But in fact I did not ask her to do that. The rubber ball contained a mixture of Ketalar and Dormicum, a fast-acting anaesthetic which is so strong that, to be sure, it is not without risk. The plan was that you would be knocked out when you got into your car in the morning and that Diana would drive the car, with you in it, to a preordained place.'

'What sort of place?'

'A cabin I had rented. Not unlike the one where I had hoped to find you last night, in fact. Albeit with a more likeable and less inquisitive owner.'

'And once there I would be . . .'

'Persuaded.'

'How?'

'You know. Coaxed a bit. Little threats if necessary.'

'Torture?'

'Torture has its entertaining sides, but firstly I hate to inflict physical pain on anyone. And secondly after a certain stage it is less effective than one might suppose. So, no, not torture as such. Just enough for you to have a taste, enough to evoke that uncontrollable fear of pain all of us carry inside. You see, it's fear, not pain, that makes you malleable. For that reason the business-like, professional interrogator does not depart from light associative torture . . .' He grinned. '. . . at least according to the CIA's manuals. Better than the FBI model you use, eh, Roger?'

I could feel sweat forming under the bandage around my throat. 'And what was it you would've wanted to achieve?'

'We would've wanted you to write and

sign a report the way we liked. We would even have put a stamp on and posted it for you.'

'And if I had refused? More torture?'

'We're not inhuman, Roger. If you had refused, we would've just kept you there. Until Alfa had given the job of writing a report to one of your colleagues. Presumably Ferdinand — isn't that his name?'

'Ferdy,' I said fiercely.

'Exactly. And he seemed very positive. And so did the chairman of the board and the public relations manager. Does that tally with your impression, Roger? Don't you agree that basically the only thing that could have stopped me was a negative report, and only then from Roger Brown himself? As you will appreciate we wouldn't have needed to hurt you.'

'You're lying,' I said.

'Am I?'

'You had no intention of letting me live. Why would you let me go afterwards and risk being exposed?'

'I could have made you a good offer. Eternal life for eternal silence.'

'Rejected husbands are not rational business partners, Greve. And you know that.'

Greve stroked the gun barrel against his chin. 'True enough. Yes, you're right. We would probably have killed you. But this at any rate was the plan I put before Diana. And she believed me.'

'Because she wanted to.'

'Oestrogen makes you blind, Roger.'

I couldn't think of anything else to say. Why the hell didn't someone . . . ?

'I found a DO NOT DISTURB sign in the same wardrobe as this coat,' Greve said as if he had been reading my mind. 'I think they hang up the sign outside when the patient's using the bedpan.'

The barrel was pointing straight at me now, and I saw his finger curl round the trigger. He hadn't raised the gun: he was obviously going to shoot from the hip the way James Cagney had done in the gangster films of the forties and fifties, with unrealistic accuracy. Regrettably, something told me that Clas Greve belonged to this group of unrealistic expert marksmen.

'I think this qualifies, too,' Greve said, already squinting, in preparation for the bang. 'Death is a private matter after all, isn't it?'

I closed my eyes. I had been right all along: I was in heaven.

'Apologies, Doctor!'

The voice rang out round the room.

I opened my eyes. And saw that three men

were standing behind Greve, just inside the door that was closing gently behind them.

'We're from the police,' said the voice belonging to the one in civilian clothes. 'This is about a murder case, so I'm afraid we had to ignore the sign on the door.'

I could see that in fact there was a certain likeness between my saving angel and the said James Cagney. But perhaps that was just down to the grey raincoat, or the medicine they had been giving me, for his two colleagues wearing black police uniforms with checked reflective bands (which reminded me of jumpsuits) looked just as improbable: like two peas in a pod, as fat as pigs, as tall as houses.

Greve had stiffened and stared at me ferociously without turning. The gun, which was hidden from the policemen's eyes, was still pointing straight at me.

'Hope we aren't disturbing you with this little murder of ours, Doctor?' said the plain-clothes officer, not bothering to conceal his annoyance that the man in white seemed to be ignoring him completely.

'Not at all,' Greve said, still with his back to him. 'The patient and I had just finished.' He pulled his white coat to the side and stuffed the pistol into the waistband of his trousers.

'I . . . I —' I began, but was interrupted by Greve.

'Take it easy now. I'll keep your wife posted about your condition. Don't worry, we'll see that she's all right. Do you understand?'

I blinked several times. Greve bent forward over the bed and patted the duvet over my knee.

'We'll be gentle, OK?'

I nodded mutely. It had to be the medicine, no question. This was just not happening.

Greve straightened up with a smile. 'By the way, Diana's right. You really do have wonderful hair.'

Greve turned, lowered his head, stared at the paper on the clipboard, and whispered to the policemen as he passed: 'He's all yours. For the time being.'

After the door slid to, James Cagney stepped forward.

'My name's Sunded.'

I nodded slowly and felt the bandage cutting into the skin of my throat. 'You came in the nick of time, Sundet.'

'Sunded,' he repeated gravely. '*Ded* at the end. I'm a murder investigator and have been called here from Kripos in Oslo. Kripos is —'

'Kriminalpolitisentralen, serious crime squad, I know,' I said.

'Good. This is Endride and Eskild Monsen from the Elverum police force.'

Impressed, I inspected them. Two twin walruses dressed in identical uniforms with identical moustaches. It was a lot of policeman for the money, no question.

'First I would like to read your rights to you,' Sunded began.

'Hang on!' I exclaimed. 'What's that supposed to mean?'

Sunded gave a weary smile. 'That means, herr Kjikerud, that you are under arrest.'

'Kji—' I bit my tongue. Sunded was waving what I recognised as a credit card. A blue credit card. Ove's card. From my pocket. Sunded raised a quizzical eyebrow.

'Sh . . . it,' I said. 'What are you arresting me for?'

'For the murder of Sindre Aa.'

I stared at Sunded as he, in everyday language, and using his own words, rather than the Lord's Prayer–like rigmarole from American films, explained to me that I had a right to a lawyer and the right to keep my mouth shut. He concluded by explaining that the consultant had given him the go-ahead to take me with them as soon as I was conscious. After all, I only had a few stitches in the back of my neck.

'That's fine,' I said before he was finished explaining. 'I'm more than happy to go with you.'

16
PATROL CAR ZERO ONE

The hospital was set in rural surroundings some way outside Elverum, it transpired. I was relieved to see the mattress-like white buildings disappear behind us. Even more because I couldn't see a silver-grey Lexus.

The car we were in was an old, but well-kept Volvo with such a wonderful-sounding engine that I suspected it had been a hot rod before it was repainted in police colors.

'Where are we?' I asked from the back seat, wedged in between the impressive physiques of Endride and Eskild Monsen. My clothes, Ove's, that is, had been sent to the dry-cleaner's but a nurse had brought me a pair of tennis shoes and a green track-suit bearing the hospital's initials, with strict instructions to return it washed. Furthermore, I had been given back all the keys and Ove's wallet.

'Hedmark county,' said Sunded from what Afro-American gang milieus reportedly call the shotgun seat: the passenger seat.

'And where are we going?'

'That's none of your business,' snarled the young, pimply driver, sending me an ice-cold glance via the rear-view mirror. Bad cop. Black nylon jacket with yellow letters on the back. ELVERUM KO-DAW-YING CLUB. I assumed it was a very mysterious, brand-new yet ancient martial art. And that it was his frenetic gum-chewing which had so disproportionately enhanced his jaw musculature. Pimples was so thin and narrow-shouldered that his arms formed a V when he had both hands on the wheel, as now.

'Keep your eyes on the road,' Sunded said in a low voice.

Pimples mumbled and glowered at the ramrod-straight strip of tarmac that sliced through the cultivated land, which was as flat as a pancake.

'We're going to the police station in El-verum, Kjikerud,' said Sunded. 'I've come up from Oslo and will interrogate you today and if necessary tomorrow. And the following day. I hope you're a reasonable fellow because I don't like Hedmark.' He drummed his fingers on an overnight bag that Endride had passed forward to him because there simply wasn't room with us

249

three in the back.

'I'm reasonable,' I said, feeling both of my arms going to sleep. The Monsen twins breathed in rhythm, which meant that I was squeezed like a tube of mayonnaise every fourth second. I wondered whether to ask one of them to change their breathing pattern, but refrained. In a way, after standing in front of Greve's pistol, this felt secure. It took me back to the time when I was small and had had to go to work with Dad because Mum was ill, and I sat between two serious but kind grown-ups on the back seat of the embassy's limousine. And everyone had been elegantly dressed, but no one as elegantly as Dad, who wore a chauffeur's cap and drove the car with such style and grace. And afterwards Dad had bought me an ice cream and told me I had behaved like a true gentleman.

The radio hissed.

'Shh.' Pimples broke the silence in the car.

'Message to all patrol cars,' crackled a nasal female voice.

'Both patrol cars,' Pimples muttered, turning up the volume.

'Egmont Karlsen has reported a stolen truck and trailer . . .'

The rest of the message was drowned in laughter from Pimples and the Monsen twins. Their bodies shook, giving me a rather pleasant massage. I think the medicines were still working.

Pimples took the radio and spoke into it: 'Did Karlsen sound sober? Over.'

'Not entirely, no,' the female voice answered.

'Then he's been out drunk-driving again and forgotten it. Ring Bamse's. I bet it's parked outside the pub. Eighteen-wheeler with Sigdal Kitchens on the side. Over and out.'

He replaced the radio, and I thought the atmosphere had noticeably lightened, so I took advantage of the opportunity.

'I've worked out that someone has been murdered, but am I allowed to ask what this has to do with me?'

The question was met with silence, but I could see by Sunded's pose that he was thinking. Then he turned towards the back seat and his eyes bored into me. 'Fine, we might as well get this over with right away. We know you did it, herr Kjikerud, and there is no way of you wriggling out of it. You see, we have a body and a crime scene and evidence that ties you to both.'

I ought to have been shocked, horrified. I ought to have felt my heart skip a beat or sink or whatever it does when you hear a jubilant policeman tell you they have proof that will send you to prison for life. But I felt none of this. For I didn't hear a jubilant policeman, I heard Inbau, Reid and Buckley. First step. Direct confrontation. Or, to paraphrase the manual: The detective should at the outset of the interrogation make it abundantly clear that the police know everything. Say 'we' and 'the police', never 'I'. And 'know', not 'believe'. Distort the interviewee's self-image, address low-status persons with 'herr' and high-status persons by their first name.

'And between you and me,' Sunded continued, lowering his voice in a way that was clearly meant to signal confidentiality, 'from what I hear, Sindre Aa was no loss. If you hadn't used the rope on the old sourpuss, someone else hopefully would have.'

I stifled a yawn. Step two. Sympathise with the suspect by normalising the act.

When I didn't answer Sunded went on. 'The good news is that with a quick confession I could reduce your sentence.'

Oh my goodness, the Explicit Promise! It was a ploy Inbau, Reid and Buckley absolutely forbade, a legal trap that only the most desperate detective would use. This man really did want to get back home from Hedmark in a hurry.

'So why did you do it, Kjikerud?'

I looked through the side window. Fields. Farms. Fields. Farms. Fields. Stream. Fields. Wonderfully sleep-inducing.

'Well, Kjikerud?' I heard Sunded's fingers drumming on the overnight bag.

'You're lying,' I said.

The drumming stopped. 'Repeat.'

'You're lying, Sunded. I have no idea who Sindre Aa is, and you've got nothing on me.'

Sunded gave a brief lawnmower laugh. 'Haven't I? So tell me where you've been for the last twenty-four hours. Would you be so kind, Kjikerud?'

'Maybe,' I said. 'If you tell me what this case is all about.'

'Smack 'im!' Pimples spat. 'Endride, smack —'

'Shut up,' Sunded said calmly, turning to me. 'And why should we tell you, Kjikerud?'

'Because then perhaps I'll talk to you. If not, I'll keep my mouth shut until my lawyer comes. From Oslo.' I saw Sunded's mouth tighten, and I upped the ante: 'Sometime tomorrow if we're lucky . . .'

Sunded angled his head and studied me as if I were an insect he was considering whether to add to his collection or just crush.

'Fine, Kjikerud. It all started when the

person sitting next to you received a phone call about a tractor abandoned in the middle of the road. They found the tractor and a flock of crows which had met for lunch on the rear loader. They had already made short work of the soft bits of a dog. The tractor belonged to Sindre Aa, but naturally he didn't respond when we rang, so one of us popped over and found him in the rocking chair where you had put him. We found a Mercedes in the barn with a dead engine and number plates that we traced to you, Kjikerud. At length Elverum police station made a connection between the dead dog and a routine report from the hospital about a semi-conscious man covered in muck who had been admitted with a nasty dog bite. They rang, and the duty nurse told us that the man had been unconscious, but in his pocket they had found a credit card bearing the name Ove Kjikerud. And hey presto — here we are.'

I nodded. So I knew how they had found me. But how on earth had Greve managed it? The question had been churning around in my admittedly dopey brain without yielding a result. Could Greve have contacts inside the local police as well? Someone who had made sure Greve could get to the hospital before the police? Wrong! They had just strolled into the room and saved me. Wrong! Sunded had done that, the uninitiated outsider, the Kripos man from Oslo. I could feel a headache coming on as the next thought announced its arrival: Suppose things were as I feared, what sort of protection would I have then in a holding cell? Suddenly the Monsen twins' synchronised breathing did not feel so reassuring. Nothing was reassuring. I felt as though there was no one in this world I could trust any more. No one. Apart from perhaps one person. The outsider with the overnight bag. I would have to lay my cards on the table, tell Sunded everything, ensure he took me to a different police station. Elverum was corrupt, no doubt about that, probably there was more than one undercover schemer in this car.

The radio crackled again. 'Patrol car zero one, come in.'

Pimples grabbed the radio. 'Yes, Lise?'

'There's no truck outside Bamse's. Over.'

Telling Sunded everything would of course involve revealing that I was an art thief. And how would I convince them that I had shot Ove in self-defence, indeed, almost by accident? A man who was so doped up by Greve's potion that he must have been cross-eyed.

'Get a grip, Lise. Ask around. No one can hide an eighteen-metre-long vehicle in this district, OK?'

The voice that answered sounded miffed. 'Karlsen says you usually find his truck for him, since you're a policeman and his brother-in-law. Over.'

'I bloody well do not! You can forget that one, Lise.'

'He says it's not much to ask. You got the least ugly of his sisters.'

I was being shaken by the Monsen twins' laughter.

'Tell the idiot that we've got proper police work to do today for once,' Pimples snarled. 'Over and out.'

I really had no idea how to play this game. It was just a question of time before my true identity would be revealed. Should I tell them straight away or was it a card I could keep up my sleeve for later?

'Now it's your turn, Kjikerud,' Sunded said. 'I've done a bit of checking up on you. You're an old acquaintance of ours. And according to our documents you're unmarried. So what did the doctor mean when he said he would look after your wife? Diana, wasn't it?'

That card went up in smoke. I sighed and looked through the side window. Wasteland, cultivated land. No oncoming traffic, no houses, just a cloud of dust from a tractor or a car on the distant horizon.

'I don't know,' I answered. I had to think more clearly. More clearly. Had to see the whole chessboard.

'What was your relationship with Sindre Aa, Kjikerud?'

Being addressed by this alien name was beginning to wear me down. I was about to reply when I realised that I had been wrong. Again. The police really did think I was Ove Kjikerud! That was the name they had been given of the person admitted to hospital. But if they had passed the same message on to Greve, why had Greve visited this Kjikerud at the hospital? He had never heard of any Kjikerud; no one in the whole world knew that Kjikerud had anything to do with me — Roger Brown! It simply didn't make sense. He must have found me via a different channel.

I saw the cloud of dust on the road approaching.

'Did you hear my question, Kjikerud?'

First of all Greve had found me in the cabin. Then at the hospital. Even though I didn't have the mobile on me. Greve didn't have any contacts, either in Telenor or in the police. So how was that possible?

257

'Kjikerud! Hello!'

The cloud of dust on the side road was travelling much faster than it had seemed from a distance. I saw the crossroads ahead of us and had a sudden sensation that it was bearing down on us and that we were on a collision course. I hoped the other car was aware that we had right of way.

But perhaps Pimples should give him a hint and use the horn. Give him a hint. Use the horn. What was it Greve had said at the hospital? *'Diana's right. You really do have wonderful hair.'* I closed my eyes and felt her hands running through my hair in the garage. The smell. She had smelt different. She had smelt of him, of Greve. No, not Greve. Of HOTE. Bearing down on us. And in slow motion everything fell into place. Why hadn't I twigged before? I opened my eyes.

'We're in mortal danger, Sunded.'

'The only person in danger here is you, Kjikerud. Or whatever your name is.'

'What?'

Sunded peered into the mirror and raised the credit card he had shown me at the hospital.

'You don't look like this Kjikerud on the photo. And when I checked Kjikerud out in the files it said he was one metre seventy-three. And you are . . . what? One sixty-five?'

It had gone quiet in the car. I stared at the cloud of dust that was drawing near at speed. It was not a car. It was a lorry with a trailer behind. It was so close now that I could read the letters on the side. SIGDAL KITCHENS.

'One sixty-eight,' I said.

'So who the hell are you?' Sunded growled.

'I'm Roger Brown. And on the left is Karlsen's stolen lorry.'

All heads turned left.

'What the hell's going on?' growled Sunded.

'What's going on,' I said, 'is that that lorry is being driven by a guy called Clas Greve. And he knows I'm in this car and is aiming to kill me.'

'How . . . ?'

'He has a GPS tracker which means he can find me wherever I am. And he's been doing that ever since my wife stroked my hair in the garage. With a handful of gel containing microscopic transmitters that adhere to your hair and are impossible to wash off.'

'Cut the crap!' the Kripos detective snarled.

'Sunded . . .' Pimples began. 'It *is* Karl-sen's truck.'

'We have to stop this car now and turn round,' I said. 'Otherwise he'll kill all of us. Stop!'

'Keep going,' Sunded said.

'Can't you see what's going to happen?!' I shouted. 'You'll soon be dead, Sunded.'

Sunded started his lawnmower laugh, but the lawn seemed to be too high. He saw that now, too. That it was already too late.

17
SIGDAL KITCHENS

A collision between two vehicles is basic physics. It all comes down to chance, but chance phenomena can be explained by the equation Energy × Time = Mass × difference in Velocity. Add values to the chance variables and you have a story that is simple, true and remorseless. It tells you, for example, what happens when a fully loaded juggernaut weighing 25 tons and travelling at a speed of 80 kph hits a sedan weighing 1,800 kilos (including the Monsen twins) and moving at the same speed. Based on chance with respect to point of impact, construction of bodywork and the angle of the two bodies relative to one another, a multitude of variants to this story are possible, but they share two common features: they are tragedies. And the sedan is in trouble.

When, at 10.13, the truck and trailer driven by Greve hit patrol car zero one, a

Volvo 740 manufactured in 1989, just in front of the driver's seat, the car engine, both front wheels and Pimples' legs were pushed sideways through the car body as the car was launched into the air. No airbags were activated as these had not been installed in Volvos before 1990. The police car — which was already a total wreck — sailed over the road, high above the crash barrier and landed on the compact clump of spruce trees lining the river at the bottom of the slope. Before the police car burst through the first treetops it had performed two and a half somersaults with one and a half twists. There were no witnesses present to confirm what I have said, but this is exactly what happened. It is — as I mentioned before — simple physics. The same as the fact that the relatively undamaged truck continued straight over the deserted crossroads where it braked with a screech of bare metal. It snorted like a dragon as the brakes were finally released, but the smell of scorched rubber and burnt disc brake linings hung over the landscape for several minutes afterwards.

At 10.14 the spruce trees had stopped swaying, the dust had settled, the truck stood with the engine idling as the sun continued to shine steadily down on the

Hedmark fields.

At 10.15 the first car passed the crime scene, and the driver probably noticed nothing except for the truck standing on the gravel side road and what might have been fragments of broken glass crunching under the car tires. He would not have seen a trace of a police car lying on its roof down under the trees by the river.

I know all of this because I was in a position that enabled me to state that we were lying on the car roof, hidden from the road by the trees alongside the river. The times given depend on the accuracy of Sunded's watch, which was ticking away right in front of me. At least I think it was his; it hung from the wrist of a severed arm protruding from a piece of grey raincoat.

A puff of wind wafted over carrying with it the resin smell of brake linings and the sound of a diesel engine idling.

The sunshine flickered down through the trees from a cloudless sky, but around me it was raining. Petrol, oil and blood. Dripping and draining away. Everyone was dead. Pimples no longer had any pimples. Or any face for that matter. What was left of Sunded was squashed flat like a cardboard figure; I could see him peering out from between his own legs. The twins seemed more or less whole but had stopped breathing. That I was alive myself was solely down to the Monsen family's aptitude for amassing body weight and forming it into perfect airbags. But those same bodies which had saved my life were now wresting it from me. The whole of the car body was crushed and I was hanging upside down from my seat. One arm was free, but I was squeezed in between the two policemen so tightly that I could neither move nor breathe. For the time being, however, my senses were functioning perfectly. Such that I could see petrol trickling out, feel it running down my trouser legs, along my body and out of my tracksuit neck. And hear the truck up on the road, hear it snorting and clearing its throat and jerking. I knew he was sitting there, Greve, thinking, appraising. He could see on the GPS tracker that I wasn't moving. He was thinking that he still ought to go down and make sure everyone was dead. On the other hand, it would be tricky getting down the slope and even trickier getting back up. And surely no one could have survived that crash? But you slept so much better knowing you had seen it with your own eyes . . .

Drive, I begged. Drive.

The worst thing about being fully conscious was that I could imagine what would happen if he found me soaked in petrol.

Drive. Drive!

The truck's diesel engine was chuntering away as though carrying on a conversation with itself.

Everything that had happened was clear to me now. Greve had not gone up to Sindre Aa on the steps to ask where I was, he could see that on the display of his GPS tracker. Aa had to be got rid of simply because he had seen Greve and his car. But while Greve had been walking up the path to the cabin, I had moved to the outside toilet, and as he hadn't found me in the cabin, he had checked the tracker again. And discovered to his amazement that the signal had gone. Because the transmitters in my hair at that point were submerged under crap, which HOTE's transmitters, as has been mentioned before, do not have signals powerful enough to penetrate. Idiot that I am, I had had more luck than I deserved.

Greve had then sent out the dog to find me while he waited. Still without a signal. Because the crap that dried round the transmitters was still blocking the signals while I was checking Aa's body and then fleeing on the tractor. It was not until the middle of the night that Greve's GPS tracker would have begun to receive signals again. Which was when I was lying on a stretcher in the hospital shower and the crap was being washed out of my hair. Greve had jumped into his car and was at the hospital by dawn. God knows how he had stolen the truck, but anyway he had no problem finding me again, me, Brown, the babbling nutter who was veritably imploring to be caught.

The fingers on Sunded's severed arm were still curled around the handle of his overnight case. His wristwatch was ticking. Ten sixteen. In a minute I would lose consciousness. In two I would be suffocated. Make up your mind, Greve.

And then he did.

I heard the truck belch. The rpm sank. He had switched off the ignition; he was on his way here!

Or . . . had he put it into gear?

A low rumble. The crunch of gravel under the tires bearing twenty-five tons. The rumble increased in volume. And increased. And became quieter. Disappeared into the countryside. Died away.

I closed my eyes and offered up my thanks. For not being burned, but only dying from a lack of oxygen. Because that is by no means the worst way to die. The brain closes down chambers one by one, you become dopey, you are numbed, stop thinking, and with that your problems cease to exist. In a way it is like taking a few stiff drinks. Yep, I thought, I can live with dying like that.

The idea of it almost made me laugh.

Me, who had spent my whole life trying to be my father's opposite, would end my life as he had, in a wrecked car. And how different from him had I actually been? When I was too old for the bloody drunkard to hit me, I had begun to hit him. In the same way that he had hit Mum, without leaving any visible marks. As another example, when he had offered to teach me to drive, I had politely refused and informed him that I was not interested in having a driver's licence. And I had got together with the ugly, pampered ambassador's daughter Dad had driven to school every day, just so I could take her home for dinner and humiliate him. When I saw my mother in the kitchen crying between the main course and dessert, I had regretted that. I had applied to a college in London I had heard Dad say was a posh place for social parasites. But he hadn't taken it as badly as I had hoped. He had even managed to put on a smile, seemed proud when I told him about it, the crafty bastard. So when later that autumn he had asked if he and my mother could travel from Norway to visit me on campus, I had said no, on the basis that I didn't want my fellow students to discover that my father was not someone high up in the diplomatic corps but a plain chauffeur. That seemed to hit a tender spot. Not tender as in tenderness, of course, but sore.

I had rung my mother two weeks before the wedding to say that I was getting married to a girl I had met, explained that it would be a simple affair, just us and two witnesses. But my mother was welcome to come so long as she came without Dad. Mum had lost her temper and said that of course she wouldn't come without him. Noble, loyal souls are often handicapped by loyalty to even the basest of individuals. Well, especially the base individuals.

Diana was going to meet my parents after the end of the semester that summer, but three weeks before we left London I had received news of the car accident. On the way home from their cabin, the policeman had said on the crackly telephone line. Evening, rain, the car had been going too fast. The old road had been temporarily rerouted, motorway extension. A new, perhaps somewhat illogical bend, but marked with danger signs. The newly laid tarmac absorbed light, naturally enough. A parked road-laying machine. I had interrupted the policeman and said they should breath-test my father. Just so that they could confirm what I already knew: that he had killed my mother.

That evening, alone in a pub in Barons Court, had been the first time I had tasted alcohol. And cried in public. The evening when I washed away my tears in the stinking urinals I saw my father's limp, drunken face in the cracked mirror. And remembered that calm, attentive glow in his eyes when he had hit out at the chess pieces, hitting the queen which had whirled through the air — two and a half somersaults — before landing on the floor. Then he had hit me. Just the once, but he had raised his hand. Slapped me below the ear. And I had seen it then, in his eyes; what Mum called the Sickness. And it was a hideous, graceful and bloodthirsty monster that resided behind his eyes. But it was also him, my father, my own flesh and blood.

Blood.

Something which lay deep, that had lain under all the layers of denial for a long time, rose to the surface. A hazy memory of a thought that had gone through my head which would not let itself be held down any longer. It took a more concrete form. Became articulated through pain. Became the truth. The truth that hitherto I had managed to hold at arm's length by lying to myself. For it wasn't the fear of being supplanted by a child that made me not want to have children. It was the fear of the Sickness. The fear that I, the son, also had it. That it was there, behind my eyes. I had lied to everyone. I had told Lotte I didn't want the child because it had a flaw, a syndrome, a chromosome irregularity. While the truth was that the irregularity was in me.

Everything was flowing now. My life had been a property left by the deceased, and now my brain had draped the furniture with dust sheets, closed the doors, prepared itself to switch off the current. My eyes dripped, ran and flooded, over my forehead, into my scalp. I was being suffocated by two human balloons. I thought about Lotte. And there, on the threshold, it dawned on me. I saw the light. I saw . . . Diana? What was the traitor doing here now? Balloons . . .

My free, dangling hand moved towards the overnight bag. My numb fingers loosened Sunded's from the handle and opened it. Petrol was dripping off me into the bag as I rummaged around, pulled out a shirt, a pair of socks, underpants and a toilet bag. That was all. I opened the toilet bag with my free hand and emptied the contents on the roof. Toothpaste, an electric shaver, plasters, shampoo, a transparent plastic bag he must have used at airport security checks, Vaseline . . . there! A pair of scissors, the little pointed kind that bend upwards at the tip and which a number of people for some reason or another prefer to modern nail clippers.

My hand groped its way up one of the twins, over his gut, his chest, trying to find a zip or buttons. But I was losing sensation in my fingers and they would neither obey orders from nor send information to the brain. Then I grabbed the scissors and stuck the point in the belly of, well . . . let's say it was Endride.

The nylon material gave with a liberating rip, slid back and revealed a bulging stomach packed into the light blue material of the police shirt. I snipped open the shirt and the flab covered in hairy, blue-white skin rolled forward. Now I had come to the part I dreaded most. But the thought of the possible reward — being able to live, to breathe — repressed all others, and I swung the scissors with maximum power, thrusting them into his stomach right above the navel. Retracted them. Nothing happened.

Strange. There was a clear hole in his stomach, but nothing came out, nothing that I hoped would relieve the pressure on me. The balloon was still as airtight as before.

I stabbed again. Another hole. Another dry well.

Like a madman, I swung the scissors again. Squelch, squelch. Nothing. What the hell were these twins actually made of? Were they lard right through? Was the obesity epidemic going to kill me, too?

Another car passed, on the road above.

I tried to scream but had no air.

With the last of my strength I slammed the scissors into his gut, but this time I didn't retract them, I simply didn't have the energy. After a pause I began to move them. Stretched my thumb and first finger and brought them back. Cut my way inside. It was surprisingly easy. And then something happened. A stream of blood ran from the hole, down the stomach, disappeared under the clothes, reappeared on the bearded throat, ran over the chin, over the lips and vanished up one nostril. I continued to cut. Frenzied now. And discovered that humans in reality are fragile creatures, because the body opened, slid open the way I had seen happen when they carved up whales on TV. And this was with a tiny pair of nail scissors! I didn't stop until the stomach had a gash running from the waist to the ribs. But the mass of blood and intestines I had expected would pour out was not forthcoming. And the strength in my arm died, I dropped the scissors and an old friend, tunnel vision, was back. Through the opening I could see the inside of the roof. There was a grey chessboard pattern. The broken chess pieces lay scattered around me. I gave up. Closed my eyes. It was wonderful to have given up. I felt gravity dragging me down to the centre of the earth, head first, like a baby on its way out of its mother's incubator, I would be squeezed out, death was rebirth. I could even feel the labour pains now, the quivering pains massaging me. Then the white queen. Heard the sound and the amniotic fluid splashing onto the floor.

And the smell.

My God, the smell!

I was born, and my life started with a fall, a bang on the head and then total darkness.

Total darkness.

Darkness.

Oxygen?

Light.

I opened my eyes. I was lying on my back and above me I saw the back seat where the twins and I had been sitting clamped together. I must have been lying on the inside of the car roof, on the chessboard. And I was breathing. There was a stench of death, of human viscera. I peered around. It looked like a slaughterhouse, a sausage-making factory. But the strange thing was that instead of doing what my nature is predisposed to do — repressing, denying, fleeing — it seemed that my brain had expanded in order to take in the full range of sensual impressions. I decided to stay here. I breathed in the smell. I looked. I listened. Picked up the chess pieces from the floor. Put them into position on the board, one by one. Finally, I raised the chipped white queen. Studied her. Then I put her directly opposite the black king.

■ ■ ■ ■

PART FOUR:
THE SELECTION

■ ■ ■ ■

18
WHITE QUEEN

I sat in the wreckage of the car gazing at the electric shaver. We have bizarre thoughts. The white queen was broken. She whom I had used to keep my father, my background, yes, the whole of my life in check. She who had said she loved me, and to whom I had vowed, even if it was a lie, that a part of me would always love her merely for saying that. She whom I had called my better half because I had really believed she was my Janus face: the good part. But I had been mistaken. And I hated her. No, not even that; Diana Strom-Eliassen no longer existed for me. Yet I was sitting in a wrecked car with four corpses around me, an electric shaver in hand and one single thought in my head:

Would Diana have loved me without my hair?

We have — as I said — bizarre thoughts. Then I dismissed the thought and pressed the *on* button. The shaver — which had belonged to Sunded, the man with the prophetic name that sounded like soon dead — vibrated in my hand.

I would change. I wanted to change. The old Roger no longer existed anyway. I set to work.

A quarter of an hour later I examined myself in the fragment that was left of the mirror. It was — as I had feared — not a pretty sight. My head looked like a peanut with the shell on, oblong with a slight kink in the middle. The shaven skull glistened, white and pale, above the more tanned skin of my face. But I was me: the new Roger Brown.

My hair lay between my legs. I swept it into the transparent plastic bag, which I then stuffed into the back pocket of Eskild Monsen's uniform trousers. There I also found a wallet. Which contained some money and a credit card. And since I had no intention of allowing myself to be traced after using Kjikerud's card, I decided to take the wallet with me. I had already found a lighter in the pocket of the black nylon jacket belonging to Pimples and once again I considered whether to set fire to the petrol-marinated wreck. It would delay the job of identifying the bodies and perhaps give me a day's respite. On the other hand, the smoke would trigger the alarm before I had a chance to get out of the area, whereas without the smoke and with a bit of luck several hours could pass before anyone found the car. I eyed the meat-like surface where Pimples' face had been and made my decision. I spent almost twenty minutes getting his trousers and jacket off and then dressing him in my green jogging outfit. And it is strange how quickly you get used to cutting people up. When I snipped the skin off both of his index fingers (I couldn't remember whether fingerprints were taken from the left or the right hand) it was with the concentrated efficiency of a surgeon. Finally, I snipped at the thumb too so that the damage to his hands looked more random. I took two steps back from the wreck and studied the result. Blood, death, silence. Even the brown river beside the copse seemed frozen in mute immobility. It was worthy of a Morten Viskum installation. If I'd had a camera I would have taken a picture, sent it to Diana and suggested she hang it in the gallery. As an augury of what was to come. For what was it Greve had said? It's the fear, not the pain, that makes you malleable.

I walked along the main road. Of course I ran the risk of being seen by Greve if he drove this way. But I was not concerned. First of all, he wouldn't have recognised the bald-headed guy in a black nylon jacket with ELVERUM KO-DAW-YING CLUB on the back. Secondly, this person walked differently from the Roger Brown he had met; with a more erect back and at a slower pace. Thirdly, the GPS tracker would show in all its clarity that I was still in the wreck and hadn't moved a metre. Obviously. After all, I was dead.

I passed a farm, but continued on my way. A car passed me, braked, wondering perhaps who I was, but accelerated again and disappeared into the sharp autumn light.

It smelt good out here. Earth and grass, coniferous forest and cow muck. My neck wounds ached a little, but the stiffness in my body was receding. I strode out, taking deep breaths, deep and life-affirming.

After half an hour's walking I was still on the same endless road, but I saw a blue sign and a hut in the distance. A bus stop.

A quarter of an hour later I got onto a grey country bus, paid cash from Eskild

Monsen's wallet and was told that the bus went to Elverum, from where there was a train connection to Oslo. I sat down opposite two platinum blondes in their thirties. Neither of them graced me with a glance.

I dozed off, but woke up to the sound of a siren and the bus slowing down and pulling in. A police car with a blue light flashing passed us. Patrol car zero two, I mused, noticing one of the blondes look at me. Meeting her gaze, I noted that she instinctively wanted to avert her eyes — I was too direct; she thought I was ugly. But she couldn't do it. I sent her a wry smile and turned to the window.

The sun was also shining on the old Roger Brown's home town when the new one alighted from the train at ten minutes past three. But an icy cold wind was blowing into the snarling mouths of the disfigured tiger sculptures in front of Oslo Central Station as I crossed the square and continued towards Skippergata.

The dope dealers and whores in Tollbugata looked at me, but didn't yell after me with their offers as they had done for the old Roger Brown. I stopped in front of the entrance to Hotel Leon and glanced up at the facade where the plaster had crumbled, leaving white sores. Beneath one of the windows hung a poster promising a room for four hundred kroner a night.

I went inside to the reception desk. Or RESEPTION as the sign hanging above the man behind the counter said.

'Yes?' he said instead of the usual warm welcome I was used to from the hotels the old Roger Brown frequented. The receptionist's face was covered in a veneer of sweat as though he had been working hard. Had drunk too much coffee. Or was just nervous by nature. The roaming eyes suggested the latter.

'Have you got a single room?' I asked.

'Yes. How long for?'

'Twenty-four hours.'

'All of them?'

I had never been to a hotel like the Leon before, but I had driven past a few times, and I had an inkling they offered rooms on an hourly basis for those who made love on a professional basis. In other words, those women who didn't have the beauty or the wit to use their bodies to acquire a house designed by Ove Bang and their own gallery in Frogner.

I nodded.

'Four hundred,' said the man. 'Payment

in advance.' He had a kind of Swedish accent, the kind preferred by dance band vocalists and preachers for some reason.

I threw Eskild Monsen's credit card on the desk. I know from experience that hotels don't give a damn whether the signature is a match or not, but to be on the safe side I had been working on a passable imitation on the train. The problem was the photograph. It showed a round-jowled man with long, curly hair and a black beard. Not even under-exposure could hide the fact that he bore absolutely no resemblance to the person standing in front of him with a thin face and a recently shaven skull. The receptionist studied the card.

'You don't look like the guy in the photo,' he said without looking up from the card.

I waited. Until he raised his eyes and they met mine.

'Cancer,' I said.

'What?'

'Cytotoxin.'

He blinked three times.

'Three courses of treatment,' I said.

His Adam's apple gave a jump as he swallowed. I could see he had severe doubts. Come on! I had to lie down soon, my throat was hurting like hell. I didn't relinquish his gaze. But he relinquished mine.

'Sorry,' he said, holding the credit card out to me. 'I can't afford to get into trouble. They're keeping an eye on me. Have you got any cash?'

I shook my head. A two-hundred-krone note and a ten-krone coin was all I had left after the train ticket.

'Sorry,' he repeated, stretching out his arm — as if begging — so that the card was touching my chest.

I took it and marched out.

There was no point trying other hotels; if they wouldn't take the card at the Leon, they wouldn't anywhere else either. And in the worst-case scenario they would sound the alarm.

I switched to plan B.

I was a new person, a stranger in town. Without money, without friends, without a past or an identity. The facades, the streets and the people who walked in them, appeared different to me from how they had to Roger Brown. A thin strip of cloud had glided in front of the sun and the temperature had sunk another few degrees.

At Oslo Central Station I had to ask which bus went to Tonsenhagen, and as I got onto the bus, for some reason the driver spoke English to me.

From the bus stop to Ove's house there were a couple of steep hills, yet I was still frozen when I finally passed his place. I circled round the area for a few minutes to make sure there were no policemen in the vicinity. Then I went up to the door and let myself in.

It was warm inside. Time- and thermostat-controlled radiators.

I tapped in *Natasha* to deactivate the alarm and walked into the sitting room-cum-bedroom. It smelt as it had before. Washing-up not done, unwashed bedlinen, gun oil and sulphur. Ove was lying on the bed as I had left him. It felt like it was a week ago.

I found the remote control, got into bed beside Ove and switched on the TV. Flicked through teletext, but there was nothing about missing patrol cars or dead police-men. The Elverum police must have had their suspicions for some time and must have launched a search, but they would probably wait for as long as possible before announcing that a patrol car had gone miss-ing in case the whole thing was down to a banal misunderstanding. However, sooner or later they would find it. How long from then until they discovered that the body without fingertips in the green tracksuit was not the detainee, Ove Kjikerud? Twenty-four hours? Forty-eight max.

These were matters, of course, which I was not qualified to judge. I didn't have the vaguest notion of the process. And the new Roger Brown knew no more about police procedures, but he did at least realise that the situation demanded firm decisions based on uncertain information, risky action instead of hesitation, and toleration of enough fear for the senses to be sharpened, but not so much that you were paralysed.

For that reason I closed my eyes and slept.

When I awoke, the clock on teletext showed 20:03. And beneath it a line about at least four people, of whom three were police officers, killed in a traffic accident outside Elverum. The patrol car had been reported missing in the morning and was located in the afternoon next to a copse by the River Trekk. A fifth person, also a policeman, was missing. The police thought he may have been hurled out of the car into the river and a search had been mounted. The police asked the public for information about the driver of a stolen Sigdal Kitchens lorry that had been found parked on a woodland road twenty kilometres from the accident scene.

When they knew that Kjikerud was the

missing person they would sooner or later come here. I had to find myself somewhere else to sleep tonight.

I took a deep breath. Then I leaned across Ove's body, picked up the phone on the bedside table and dialled the only number I knew by heart.

She answered on the third ring.

Instead of her usual shy but warm 'Hi', Lotte answered with an almost inaudible 'Yes?'

I put down the phone immediately. All I wanted to know was that she was at home. I hoped she would be later that night as well.

I switched off the TV and got up.

After searching for two minutes I had found two guns: one in the bathroom and one squeezed behind the TV. I chose the small black one from behind the TV and went to the kitchen drawer, took out two boxes, one with live ammunition and one labelled 'blanks', filled the magazine with live cartridges, loaded the gun and engaged the safety catch. Then I stuffed the gun into my waistband as I had seen Greve do. I went into the bathroom and put the first gun back. After closing the cabinet door, I stood inspecting myself in the mirror. The fine shape of the face and the deep lines, the head's brutal nakedness, the intense gaze, the almost feverish skin and mouth; relaxed and determined, silent and expressive.

Wherever I woke up tomorrow morning, it would be with murder on my conscience. *Premeditated* murder.

19
PREMEDITATED MURDER

You walk along your own street. You stand in the evening gloom under a cluster of trees looking up at your own house, at the lights in the window, at a movement by the curtains which might be your wife. A neighbour out walking his English setter passes by and sees you, sees a stranger in a street where most people know each other. The man is suspicious, and the setter lets out a low growl; they can both smell that you hate dogs. Animals, like humans, stick together against intruders and trespassers up here on the mountainside where they have entrenched themselves, raised high above the confusion of the town and the chaotic jumble of interests and agendas. Up here they just want things to continue as they are, for things are good, everything's fine, the cards should not be re-dealt. No, let the aces and kings remain in the hands they are in now: uncertainty damages investor confidence, stable economic conditions ensure productivity, which in turn serves the community. You have to create something before you can distribute it.

It is odd to think that the most conservative person I have ever met was a chauffeur who drove people earning four times as much as he did and addressed him with the condescension that only the most painfully correct politeness can express.

Dad once said that if I became a socialist I would no longer be welcome in his house, and the same applied to my mother. He was, it is true, not sober when he made that threat, but that was all the more reason to assume that he meant quite literally what he said. He thought that the caste system in India had a lot to recommend it, that we were born into our station in life in accordance with God's will and it was our damned duty to spend our wretched lives there. Or as the sexton says in Johan Falkberget's *The Fourth Night Watch:* 'Sextons are sextons. And priests are priests.'

My rebellion, a chauffeur's son's rebellion, had therefore been: education, a rich man's daughter, Ferner Jacobsen−branded suits and a house on Voksenkollen. It had gone wrong. Dad had had the impudence to forgive me; he had even been so crafty as to act proud. And I knew, when I sobbed like a baby at their funeral, that I was not grieving over my mother; I was furious at my father.

The setter and the neighbour (strange that I could no longer remember what his name was) were swallowed up by the darkness and I crossed the road. There had been no unfamiliar cars in the street, and, pressing my face against the garage window, I could see that it too was empty.

I sneaked quickly into the raw, almost palpably black night of the garden and took up position under the apple trees where I knew it was impossible to see anyone from the living room.

But I could see her.

Diana was pacing the floor. The impatient movements combined with the Prada phone pressed to her ear led me to infer that she was trying to ring someone who was not answering. She was wearing jeans. No one could wear jeans the way Diana did. Despite her white woollen sweater, she walked with her free arm across her chest as though she were freezing. A big house built in the 1930s takes time to warm up after a plunge in temperature, however many radiators you turn on.

I waited until I was quite sure she was

alone. Felt for my gun lodged in my waistband. Took a deep breath. This would be the most difficult thing I had ever done. But I knew I would succeed. The new man would succeed. That was perhaps why the tears flowed, because the outcome was already a given. I did nothing to restrain the tears. They ran like hot caresses down my cheeks while I concentrated on being still, not losing control of my breathing, and not sobbing. After five minutes I was empty and dried my cheeks. Then I walked to the door with rapid strides and let myself in as quietly as I could. Inside, in the corridor, I stood listening. It was as though the house was holding its breath: the silence was broken only by the click of her footsteps on the parquet floor upstairs in the living room. And soon they would stop, too.

It was ten o'clock in the evening, and behind the barely open door I glimpsed a pale face and a pair of brown eyes.

'Could I sleep here?' I asked.

Lotte didn't answer. She didn't usually. But she was staring as if I were a ghost. She didn't usually stare or look frightened, either.

I smirked and ran a hand across my smooth scalp.

'I've shaved off . . .' I searched for the word. '. . . the lot.'

She blinked twice. Then she pulled back the door and I slipped in.

20
RESURRECTION

I awoke and glanced at my watch. Eight. It was time to begin. I had what they call a big day in front of me. Lotte lay on her side with her back to me, swathed in the sheets that she preferred to a duvet. I slid out on my side of the bed and dressed at top speed. It was bitterly cold, and I was frozen to the marrow. I crept into the hall, put on my jacket, hat and gloves and went into the kitchen. In one of the drawers I found a plastic bag which I shoved into my trouser pocket. Then I opened the fridge, thinking it was the first day I had woken up as a murderer. A man who had shot a woman. It sounded like something from the newspaper, the kind of case I ignored because criminal cases were always so painful and banal. I grabbed a carton of grapefruit juice and was about to put it to my mouth. But changed my mind and fetched a glass from the overhead cabinet. You don't need to let all your standards decline just because you have become a murderer. After finishing the juice, rinsing the glass and putting the carton back, I went into the living room and sat down on the sofa. The small black gun in my jacket pocket poked me in the stomach, and I took it out. It still smelt, and I knew the smell would come to remind me of the murder for ever. The execution. One shot had been sufficient. At point-blank range, as she was about to embrace me. I had shot during the embrace and hit her in the left eye. Was it intentional? Maybe. Maybe I had wanted to take something from her in the same way that she had tried to take everything from me. And the lying traitor had embraced the lead, the phallic bullet had penetrated her as I had once done. Never again. Now she was dead. Thoughts came like that, in short sentences confirming facts. Good. I would have to continue thinking like that, maintaining the chill, not letting my emotions have a chance. I still had something to lose.

I raised the remote control and switched on the TV. There was nothing new on teletext; the editors weren't in the office that early, I supposed. It still said the four bodies would be identified in the course of the following day, today in other words, and that one person was still missing.

One person. They had changed that from 'one policeman', hadn't they? Did that mean then that they now knew that the missing person was the detainee? Maybe, maybe not; there was no mention of them searching for anyone.

I leaned over the armrest and picked up the receiver from her yellow landline phone, the one I always visualised by Lotte's red lips when I rang. The tip of her tongue was next to my ear as she was wetting them. I dialled 1881, asked for two numbers and interrupted her when she said an automated voice would give them to me.

'I would like to hear them from you personally in case the speech is unclear and I have any problems understanding,' I said.

I was given the two numbers, memorised them and asked her to put me through to the first. The central switchboard at Kripos answered on the second ring.

I introduced myself as Runar Bratli and said I was a relative of Endride and Eskild Monsen and that I had been asked by the family to collect their clothes. But no one had told me where to go or who to see.

'Just a moment,' said the switchboard lady, putting me on hold.

I listened to a surprisingly good pan-pipe

version of 'Wonderwall' and thought about Runar Bratli. He was a candidate I had once decided not to recommend for a top management job even though he had been the best qualified by far. And tall. So tall that during the final interview he had complained that he had to sit doubled up in his Ferrari, an investment he had conceded with a boyish smile that had been a childish caprice; more like a midlife crisis I thought. And I had jotted down: *Open, enough self-assurance to expose own foolishness.* Everything had been, in other words, textbook stuff. Just not the comment he had followed up with: 'When I think about how I hit my head on the roof of the car, I almost env—'

He had cut off the sentence there, shifted his gaze away from me and on to one of the customer's representatives and chatted about exchanging the Ferrari for a SUV, the kind you allow your wife drive. Everyone round the table had laughed. I had, too. And not so much as a twitch revealed that I had completed the sentence for him: '. . . envy you for being so small.' And that I had just put a line through his name as a contender. Unfortunately, he didn't possess any interesting art.

'They're in the Pathology Unit.' It was the switchboard again. 'At Rikshospital in Oslo.'

'Oh?' I said, trying not to overdo my naivety. 'Why's that?'

'It's a routine procedure when there's a suspicion that a crime may have been committed. It looks like the car was rammed by this truck.'

'I see,' I said. 'I suppose that's why they asked me to help them. I live in Oslo, you see.'

The lady didn't answer. I could visualise her rolling eyes and long, carefully painted nails drumming on the table with impatience. But I might have been wrong, of course. Being a headhunter doesn't necessarily mean you're a good judge of character or particularly empathetic. To get to the top in this business I think the opposite is true, that it can be a disadvantage.

'Could you inform the relevant person that I'm on my way to the Pathology Unit now?' I asked.

I could hear her hesitate. This task apparently didn't come under her job description. Job descriptions in public service are a mess, as a rule, believe me, I still read them.

'I don't have anything to do with this. I'm just trying to help out,' I said. 'So I hope to be in and out quickly.'

'I'll try,' she said.

I put down the receiver and dialled the

second number. He answered on the fifth ring.

'Yes?' His voice sounded impatient, almost irritated.

I tried to work out from the background noise where he was. In my house or in his own apartment.

'Boo,' I said and rang off.

Clas Greve was hereby warned.

I didn't know what he would do, but he was bound to switch on the GPS and check where the ghost was.

I returned to the opened door. In the dark of the bedroom I could just make out the contours of her body under the sheet. I resisted a sudden impulse: to get undressed, slip back into the bed and snuggle up to her. Instead I felt an odd sensation that everything that had happened had not been about Diana, but about me. I closed the bedroom door softly and left. Just as when I had arrived, there was no one on the staircase to greet. Nor when I got out onto the street did I meet anyone who would respond to my friendly nods; no one looked at me or acknowledged my existence in any other way. Now it had dawned on me what the sensation was: I didn't exist.

It was time to find myself again.

■ ■ ■ ■

Rikshospital is situated on one of Oslo's many sloping ridges, raised high above the town. Before it was built there had been a small madhouse here. A name that was changed to an institute for the insane. And then to asylum, and finally to psychiatric hospital. And so on as the general population caught on to the fact that the new phrase just meant quite ordinary mental derangement, too. Personally, I have never understood this word game, although those in charge must believe the general public are a bunch of prejudiced idiots who have to be wrapped in cotton wool. They might be right, but it was nevertheless refreshing to hear the woman behind the glass partition say: 'Corpses are on the lower ground floor, Bratli.'

Being a corpse is apparently all right. No one highlights the outrage of calling a person who is dead a corpse, or says that, in spite of everything, there is more merit in being a dead person than there is in being dead, or that the word 'corpse' reduces people to being a lump of flesh in which the heart happens to beat no longer. And so what? Or perhaps it is all down to the fact that corpses cannot plead minority status; after all, they are in the woeful majority.

'Down the staircase over there,' she said, pointing. 'I'll ring down and tell them you're on your way.'

I did as instructed. My footsteps resounded through the bare white walls; otherwise it was very quiet here. At the far end of a long, narrow, white corridor on the floor below, with one foot inside an open door, stood a man dressed in a green hospital uniform. He could have been a surgeon, but something about his exaggeratedly relaxed posture, or perhaps it was his moustache, told me he was lower down the hierarchy.

'Bratli?' he shouted, so loud that it seemed like a conscious insult to those sleeping on this floor. The echo rolled menacingly backwards and forwards in the corridor.

'Yes,' I said, hurrying towards him so that we wouldn't have to take any more of this shouting.

He held the door open for me, and I stepped in. It was a kind of locker room. The man walked ahead of me to a locker, which he opened.

'Kripos rang to say you would be coming to pick up the Monsen boys' things,' he said, still with this exaggeratedly powerful voice.

I nodded. My pulse was racing faster than I had liked. But not as fast as I had feared. This was, after all, a critical phase, the weak point in the plan.

'And so who are you?'

'Third cousin,' I said airily. 'The next of kin asked me to pick up their clothes. Just the clothes, no valuables.'

I had decided on 'next of kin' with care. It might indeed sound conspicuously formal, but as I didn't know whether the Monsen twins had been married or their parents were still alive, I had to choose words which covered all eventualities.

'Why doesn't fru Monsen come and collect them herself?' the man said. 'She's coming here at twelve anyway.'

I gulped. 'I suppose she can't bear the thought of all that blood.'

He grinned. 'But you can?'

'Yes,' I said simply, hoping with a passion that there would be no more questions.

The man shrugged and passed over a sheet of paper on a clipboard. 'Sign here to confirm receipt.'

I scribbled an R with a wavy line followed by a B with a corresponding squiggle and a final dot over the 'i'.

The porter scrutinised the signature thoughtfully. 'Have you got any ID, Bratli?'

The plan was creaking at the joints.

I patted my trouser pockets and put on an apologetic smile. 'Must have left my wallet in the car down in the car park.'

'Up in the car park, don't you mean?'

'No, down. I parked in the Research Car Park.'

'All the way down there?'

I could see his hesitation. Naturally, I had thought this scenario through beforehand. In the event that I was sent off to fetch ID, I would just leave without returning. It wouldn't be a disaster, but I wouldn't have achieved what I had come for. I waited. And from the two first words knew that the decision had gone against me.

'Sorry, Bratli, but we have to be on the safe side. Don't take this the wrong way but murder cases attract a huge number of weird individuals. With extremely weird interests.'

I acted astonished. 'Do you mean to say that . . . people collect murder victims' clothing?'

'You wouldn't believe what some get up to,' he said. 'For all I know you may never have met the Monsen boys, just read about them in the papers. Sorry, but I'm afraid that's the way it is.'

'Fine, I'll be back in a bit,' I said, moving towards the door. Where I paused as though I had remembered something and played my last card. To be precise: the credit card.

'Now I think about it,' I said, plunging my hand into my back pocket, 'the last time Endride was at my place, he left his credit card. Perhaps you could give it to his mother when she comes . . .'

I passed it to the porter, who held it and studied the name and photo of the bearded young man. I bided my time but was already halfway out of the door when I finally heard his voice behind me.

'That's good enough for me, Bratli. Here, take the togs.'

Relieved, I turned back. Took out the plastic bag I had stuffed into my trouser pocket and shoved the clothes in.

'Got everything?'

I fingered the back pockets of Endride's uniform trousers. Could feel it was still there, the plastic bag with my shorn hair. I nodded.

I had to stop myself from running as I left. I was resurrected, I existed once more, and inside me this created a strange exultation. The wheels were spinning again, my heart was beating, my blood was circulating and my fortunes turning. I hurried up the stairs two at a time, passed the woman behind the glass partition at a more sedate pace and was almost at the door when I heard a familiar voice behind me.

'Hello there, mister! Hold on a minute.'

Of course. It had been too easy.

I turned slowly. A man, familiar too, came towards me. He was holding up an ID card. Diana's secret love. And the heretical thought flashed through my mind: I've had it.

'Kripos,' said the man in a deep pilot's voice. Atmospheric noise, specks of outage. 'May I have a few words with you, mis-er?' Like a typewriter with a worn letter.

It is said that unconsciously we create an image of people we see in films or on TV that is bigger than they are in reality. This was not the case with Brede Sperre. He was even bigger than I had imagined. I forced myself to stand still as he walked towards me. Then he towered over me. From on high, under blond, boyish locks, cut so that his hair would seem wild in a trustworthy way, a pair of steel-grey eyes looked down at me. One of the things I had picked up about Sperre was that he was supposed to be having a relationship with a very well-known and very masculine Norwegian politician. Now rumours of homosexuality are, of course, the final proof that you have become a celebrity, the very hallmark so to speak. It was just that the person who'd told me this — one of the male models used by the designer Baron von Bulldog who had begged his way into Diana's private view — claimed that he had allowed himself to be sodomised by the 'police god', as he reverentially called him.

'Oh, that's just talk, that is,' I had said with a rigid smile, hoping the penetration angst did not show in my eyes.

'Right, mister. I've jus-heard that you're the third cousin of the Monsen boys and know them well. Perhaps you might be so kind as to help us iden-ify the bodies?'

I swallowed. The polite form of address and the semi-jocular 'mister' in the same utterance. But Sperre's eyes were neutral. Was he playing the status game or did he just do that automatically, almost like a professional reflex action? I heard myself repeating 'identify' with a stammer as though the concept were totally unfamiliar to me.

'Their mother will be here in a few hours,' Sperre said. 'But any time we could save . . . We would app-eciate that. It'll on-y take a couple of se-onds.'

I didn't want to. My body bristled and my brain insisted I refuse and get the hell out of there. For I had been reawakened. I — that is the plastic bag of hair I was carrying — was now a person who was active again on Greve's GPS receiver. It was only a question of time before he would resume the hunt; I could already scent the dog in the air, sense the panic mounting. But another part of my brain, the one with the new voice, said that I should not refuse. That it would arouse suspicion. That it would only take a few seconds.

'Of course,' I said and was about to smile, until I realised that would be perceived as an inappropriate reaction to having to identify the corpses of your own relatives.

We went back the same way as I had come.

The porter nodded to me with a grin as we went through the locker room.

'You should prepare yourself. The deceased are in pretty bad shape,' Sperre said, opening a heavy metal door. We stepped into the mortuary. I shivered. Everything in the room suggested the inside of a fridge: white walls, roof and floor, a few degrees above zero and meat that was past its sell-by date.

The four bodies lay in a line, each on its own metal table. Feet stuck out from under white sheets, and I could see that film conventions were rooted in reality; they did in fact each have a metal tag attached to a big toe.

'Ready?' said Sperre.

I nodded.

He whipped back two sheets with a flourish, like a magician. 'Traffic accidents,' the policeman said, rocking on his heels. 'The worst. Hard to identify, as you can see.' I had the sudden impression Sperre was speaking abnormally slowly. 'There should have been five people in the car, but we found only these four bodies. The fifth must have landed in the river and floated away.'

I stared, swallowed and breathed heavily through my nose. I was play-acting, of course. For even naked, the Monsen twins looked better now than they had in the wrecked car. Moreover, it didn't reek in here. No gaseous faeces, no smells of blood and petrol or the stench of human intestines. It occurred to me that visual impressions are overrated, that sound and smell terrorise the sense mechanisms in a much more effective way. Like the crunching sound a woman's head makes as it hits the parquet floor, after being shot through the eye.

'It's the Monsen twins,' I whispered.

'Yes, we've managed to work that out, too. The question is . . .'

Sperre paused for a long — a really long — dramatic pause. My God.

'Which is Endride and which is Eskild?'

Despite the wintry temperature in the room I was soaked with sweat under my clothes. Was he speaking so slowly on purpose? Was it a new interrogation method, of which I knew nothing?

My gaze hovered over the naked bodies and found the mark I had made. The wound running from the ribs down the stomach was still open and had black scabs along the edges.

'That's Endride,' I stated, pointing. 'The other's Eskild.'

'Hm,' Sperre purred with satisfaction, making a note. 'You must've known the twins very well. Not even their colleagues, who have been here, could tell them apart.'

I answered with a sorrowful nod. 'The twins and I were very close. Especially of late. Can I go now?'

'Sure,' Sperre said, but continued to make notes in a way that did not invite a dismissal.

I looked at the clock behind his head.

'Identical twins,' Sperre said, continuing to write. 'Ironic, isn't it?' What the hell was he writing? One was Endride, the other Es-

309

kild, how many words did you really need to say that?

I knew I ought not to ask, but I couldn't resist. 'What's ironic?'

Sperre stopped writing and looked up. 'Born in the same second from the same egg. Dead in the same second in the same car.'

'No irony in that, is there?'

'None?'

'None that I can see.'

'Mm. You're right. "Paradox" is probably the word I was looking for.' Sperre smiled.

I felt my blood beginning to bubble. 'It's not a paradox, either.'

'Well, it is strange anyway. There is a sort of cosmic logic to it, don't you think?'

I lost control, saw my knuckles go white as I squeezed the bag and heard my quivering voice say: 'No irony, no parody, no cosmic logic.' The volume increased. 'Just an arbitrary symmetry of life and death, which is not even that arbitrary since they, like many other identical twins, chose to spend a lot of their time in the immediate vicinity of each other. Lightning struck and they were together. End of story.'

I had almost shouted the last part.

Sperre looked at me with a thoughtful gaze. He had a finger and thumb placed at opposite corners of his mouth and now he ran them down to his chin. I knew that look. He was one of the few. He had the interrogator look, the eyes that could expose lies.

'Well, Bratli,' he said, 'something bothering you, is there?'

'Sorry,' I said with a wan smile and knew I had to say something truthful now, something that did not register on the lie detector staring at me. 'I had a bit of a disagreement with my wife last night, and now this accident. I'm a bit off-kilter. My deepest apologies. I'll remove myself this minute.'

I turned on my heel and left.

Sperre said something, perhaps goodbye, but it was drowned by the metal door slamming behind me and a bass tone booming through the mortuary.

21
INVITATION

I caught the tram at the stop outside Riks-hospital, paid the conductor in cash and said, 'To the centre.' He smirked as he gave me change, presumably the price was the same wherever I went. I had caught the tram before, of course, as a boy, but I didn't recall the routine so well. Get out through the back door, have your ticket ready to be checked, press the stop button in good time, don't disturb the driver. A lot had changed. The noise from the rails was less deafening, the advertising more deafening and extrovert. People on the seats more introvert.

In the centre I switched mode of transport, to a bus which took me north-east. Was told I could travel on the tram ticket. Fantastic. For peanuts I could navigate my way through the town in a way I had never known was possible. I was in motion. A flashing dot on Greve's GPS thingy. I seemed to be able to sense his confusion:

What the fuck is going on? Are they moving the body?

I got off the bus at Årvoll and began to climb the hills towards Tonsenhagen. I could have got off closer to Ove's place, but everything I was doing now had a point. In these residential areas it was a quiet morning. A stoop-shouldered old lady was tottering along the pavement pulling a shopping cart behind her with screaming, unlubricated wheels. Nevertheless she smiled at me as if it was a wonderful day, a beautiful world, a lovely life. What was Greve thinking now? That there was a hearse driving Brown to his childhood home or something like that, but it suddenly seemed to be going so slowly — was there a traffic jam?

Two gum-chewing, heavily made-up teenage girls with school bags, tight trousers and muffin tops came towards me. They glared briefly, but didn't stop talking in loud voices about something that obviously annoyed them. As they passed, I caught a 'I mean . . . so unfair!' I guessed that they were skipping school, were on their way down to a cake shop in Årvoll, and that the unfairness was not directed at the fact that eighty per cent of the earth's population could not afford the cream buns they were about to tuck away. And it struck me that if Diana and I had had the child, she would — I was convinced it would be a girl even though Diana had already called it Damien — have looked at me one day with the same mascara-heavy eyes, shouted that it was unfair, for Chrisssake, she and her girlfriend wanted to go to Ibiza and after all they were old enough and would soon be leaving school! And that I . . . I could have managed, I think.

The road passed a park with a large pond in the middle, and I took one of the brown paths leading to a group of trees on the other side. Not because it was a short cut, but to get the dot on Greve's GPS to move off the street map. Bodies can be moved around in cars, but they don't move through the landscape. It was confirmation of the suspicion that my wake-up call from Lotte's place this morning would have planted in the Dutch headhunter's head: that Roger Brown had risen from the dead. That Brown had not been lying in the mortuary at Riks-hospital as it had seemed from the GPS, but presumably in a bed in the same building. But they had said on the news that everyone in the car was dead, so how . . . ?

I may not be particularly empathetic, but I am a good judge of intelligence, so good that I am used to hiring leaders for Nor-

way's biggest companies. So while I plod-
ded around the pond, I again went through
Greve's probable reasoning at this moment.
Which was simple. He would have to come
after me, have to exterminate me, even if it
involved much greater risk than before. For
I was no longer just someone who could
put a stop to HOTE's plans for taking over
Pathfinder, I was a witness who could put
him in the slammer for the murder of Sindre Aa. If I was allowed to live long enough
for the case to come to court.

In short, I had sent him an invitation he
could not refuse.

I had arrived at the other side of the park,
and as I passed the clump of birch trees, I
stroked my fingers along the thin, white,
peeling bark, pressed them lightly against
the hard trunk, bent my fingers and scraped
my nails across the surface. Smelt my
fingertips, stopped, closed my eyes and
breathed in the aroma as memories of childhood, play, laughter, wonder, gleeful horror
and discovery flooded back. All the tiny
things I thought I had lost but which were
there, of course, encapsulated, they didn't
disappear, they were water children. The
old Roger Brown had been unable to recap-
ture them, but the new one could. How long
would the new one live? Not much longer

now. But it didn't matter, he would live his last hours more intensely than the old one had lived all his thirty-five years.

I was hot when I finally saw Kjikerud's place. I walked up into the edge of the forest and sat down on a tree stump where I had a good view of the terraced houses and blocks of flats along the road. And established that people in east Oslo do not have the same wide array of views that those living in west Oslo have. We could all see the Post Giro building and the Plaza Hotel. The town didn't come across as any uglier or more attractive. The only difference was that basically you could see the western side from here. Which made me think of the story about Gustave Eiffel and the famous tower he had built for the World Expo in Paris in 1889; the critics said the finest view in Paris was from the Eiffel Tower because that was the only place in Paris where you couldn't see it. And I wondered if perhaps that was what it was like being Clas Greve; that the world for him had to seem a slightly less hideous place. Because he couldn't see himself through other people's eyes. Mine for example. I saw him. And I hated him. Hated him with such a surprising intensity and passion that it almost frightened me. But it was not a muddied hatred, quite the contrary, it was a pure, decent, almost innocent hatred, in the same way that the crusaders must have hated the blasphemers. And that was why I could sentence Greve to death with the same measured, naive hatred that allows the devout Christian American to send his death-row neighbour to the execution chamber. And in many ways this hatred was a purifying sensation.

It made me understand, for example, that what I had felt for my father was not hatred. Anger? Yes. Contempt? Maybe. Pity? Definitely. And why? Many reasons, to be sure. But I saw now that my fury originated from my feeling, deep down, that I was like him, that I had it in me to be exactly like him: a drunken, penniless wife-beater who thought east was east and could never be west. And now I had become him, definitively and in full measure.

The laughter bubbled up inside me, and I did nothing to stop it. Not until it resounded among the tree trunks, a bird took off from a branch above me and I saw a car coming down the road.

A silver-grey Lexus GS 430.

He had come faster than I had expected.

I got up instantly and walked down to Kjikerud's house. Standing on the step, about to insert the key into the lock, I looked at my hand. The shaking was imperceptible, but I saw it.

It was instinct, an ur-fear. Clas Greve was the kind of animal who made other animals afraid.

I found the keyhole at first attempt. Turned the key, opened the door and went quickly into the house. Still no smell. Sat up on the bed, shifted backwards until I was sitting with my back against the headboard and to the window. Checked that the duvet covered Ove lying beside me.

Waited. The seconds were ticking. And my heart was, too. Two heartbeats a second.

Greve was cautious, that went without saying. He wanted to make sure I was alone. And even though I was alone, he knew now that I was not as harmless as he had initially thought. Firstly, I must have had something to do with his dog's death. Secondly, he must have been there, seen her body and known that I was capable of killing.

I didn't hear the door open. Didn't hear his footsteps. Only saw him standing in the doorway in front of me. His voice was gentle and the smile genuinely apologetic.

'Sorry to burst in on you like this, Roger.'

Greve was dressed in black. Black trousers, black shoes, black roll-neck, black gloves. On his head a black woollen hat. The

only thing that was not black was the gleam-
ing silver Glock.

'That's fine,' I said. 'It's visiting time.'

22
SILENT FILM

It is said that a fly's perception of time, the reason it experiences the palm of a hand zooming towards it as yawningly slow, is due to the fact that the information it receives through its facet eyes contains such a large amount of data that nature has had to equip it with an extra-fast processor so as to be able to deal with everything in real time.

For several seconds there was total silence in the sitting room. How many I don't know. I was a fly and the hand was on its way. Kjikerud's Glock pistol was directed at my chest; Greve's eyes at my shiny pate.

'Aha,' he said at length.

This one word contained everything. Everything about how we humans have been able to conquer the earth, rule over the elements, kill creatures that are greater than ourselves in speed and strength. Processor capacity. Greve's 'Aha' came at the end of an avalanche of thoughts, the search for and filtering of hypotheses, relentless deductive powers that together led to an inevitable conclusion: 'You've shaved off your hair, Roger.'

Greve was — as suggested earlier — an intelligent person. Of course he had done more than state the banal fact that my hair had been removed, but also when, how and why it had happened. Because that cleared up all the confusion, answered all the questions. That was why he added, more as a fact than as a question: 'In the wrecked car.'

I nodded.

He sat down in the chair at the foot of the bed, rocked it back against the wall, without the barrel of the gun deviating an inch from me.

'And then? Did you plant the hair on one of the bodies?'

I thrust my hand in the jacket pocket.

'Freeze!' he screamed, and I saw the finger pressing the trigger. No cocked hammer. Glock 17. A dame.

'It's my left hand,' I said.

'OK. Slowly does it.'

I took my hand out slowly and slung the bag of hair on the table. Greve nodded gently without taking his eyes off me.

'So you knew,' he said. 'That the transmitters were in your hair. And that she had put them there for me. That was why you killed her, wasn't it?'

'Did it feel like a loss, Clas?' I asked, leaning back. My heart was pounding, yet I felt remarkably mellow in this, my final hour. The flesh's mortal dread and the spirit's serenity.

He didn't answer.

'Or was she just — what did you call it? — a means to an end? A necessary expense to acquire income?'

'Why do you want to know, Roger?'

'Because I want to know if people like you really exist or whether they're just fiction.'

'Like me?'

'People who are unable to love.'

Greve laughed. 'If you wanted an answer to that you only needed to look in the mirror, Roger.'

'I loved someone,' I said.

'You might have imitated love,' Clas said. 'But did you really love? Do you have any proof of that? I see only proof of the opposite, that you denied Diana the one thing she wanted besides you: a child.'

'I would've given her that.'

He laughed again. 'So you've changed your mind? When did that happen? When did you become the contrite husband? When you discovered that she was fucking another man?'

'I believe in contrition,' I said quietly. 'In contrition. And in forgiveness.'

'And now it's too late,' he said. 'Diana got neither your forgiveness nor your child.'

'Not yours either.'

'It was never my intention to give her a child, Roger.'

'No, but if you'd wanted it, you'd never have been able to do it, would you?'

'Of course I would. Do you think I'm impotent?'

He spoke quickly. So quickly that only a fly could have perceived the nanosecond of hesitation. I breathed in. 'I've seen you, Clas Greve. I've seen you from . . . a frog's-eye view.'

'What the fuck are you on about now, Brown?'

'I've seen your reproductive organs at a closer range than I would've chosen of my own accord.'

I watched his mouth slowly drop, and went on.

'In an outside toilet near Elverum.'

Greve's mouth seemed poised to formulate something, but nothing emerged.

'Was that how they made you talk when you were in the cellar in Suriname? By targeting your testicles? Battering them? A knife? They didn't take the desire, only the reproductive capacity, didn't they? What was left of your balls was sewn together with rough thread.'

Greve's mouth was closed now. A straight line in a stony face.

'That explains the fanatical hunt for what you yourself said was a pretty insignificant drug smuggler in the jungle, Clas. Sixty-five days, wasn't it? Because it was him, wasn't it? He was the one who'd slashed your manhood. Taken from you the ability to make replicas of yourself. He'd taken everything from you. Almost. So you took his life. And I can understand that.'

Yes, indeed, this was Inbau, Reid and Buckley's sub-point in step two: suggest a morally acceptable motive for the crime. But I no longer needed his confession. Instead he got mine. In advance. 'I understand, Clas, because I've decided to kill you for the same reason. You took everything from me. Almost.'

Greve's mouth made a sound I interpreted as laughter. 'Who's sitting with the gun here, Roger?'

'I'm going to kill you the way I killed your damned dog.'

I saw his jaw muscles tighten as he clenched his teeth, saw the white of his knuckles.

'You never saw that, did you, now? It ended its days as crow fodder. Transfixed on the prongs of Aa's tractor.'

'You make me sick, Roger Brown. You sit there moralising while you yourself are an animal killer and a child murderer.'

'You're right. But wrong about what you said to me at the hospital. That our child had Down's syndrome. Quite the opposite, all the tests showed that it was healthy. I persuaded Diana to have an abortion simply because I didn't want to share her with anyone. Have you ever heard anything so childish? Pure, unadulterated jealousy towards an unborn baby. I assume I didn't get enough love when I was growing up. What do you think? Perhaps it was the same for you, Clas? Or were you evil from birth?'

I don't think Clas took the questions in because he was staring at me with that gawping expression that showed his brain was working at full capacity again. Reconstructing, following the branches on the tree of decisions back down to its trunk, to the truth, to where it had all started. And found it. One single sentence at the hospital. Something he had said himself: '. . . have an abortion because the baby has Down's syndrome.'

325

'So tell me,' I said when I saw that he had understood, 'have you loved anyone else apart from your dog?'

He raised the gun. There were only seconds left of the new Roger Brown's short life. Greve's ice-blue eyes sparkled and the gentle voice was just a whisper now.

'I had been thinking of putting a single bullet through your head as a mark of respect for being a prey worthy of a hunter, Roger. But I think I'll go back to the original plan after all. Shooting you in the stomach. Have I told you about stomach shots? How the bullet bores through your spleen causing the gastric acid to leak out and burn its way through the rest of the intestines? Then I have to wait until you beg me to kill you. And you will, Roger.'

'Perhaps you ought to cut the chat and shoot, Clas? Perhaps you shouldn't wait as long as you did at the hospital?'

Greve laughed again. 'Oh, I don't think you've invited the police here, Roger. You've killed a woman. You're a murderer like me. This is between you and me.'

'Think again, Clas. Why do you reckon I risked going to the Pathology Unit and tricking them into handing over the bag of hair?'

Greve rolled his shoulders. 'Simple. It's

the DNA evidence. Probably the only thing they had which they could have used against you. They still think the name of the person they're looking for is Ove Kjikerud. Unless you wanted your beautiful mane back, that is. Make a wig out of it? Diana told me your hair was very important to you. That you used it to compensate for your height?'

'Correct,' I said. 'But incorrect. Sometimes the headhunter forgets that the head he is hunting can think. I don't know if it thinks better or worse without hair, but in this case it has enticed the hunter into a trap.'

Greve blinked slowly while I observed his body tense up; he sensed mischief.

'I don't see a trap, Roger.'

'It's here,' I said, whisking aside the duvet next to me. I saw his eyes fall on the body of Ove Kjikerud. And on the Uzi machine gun that lay on his chest.

He reacted with lightning speed, pointing the pistol at me. 'Don't try anything, Brown.'

I moved my hands towards the machine gun.

'Don't!' Greve screamed.

I raised the weapon.

Greve fired. The explosion filled the room.

I pointed my gun at Greve. He had half

risen to his feet in the chair and loosened off another round. I pressed the trigger. Pressed it all the way. A hoarse roar of lead tore through the air, Ove's walls, the chair, Clas Greve's black trousers, the perfect thigh muscles beneath, tore open his groin and, I hoped, his genitals which had been inside Diana, his well-developed abdominal muscles and the organs they were supposed to protect.

He fell back in the chair and the Glock thudded to the floor. There was an abrupt silence, then the sound of a cartridge rolling over the parquet. I angled my head and peered down at him. He returned the look, his eyes black with shock.

'Now you won't pass the medical for Pathfinder, Greve. Sorry about that. You will never steal the technology. However thorough you are. In fact, that bloody thoroughness was your undoing.'

Greve's groan was barely audible, something Dutch.

'It was the thoroughness that tempted you here,' I said. 'To the final interview. Because do you know what? You're the man I've been seeking for this job. A job for which I not only think but know you are perfect. And that means the job is perfect for you. Believe me, herr Greve.'

Greve didn't answer, just stared down at himself. The blood had made the black rollneck even blacker. So I went on.

'You are hereby appointed as the scapegoat, herr Greve. As the man who killed Ove Kjikerud, the body lying next to me.' I patted Ove on the stomach.

Greve groaned again and raised his head. 'What the fuck are you babbling on about?' His voice sounded desperate and at the same time groggy, sleepy. 'Ring for an ambulance before you murder someone else, Brown. Think about it, you're an amateur, you'll never get away from the police. Ring now, and I'll save you, too.'

I looked down at Ove. He seemed peaceful where he lay. 'But it's not me who will kill you, Greve. It's Kjikerud here, don't you understand?'

'No. Christ, ring for a bloody ambulance now. Can't you see I'm bleeding to death here!'

'Sorry, it's too late.'

'Too late? Are you going to let me die?'

Something different had crept into his voice. Could it have been tears?

'Please, Brown. Not here, not like this! I implore you, I beg you.'

It was tears indeed. They streamed down his cheeks. Not that strange perhaps, if what

329

he had said about being shot in the stomach was correct. I could see blood dripping from the inside of his trouser legs onto the polished Prada shoes. He had begged. Had not been able to maintain dignity in death. I have heard it said that no one can, that those who appear to manage it are just emotionless from shock. The most humiliating part for Greve was of course that there were so many witnesses to his breakdown. And there would be more.

Fifteen seconds after I had let myself into Kjikerud's house and entered the sitting room without tapping in 'Natasha' on the alarm, the CCTV cameras would have begun to record as the alarm went off at Tripolis. I formed a mental image of how they would have flocked around the monitor, how they would have stared at the silent film in disbelief, with Greve as the only visible actor, seen him open his mouth but would have been unable to hear what he said. They would have seen him shoot and take a hit, and cursed Ove for not having had a camera that showed the person in bed.

I looked at my watch. Four minutes had passed since the alarm had gone off, and, I presumed, three minutes since they had phoned the police. They, in turn, had rung Delta, the armed unit that was used on stake-outs. And whom it took some time to assemble. Tonsenhagen was also quite some distance from the centre. Assumptions of course, but the first police cars would hardly be here in less than, at best, a quarter of an hour. On the other hand, there was no reason to let this drag on. Greve had fired two of the seventeen shots in the magazine.

'All right, Clas,' I said, opening the window behind the headboard. 'You can have a last chance. Pick up your gun. If you can shoot me, I suppose you can ring for an ambulance yourself.'

He stared at me with empty eyes. An icy cold wind swept into the room. Winter had arrived, no question.

'Come on,' I said. 'What have you got to lose?'

The logic of this seemed to penetrate his shock-addled brain. And with a swift movement, much swifter than I had believed possible with the injuries he had, he threw himself sideways to the floor and grabbed the gun. The bullets from the machine gun, *plumbum,* the soft, heavy, toxic metal, gouged up splinters from the parquet floor between his legs. But before the spray of bullets reached him again, before it swept across his chest, pierced his heart and punctured both lungs, causing him to wheeze his last, he managed to fire one shot. A single shot. The sound quivered between the walls. Then it was quiet again. Deathly quiet. Only the wind sang its low song. The silent film had become a freeze-frame, frozen in the cold temperature that seeped into the room.

It was over.

■ ■ ■ ■

Part Five:
Last Interview
One Month Later

■ ■ ■ ■

23
NEWS TONIGHT

The theme song of the news program *News Tonight* was a simple guitar riff reminiscent of a bossa nova, swaying hips and colorful drinks, not hard facts, politics and depressing social problems. Or, like this evening, crime. The tune was brief in order to signal that *News Tonight* was a program without unnecessary frills, it dealt with the nitty-gritty and went straight to the point.

That was presumably why it started with the jib camera in Studio 3 that showed the evening's guests from above, then swept down to finish with a head shot of the anchor, Odd G. Dybwad. As the music stopped, he looked up from his papers and removed his reading glasses. That had probably been the producer's idea; he or she might have thought it gave the impression that the news item they were going to discuss was hot off the press, so much so that Dybwad had only just managed to read it himself.

Dybwad had short, thick hair which was greying at the temples and one of those fortyish faces. He had looked forty when he was thirty and forty now that he was fifty. Dybwad had majored in social sciences, was analytical, verbally bright and by predilection tabloid through and through. It was probably not this attribute that had been decisive in the station manager's decision to give him his own talk show, but rather the job Dybwad had been doing as a news anchorman for half a human lifetime. By and large the task had been to read aloud prepared texts with the right intonation and facial expression, dressed in the right suit with the right tie, but in Dybwad's case the intonation, the expression and the tie had been so right that it had given him more credibility than any other living person in Norway. And it was credibility that was needed to carry a program like *News Tonight.* Strangely enough, publicly stating several times that he loved his ratings and that at editorial meetings it was he, and not the station manager, who pushed for the most commercial news items just seemed to reinforce Dybwad's impregnability. He wanted to have slants with the potential to create heat and stir emotions, not doubts, nor a variety of views and debate. That was best managed by newspaper feature articles. His stock response was: 'Why leave discussions about the royal family, homosexual foster parents and welfare abuse to frivolous media operators when we can have them on *News Tonight*?'

News Tonight was an unqualified success and Odd G. Dybwad a star. So much of a star that after an extremely painful and extremely public divorce he had been able to marry one of the channel's young female stars.

'This evening we have two items,' he said with a voice that was already trembling a fraction with suppressed emotion as he stared with piercing eyes from the TV screen. 'First we will be giving an overview of one of the most dramatic murder cases in Norway's history. After a month of intense investigation the police now believe they have unravelled all the threads of the so-called Greve case. In all, it involves eight murders. A man who was strangled on his farm outside Elverum. Four policemen whose car was rammed by a stolen juggernaut. A woman who was shot in her Oslo home. All of this before the two main protagonists in this drama gunned each other down in a house in Tonsenhagen here in Oslo. The last episode in this drama was caught on film because the house was fitted with CCTV, and copies of the video have already leaked out and have been circulating on the Internet over the last few weeks.'

Dybwad bumped up the dose of pathos.

'And, as if that were not enough, at the centre of this bizarre case is a world-famous painting. Peter Paul Rubens's *The Calydonian Boar Hunt* had been missing, feared lost, ever since the last world war. Until it was found four weeks ago in a . . .' Here Dybwad became so excited that he started to stammer. '. . . in — in an outside toilet here in Norway!'

After this introduction Dybwad had to touch down before taking off again.

'We are joined by someone who can help us get to the heart of the Greve case. Brede Sperre . . .'

Dybwad paused for a moment as this was the cue for the producer in the control room to switch to camera 2. The producer chose a side shot of the only guest in the studio, a tall, good-looking, blond man. An expensive suit for a civil servant, an open-necked shirt, mother-of-pearl buttons, probably put together by the *ELLE* stylist he was secretly — or almost secretly — shagging. None of the female viewers would be switching channels for the time being.

'You led the Kripos investigation into this murder case. You have almost fifteen years' experience in the police force. Have you ever encountered anything like this before?'

'All cases are different,' Brede Sperre said, with effortless self-assurance. You didn't need to be a fortune teller to know that his mobile phone would be crammed with texts after the broadcast. A woman wondering if he was single and fancied a coffee with an interesting person; a single mother, living just outside Oslo, with her own car and loads of free time next week. A young man who liked older, resolute men. Some skipped the preliminaries and just sent a photo. One they were pleased with, nice smile, straight from the hairdresser, nice clothes, suitably low neckline. Or without a face. Or clothes.

'But, of course, eight murders is not your usual bread-and-butter case,' Sperre said in his stilted voice. And added, hearing that an understatement was a trifle on the nonchalant side: 'Not here and not in countries which it would be na-ural to compare ourselves with.'

'Brede Sperre,' said Dybwad, who was always careful to repeat the guest's name a couple of times, so that it stuck in viewers' minds, 'this is a case which has aroused international interest. Aside from the murder of eight people, this heightened attention is primarily down to the fact that a world-famous old master has played a key role, isn't it?'

'Well, it's certainly a painting familiar to art connoisseurs.'

'Now I think we can say without fear of contradiction that it is world-famous!' Dybwad exclaimed, trying to catch Sperre's eye, perhaps to remind him about what they had discussed before the show, that they were a team, two people who should work together to tell a fantastic story. Devaluing the fame of the painting had the effect of making the story less fantastic.

'Nevertheless Rubens's painting must have been of central importance when Kripos, with no survivors or other witnesses to rely on, had to fit all the pieces of this puzzle together. Isn't that right, Inspector Sperre?'

'That is correct.'

'You will be presenting the final case report tomorrow, but I understand you can already tell our viewers what actually happened in the Greve case, the whole course of events from start to finish.'

Brede Sperre nodded. But instead of starting to speak he raised the glass of water on the desk in front of him and took a small sip. Dybwad, to the right of the picture, was beaming. The two of them might have arranged this little spot of theatricality in advance, this pause that made viewers perch on the very edge of their sofas, all eyes and ears. Or perhaps Sperre had taken over the stage management. The policeman put down his glass and took a deep breath.

'Before I joined Kripos, I was, as you know, in the Robberies Unit and had investigated the many art thefts that have occurred in Oslo over the last two years. The similarities suggested that there was a gang behind them. At a very early stage we had been focusing on the security company Tripolis as most of the residences that were burgled had alarms from there. And now we know that one of the people behind the thefts worked for Tripolis. Ove Kjikerud had access to property owners' keys at Tripolis and thus could also switch off alarms. In addition, Kjikerud had clearly found a way to delete reports of break-ins from the system's databases. We assume Kjikerud himself carried out most of the bur-laries. But he needed a person who had some insight into the art world, who spoke to other art enthusiasts in Oslo and could gain an overview of which pictures were hanging where.'

'And this is where Clas Greve came in?'

'Yes. He himself had a fine collection of art in his apartment in Oscars gate and hung out with art connoisseurs, particularly at Galleri E, where he was often observed. There he spoke to people who themselves had valuable paintings or could tell him who had. This was i-formation that Greve in turn passed on to Kjikerud.'

'What did Kjikerud do with the paintings after stealing them?'

'Through an anonymous tip-off, we have managed to trace a fence, a receiver of stolen goods, in Gothenburg, an old friend of the police who has already confessed to having been in contact with Kjikerud. In interviews this person has told our Swedish colleagues that the last time he heard anything from Kjikerud was when he called and said that the Rubens picture was on its way. The fence said he found it difficult to believe that this was true. And neither the painting nor Kjikerud turned up in Gothenburg . . .'

'No, it didn't,' Dybwad rumbled with tragic gravity. 'Because what happened?'

Sperre smirked before continuing, as though finding the anchor's melodrama rather amusing. 'It seems that Kjikerud and

Greve decided not to deal with the fence in Gothenburg. They may have decided to sell the painting themselves. Remember that the receiver rakes in fifty per cent of the sale price, and on this occasion the sums they were talking about were quite different from the proceeds from other pictures. As the former CEO of a Dutch technology company which had dealings with Russia and several ex-Eastern bloc countries, Greve had a pile of con-acts, not necessarily all on the right side of the law. And this was Greve and Kjikerud's chance to be financially secure for the rest of their lives.'

'But on the face of it Greve seemed like a person who had enough money, didn't he?'

'The technology company which he part-owned was going through a rough patch, and he had just lost his post there. Apparently he had a lifestyle which necessitated income. We know he had recently applied for a job with a Norwegian company in Horten.'

'So Kjikerud didn't turn up for the meeting with the fence because he and Greve wanted to sell the painting themselves. What happened then?'

'Until they found a buyer they had to hide the painting somewhere secure. So they went to a cabin Kjikerud had rented from

Sindre Aa for several years.'

'Outside Elverum.'

'Yes. The neighbours say that the cabin wasn't used much, from time to time there were two men around the place, but no one had ever exchanged words with them. It seemed almost as though they were in hiding.'

'And you believe this was Greve and Kjikerud?'

'They were incredibly professional and extremely par-icular in their dealings with others. And they didn't want to leave any traces that might connect the two of them. We don't have any witnesses who ever saw them together, and no phone records to show they had spoken.'

'But then an unforeseen event took place?'

'Yes. Precisely what, we don't know. They had gone to the cabin to hide the painting. Not unnaturally when the sums are so huge there is a tendency for suspicions to sneak in about the partner you trusted before . . . Perhaps they started arguing. And they must have been high: we found traces of drugs in both their blood samples.'

'Drugs?'

'A mixture of Ketalar and Dormicum. Strong stuff and very unusual among addicts in Oslo, so our guess is that Greve must have brought this with him from Amsterdam. The combination may have made them careless and in the end they totally lost control. Which ended up with them taking the life of Sindre Aa. Afterwards —'

'One moment,' Dybwad interrupted. 'Could you explain to viewers exactly what happened in connection with this first murder?'

Sperre raised an eyebrow, as if to express a certain displeasure with the anchor's undisguised bloodthirstiness. Then he gave in.

'No, we can only guess. Kjikerud and Greve may have taken the party down to Sindre Aa and boasted about the famous painting they had stolen. And Aa rea-ted by threatening to or actually trying to contact the police. Whereupon Clas Greve garrotted him.'

'And a garrotte is?'

'A thin piece of wire or nylon which is tightened around the victim's neck, block-ing the flow of oxygen to the brain.'

'And he dies?'

'Er . . . yes.'

A button in the control room was pressed and on the live monitor — the screen show-ing what was being transmitted to the thousands of TV viewers — Odd G. Dybwad was nodding slowly while staring at Sperre with a studied mixture of horror and earnestness. He let it sink in. One, two, three seconds. Three TV years. The producer was presumably sweating now. And then Dybwad broke the silence. 'How do you know it was Greve who carried out the killing?'

'Forensic evidence. We later found the garrotte on Greve's body, in the jacket pocket. Sindre Aa's blood and traces of Greve's skin were found on it.'

'And so you know that both Greve and Kjikerud were in Aa's sitting room at the time of the murder?'

'Yes.'

'How do you know that? More forensic evidence?'

Sperre squirmed. 'Yes.'

'What evidence?'

Brede Sperre coughed and shot a look at Dybwad. They might have had discussions about this point. Sperre may have asked him to skip the detail, but Dybwad had insisted it was important to fill out the story.

Sperre braced himself. 'We found some evidence in the vicinity of Sindre Aa's body. Traces of excrement.'

'Excrement?' Dybwad interrupted.

'Human?'

'Yes. We sent it to the lab for DNA analysis. Most matches the DNA profile of Ove Kjikerud. But there was also some from Clas Greve.'

Dybwad opened his palms. 'What on earth was going on here, Inspector Sperre?'

'It is difficult to form a detailed picture, of course, but it looks as if Greve and Kjikerud . . .' Another pause to brace himself. '. . . smeared their own excrement over themselves. Some people do that, don't they?'

'In other words, we're talking about some very sick individuals here?'

'They'd been taking drugs, as I mentioned before. But, yes, it is undoubtedly . . . er, deviant behaviour.'

'And it doesn't stop there, does it?'

'No.'

Sperre paused as Dybwad raised his forefinger, the agreed signal for Sperre to take a tiny break. Enough for viewers to be able to digest the information and prepare themselves for what was to follow. Then the inspector continued.

'Ove Kjikerud, in his drug-fuelled state, discovers a sadistic game to play with the dog that Greve has brought along. He skewers it on the prongs of a loader at the back of a tractor. But this is a fighting dog and in the heat of the struggle Kjikerud receives deep bites to the neck. Afterwards Kjikerud drives the tractor around the area with the dog hanging from the loader. He is obviously so high that he can barely keep the tractor on the road and is stopped by a motorist. The motorist has no idea what he has stumbled upon and does what any right-minded citizen would feel duty-bound to do — he puts the injured Kjikerud in his car and drives him to hospital.'

'What a contrast in . . . in human qualities,' exclaimed Odd G. Dybwad.

'One might indeed say that. It was this motorist who was able to tell us that Kjikerud was covered in his own excrement when he met him. He thought Kjikerud had fallen into a muck heap, but the hospital staff who washed Kjikerud said that it was human ex-rement, not animal. They have had some experience of . . . of . . .'

'What did they do with Kjikerud at the hospital?'

'Kjikerud was semi-conscious, but they showered him, bandaged the wound and put him to bed.'

'And it was at the hospital that they found traces of drugs in his blood?'

'No. They did take blood samples, but

they were routinely destroyed. We found traces of drugs in his blood during the post-mortem examination.'

'OK, but let's go back. We've got up to Kjikerud being admitted to the hospital with Greve still at the farm. What happens then?'

'Greve, naturally enough, suspects something when Kjikerud doesn't return. He discovers the tractor's gone, fetches his own car and starts driving around the district searching for his companion. We assume that Greve has a police radio in his car and through it hears that the police have found the tractor and — getting on for morning — the body of Sindre Aa.'

'Right, so now Greve is in trouble. He doesn't know where his accomplice is, the police have found the body of Sindre Aa, the farm is a crime scene and in their search for the murder weapon there is a chance the police may uncover the Rubens painting. What is going through Greve's mind?'

Sperre hesitated. Why? Police reports always avoid descriptions of what people think, keeping only to what can be proved At most, one might refer to what those involved said they were thinking. But in this case no one had said anything. On the other hand, Sperre knew he had to come up with something, had to help bring the story to life so as to . . . to . . . He probably hadn't allowed himself to think that thought through to its logical conclusion because he had an inkling what lay at the end. That he liked being the person the media rang, the one they wanted a sound bite from if a comment or an explanation was needed, the nods of recognition on the street, the unsolicited photos on the mobile phone. But if he stopped delivering, would the media stop ringing? So what did it all boil down to? A question of integrity versus media attention, respect from colleagues versus popularity with the man on the street?

'Greve is thinking . . .' Brede Sperre said, '. . . that the situation is tricky. He drives around searching, and it is morning by now. Then he hears on the police radio that Kjikerud is going to be arrested, collected from the hospital by the police and taken in for questioning. And now Greve knows the situation has gone from tricky to desperate. You see, he knows that Kjikerud is no hard-boiled thug, that the police won't need to push him very far, that Kjikerud may be offered a reduced sentence if he informs on his partner and, of course, that Kjikerud will not accept the guilt for the murder of Sindre Aa.'

'Logical,' Dybwad nodded, bending forward, egging him on.

'So Greve realises the only way out is to rescue Kjikerud from the police before the questioning starts. Or . . .'

Sperre didn't need Dybwad's discreetly raised forefinger to tell him that this was the right place for another little pause.

'. . . or kill him in the process.'

The TV signals seemed to crackle in the studio air, which was so dry from the stage lighting that it could catch fire at any point. Sperre went on.

'So Greve starts searching for a car he can borrow. And in a car park he comes across an abandoned truck with a trailer. With his background in a Dutch counter-terrorism unit he knows how to start an engine. He still has the police radio with him and has obviously studied the map to be clear which route the police car transporting Kjikerud will take from the hospital to Elverum. He waits for them in the truck on a side road . . .'

Dybwad launched himself into the story with a dramatically raised finger. 'And then the greatest tragedy in the whole case takes place.'

'Yes,' Sperre said, eyes downcast.

'I know this is painful for you, Brede,' Dybwad said.

Brede. Christian name. That was the cue.

'Close-up of Sperre now,' the producer said in the earplug to camera 1.

Sperre took a deep breath. 'Four good policemen were killed in the collision that followed, one of them a close Kripos colleague of mine, Joar Sunded.'

They had zoomed in with such care that the average viewer wouldn't have noticed that Sperre's face now took up a slightly bigger part of the screen; they only perceived it as a tenser, more intimate atmosphere, a feeling of getting inside this visibly moved stalwart policeman.

'The police car is hurled over a crash barrier and disappears beneath the trees right by the river,' Dybwad went on. 'But, miraculously, Ove Kjikerud survives.'

'Yes.' Sperre has recovered. 'He clambers out of the wreck, either on his own or with Greve's help. After dumping the truck they get into Greve's car and go back to Oslo. When the police later find the patrol car and one body is missing they believe it's landed in the river. Furthermore, Kjikerud has dressed one of the police bodies to look like himself and for a while this creates confusion about who has survived.'

'But even though Greve and Kjikerud are

safe for the moment their paranoia is in full bloom, isn't it?'

'Yes. Kjikerud is aware that when Greve drove the truck into the patrol car, he had to be indifferent as to whether Kjikerud lived or died. And Kjikerud has realised that his life is in danger; Greve has at least two good reasons to get rid of him. The first because he witnessed the murder of Aa, the second because Greve wouldn't have to share the proceeds from the Rubens painting. He knows that Greve will strike whenever the opportunity offers itself again.'

Dybwad leaned forward with excitement. 'And that's where we move into the last act of the drama. They have arrived in Oslo and Kjikerud has gone back to his house. But not to relax. He knows he has to make the first move — eat or be eaten. Then from his huge arsenal of weapons he takes out a little black pistol, a . . . a . . .'

'Rohrbaugh R9,' Sperre said. 'Nine millimetres, semi-automatic, six bullets in the magaz—'

'And he takes it with him to where he believes Clas Greve is staying. At his lover's. Right?'

'We're not sure about the relationship Greve had with this woman, but we do know that they were in regular contact, that

353

they met and that Greve's fingerprints have been found in her bedroom, among other places.'

'So Kjikerud goes to the lover's address and is standing there with the weapon when she opens the door,' Dybwad said. 'She lets him into the hall where Kjikerud shoots her. Then he searches the apartment for Greve, but he isn't there. Kjikerud puts the body of the woman into her bed and goes back to his own place. He makes sure he has the weapon to hand wherever he is, even in bed. And then Greve appears . . .'

'Yes. We don't know how he gets in, perhaps he picks the lock. At any rate he is not aware he has activated the soundless alarm when entering. But that sets off the CCTV cameras in the house.'

'Which means that the police have pictures of what happens from now on, the final showdown between these two criminals. And for those who do not have the stomach to see this on the Internet, could you tell us briefly what happens?'

'They start shooting at each other. Greve fires off two shots first, with his Glock 17. Amazingly enough, he misses with both.'

'Amazing?'

'At such a close range, yes. Greve was a trained commando after all.'

'So he hits the wall instead?'

'No.'

'No?'

'No, there were no bullets in the wall by the bed head board. He hits the win-ow. That is, he doesn't hit the window, either, because it's wide open. His shots go outside.'

'Outside? How do you know that?'

'Because we've found the bullets outside.'

'Oh?'

'In the forest behind the house. In a bird house for owls hanging from a tree trunk.' Sperre gave a wry grin, the way men do when they think they're underplaying a success story.

'I see. And then?'

'Kjikerud starts shooting back with an Uzi machine gun which he has in his bed. As we can see on the film, the bullets hit Greve in the groin and the stomach. He drops his pistol, but picks it up again and manages to fire off a third and final shot. The bullet hits Kjikerud in the forehead above his right eye. It causes massive damage to the brain. But it's not how people imagine from films — that every shot to the head inflicts instant death. You see, Kjikerud manages to fire a final salvo before dying. And this kills Clas Greve.'

A long silence followed. The producer probably raised one finger to Dybwad, the signal that there was one minute left on the schedule and it was time to summarise and round off the news item.

Odd G. Dybwad leaned back in the chair, more relaxed now. 'So Kripos has never been in any doubt that this was how it all happened?'

'No,' said Sperre, fixing his gaze on Dybwad. Then he splayed his arms. 'But it goes without saying that there will always be some uncertainty with regard to details. And a little confusion. For instance, the pathologist who was at the crime scene felt that the temperature of Kjikerud's body had fallen with surprising rapidity. On the basis of the usual charts and figures he would have put the time of death at least twenty-four hours earlier. But then the police officers at the scene pointed out that the window behind the bed had been open when they arrived. And this was, as you remember, the first day of sub-zero temperatures in Oslo. This kind of uncertainty exists all the time, it is part and parcel of our work.'

'Yes, for even though you can't see Kjikerud on the recordings, the bullet in Kjikerud's head . . .'

'Came from the Glock that Greve fired,

yes.' Sperre smiled again. 'The forensic evidence is what the press likes to call "overwhelming".'

Dybwad gave a befitting beam as he shuffled the papers together in front of him, signalling that things were being rounded up. All that was left to do now was to thank Brede Sperre, stare straight into the lens of camera 1 and see to the evening's other item: another round of agricultural subsidies. But he stopped, his mouth half open, his eyes flicked down. A message in his ear? Something he had forgotten?

'Just one last thing, Inspector,' Dybwad said, calm, deft, experienced. 'What do you actually know about the woman who was shot?'

Sperre hunched his shoulders. 'Not a lot. As I said, we believe she was Greve's lover. One of the neighbours says he saw Greve come and go. She doesn't have a criminal record, but we have found out via Interpol that she was involved in a drugs case many years ago when she and her pa-ents lived in Suriname. She was the girlfriend of one of the drug barons there, but when he was killed by a Dutch commando unit she helped them to reel in the rest of the gang.'

'But she wasn't charged?'

'She was underage. And pregnant. The

authorities sent her family back to their home country.'

'Which was . . . ?'

'Er, Denmark. And there she stayed living, as far as we know, a quiet life. Until she came to Oslo three months ago. And met a tragic end.'

'Apropos of tragic ends, I'm afraid we have to say thank you and goodbye to you, Brede Sperre.' Glasses off, look into camera 1. 'Should Norway cultivate its own tomatoes at any price? In *News Tonight* we're going to meet . . .'

The TV picture imploded as I pressed the 'off' button on the remote control with my left thumb. I would usually have done it with my right thumb, but that arm was busy. And even though it was going to sleep through poor blood circulation, I would not have moved it for anything in the world. In fact, it was supporting the most beautiful head I knew. The head turned to me, and her hand pushed away the duvet to have a good look at me.

'Did you really sleep in her bed after shooting her that night? Next to her? How wide did you say it was?'

'One hundred and one centimetres,' I said. 'According to the IKEA catalogue.'

Diana's big blue eyes stared at me in horror. But — if I wasn't mistaken — there was a certain admiration there, too. She was wearing a gauzy negligée, an Yves Saint Laurent creation which was cool when it caressed my skin like now, but burning hot when my body pressed it against hers.

She propped herself up on her elbows.

'How did you shoot her?'

I closed my eyes and groaned. 'Diana! We've agreed that we won't talk about this.'

'Yes, we did, but I'm ready for it now, Roger. I promise.'

'Darling, listen . . .'

'No! Tomorrow the police report will be out and I'll get to hear the details anyway. I'd rather hear them from you.'

I sighed. 'Sure?'

'Absolutely positive.'

'In the eye.'

'Which one?'

'This one.' I placed my forefinger against her finely formed left eyebrow.

She closed her eyes and took a slow, deep breath. In and out. 'What did you shoot her with?'

'A small black pistol.'

'Where did . . . ?'

'I found it at Ove's place.' I ran my finger along her eyebrow to the side of her face, stroked it over her high cheekbones. 'And that was where it stayed, too. Minus my fingerprints of course.'

'Where were you when you shot her?'

'In the hall.'

Diana's breathing was already noticeably faster. 'Did she say anything? Was she frightened? Did she understand what was happening?'

'I don't know. I shot her as soon as I entered.'

'What did you feel?'

'Sorrow.'

She gave a faint smile. 'Sorrow? Really?'

'Yes.'

'Even though she tried to lure you into Clas's trap?'

My finger stopped. Not even now, a month after it was all over, did I like her using his Christian name. But, of course, she was right. Lotte's mission had been to become my lover; it was she who was to introduce me to Clas Greve and persuade me to invite him to a job interview with Pathfinder and who was to make sure that I selected him. How long had it taken her to hook me? Three seconds? And I had splashed about helplessly as she had reeled me in. But then something unexpected had happened. I had dropped her. A man had loved his wife so much that he had, of his own accord, renounced a self-sacrificing and totally undemanding lover. Very surprising. And they had had to change plans.

'I suppose I felt sorry for her,' I said. 'I think I was just the last in a succession of men who had let Lotte down throughout her life.'

I felt Diana give a little jerk when I articulated her name. Good.

'Shall we talk about something else?' I suggested.

'No, I want to talk about this now.'

'OK. Let's talk about how Greve seduced you and persuaded you to take over the role of manipulating me.'

She chuckled. 'Fine by me.'

'Did you love him?'

She turned and her eyes lingered on me.

I repeated the question.

She sighed and wriggled closer. 'I was in love.'

'In love?'

'He wanted to give me a child. So I fell in love.'

'So simple?'

'Yes. But it's not simple, Roger.'

She was right, of course. It isn't simple.

'And you were willing to sacrifice everything to have this child? Even me?'

'Yes, even you.'

'Even though it meant I would have to pay with my life?'

She nudged my shoulder with her temple. 'No, not that. You know very well that I thought he would only persuade you to write the report in his favour.'

'Did you really think that, Diana?'

She didn't answer.

'Really, Diana?'

'Yes, I think so anyway. You have to understand that I wanted to believe that.'

'Enough for you to place the rubber ball filled with Dormicum on the car seat?'

'Yes.'

'And when you came down to the garage it was to drive me to the place where he would persuade me, wasn't it?'

'We've been through all this, Roger. He said this way entailed the least risk for all parties. Of course, I should have known it was madness. And perhaps I did, too. I don't know what else I can tell you.'

We lay absorbed in our own thoughts while listening to the silence. In the summer we could hear the wind and the rain on the leaves of the trees in the garden outside, but not now. Now everything was stripped bare. And quiet. The only comfort was that it would be spring again. Perhaps.

'And how long were you in love?' I asked.

'Until I realised what I was doing. The night you didn't come home . . .'

'Yes?'

'I just felt like dying.'

'I didn't mean in love with him,' I said. 'I meant with me.'

She chuckled. 'I can't know that until I've stopped loving you.'

Diana almost never lied. Not because she couldn't, Diana was a wonderful liar, but because she couldn't be bothered. Beautiful people don't need shells, are not obliged to learn all the defence mechanisms we others develop in order to protect ourselves against rejection and disappointment. But when women like Diana make up their minds to lie, they are thorough and efficient. Not because they are less moral than men, but because they have greater mastery of this aspect of the treachery. And that was precisely why I had gone to Diana that last evening. Because I knew she was the perfect candidate for the job.

After unlocking the door, standing in the hallway and listening to her footsteps on the parquet floor for a while, I had gone upstairs to the living room. I had heard her steps stop, the phone fall onto the coffee table, the whispered half-sob 'Roger . . .', seen the tears welling up in her eyes. And I had done nothing to stop her when she had thrown herself around my neck. 'Thank God you're alive! I kept ringing you all day yesterday and I've been trying all day today . . . where have you been?'

And Diana was not lying. She was crying because she thought she had lost me. Because she had sent me and my love out of her life like a dog to the vet to be put down. No, she was not lying. Said my gut instinct. But, as I have said, I am no great judge of human beings, and Diana is a wonderful liar. So when she had gone to dry her tears in the bathroom, I picked up her phone and checked that it was in fact my phone number she had been trying to ring. To be on the safe side.

When she came back, I told her everything. Absolutely everything. Where I had been, who I had been, what had happened. About the art thefts, about the phone under the bed in Greve's apartment, about Danish Lotte who had pulled the wool over my eyes. About the conversation with Greve at the hospital. The one that had made me see that he knew Lotte, that she was his closest ally, that the person who had rubbed the gel containing transmitters into my hair was not Diana but the brown-eyed pallid-faced girl with the magical fingers, the translator who spoke Spanish and liked others' stories better than her own. That I had had the gel in my hair since the evening before I had found Kjikerud in the car. Diana had stared at me in silence with wonder-filled eyes while I had told her.

'At the hospital Greve said I'd persuaded you to have an abortion because the baby had Down's syndrome.'

'Down's?' It was the first thing Diana had said for several minutes. 'Where did he get that idea from? I didn't say —'

'I know. It was something I made up when I told Lotte about the abortion. She told me her parents had forced her to have an abortion when she was a teenager. So I made up the Down's syndrome story because I thought she might see me in a better light.'

'So she . . . she . . .'

'Yes. She's the only one who could have told Greve that.'

I had waited. Let it sink in.

Then I had told Diana what would happen now.

She had stared at me in horror and shouted: 'I can't do it, Roger!'

'Yes, you can,' I had said. 'You can and

you will, my love.' Said the new Roger Brown.

'But . . . but . . .'

'He was lying to you, Diana. He can't give you a child. He's sterile.'

'Sterile?'

'I'll give you the child. I promise. Just do this for me.'

She had refused. Cried. Begged. And then she had promised.

When I went down to Lotte's to become a murderer later that evening, I had instructed Diana and knew she would accomplish the mission. I could see her before me, receiving Greve when he came, the dazzling perfidious smile, the cognac already in the glass, passing it to him, toasting the victor, the future, the as yet unconceived child. Which she insisted should be conceived as soon as possible, tonight, now!

I recoiled as Diana pinched one of my nipples. 'What are you thinking about right now?'

I pulled up the duvet. 'The night Greve came here. Him lying with you where I am now.'

'So what? You were lying with a dead body that night.'

I had desisted from asking, but now I couldn't restrain myself any longer. 'Did you have sex?'

She chuckled. 'You did well to restrain yourself for so long, darling.'

'Did you?'

'Let me put it like this: the drops of Dormicum that were left in the rubber ball and that I squeezed into his welcome drink worked faster than I had imagined. I dolled myself up and when I came in here, he was already sleeping like a baby. The following day, however . . .'

'I withdraw the question,' I said with alacrity.

Diana stroked my stomach with her hand and laughed again. 'The next morning he was very much awake. Not because of me, but because of a phone call that had woken him up.'

'My warning.'

'Yes. At any rate he was dressed and off at once.'

'Where was his gun?'

'In his jacket pocket.'

'Did he check the gun before he left?'

'I don't know. He wouldn't have noticed the difference anyway, the weight was about the same. I just exchanged the top three cartridges in the magazine.'

'Yes, but the blank cartridges I gave you have a red B on the end.'

'If he'd checked he would probably have thought it stood for "back".'

The laughter of two people filled the bedroom. I enjoyed the sound. If all went well and the litmus test was positive, the room would soon be filled by the laughter of three people. And it would suppress the other sound, the echo I could still wake up to in the night. The bangs as Greve fired, the flash of the muzzle, the fraction of a second thinking that Diana had not switched the cartridges after all, that she had changed sides again. And then, the echo, the clink of empty cartridge cases landing on the parquet floor that was already covered with cartridges, live and blank, old and new, so many that the police would not be able to tell them apart regardless of whether they suspected that the video recording was a put-up job.

'Were you frightened?' she asked.

'Frightened?'

'Yes. You never told me how it felt. And you don't appear in the pictures . . .'

'Pic—' I moved away to be able to see her face. 'Do you mean to say you've been on the Net looking at the film?'

She didn't answer. And I thought there was still a lot I didn't know about this woman. Perhaps there would be enough mysteries for a whole lifetime.

'Yes,' I said. 'I was scared.'

'What of? You knew his gun didn't have any —'

'Only the top three cartridges were blanks. I had to make sure he fired all of them so that the police wouldn't find unused blanks in the magazine and see through the plan, didn't I? But he could have fired some of the live bullets too. And he could have changed the magazine before coming. And he could also have brought along a sidekick I knew nothing about.'

Silence fell. Until she asked in a whisper: 'So there was nothing else you were frightened of?'

I knew she was thinking what I was thinking.

'Yes, there was,' I said, turning to her. 'I was frightened of one more thing.'

Her breathing on my face was fast and hot.

'He might have killed you during the night,' I said. 'Greve didn't have any plans to start a family with you, and you were a dangerous witness. I knew I was putting your life in danger when I asked you to be the decoy.'

'I knew I was in danger the whole time, darling,' she whispered. 'That was why I gave him the welcome drink as soon as he came through the door. And didn't wake him until you rang his phone. I knew he would be up and away after hearing the ghost's voice. And besides, I had swapped the first three bullets in the gun, hadn't I?'

'True,' I said. Diana, as I have said, is a woman with a relaxed relationship to prime numbers and logic.

She caressed my stomach with her hand. 'And another thing — I appreciate the fact that you knowingly and deliberately put my life in danger . . .'

'Oh?'

She ran her hand further down, over my penis. Held my balls in her hand. Weighed them, gently squeezed the two testicles. 'Balance is of the essence,' she said. 'That applies to all good, harmonious relationships. Balance in guilt, balance in shame and pangs of conscience.'

I chewed on that, tried to digest it, let my brain assimilate this somewhat weighty nugget of thought.

'You mean . . .' I began, gave up and started afresh. 'You mean to say you put yourself in mortal danger for my sake . . . that that . . .'

'. . . was an appropriate price to pay for what I had done to you, yes. The same as

370

Galleri E was an appropriate price for you to pay for the abortion.'

'And you've thought this for a long time?'

'Of course. So have you.'

'Correct,' I said. 'Penance . . .'

'Penance, yes. It's a very much underrated method of gaining peace of mind.' She squeezed my testicles a bit harder and I tried to relax, to enjoy the pain. I inhaled her fragrance. It was wonderful, but would I ever wipe out the stench of human excrement? Would I ever hear anything that would drown the sound of Greve's punctured lungs? Afterwards he had seemed to be staring at me with glazed, wronged eyes as I pressed Ove's cold fingers against the stock and the trigger of the Uzi and the small black Rohrbaugh pistol with which I had shot Lotte. Would I ever be able to eat anything that could dull the taste of Ove's dead flesh? I had bent over him there in bed sinking my canine teeth into his neck. Tightened my jaws until his skin was pierced and the corpse taste filled my mouth. There had been almost no blood, and when I had stifled my retching and wiped away the saliva, I had studied the result. It would probably pass as a dog bite to a detective looking for precisely that. Then I had crawled out of the open window behind the top of Ove's bed to make sure I wasn't recorded by the camera. Walked quickly into the forest; found paths, routes. Greeted walkers with a friendly gesture. The air, which became colder the higher I climbed, had kept me cool all the way to Grefsentoppen. There I had sat down and contemplated the autumn colors, which winter had already begun to suck from the forest beneath me, the town, the fjord and the light. The light that always presages the oncoming darkness.

I could feel the blood surging into my dick, the shaft throbbing.

'Come on,' she whispered close to my ear.

I took her. Systematically and completely, like a man who has a job to do. Who enjoys his work, but nonetheless sees it as a job. And he works until the siren goes off. The siren goes off and she places her hands with protective care over his ears, and the reins are slipped and he sprays her full of hot, life-giving seed, even though the place is already taken. And afterwards she sleeps, and he lies listening to her breathing, feeling the satisfaction of a job well done. Knowing things can never be the same as they were. But they could be similar. There could be a life ahead. He could look after her. He could love someone. And as if that alone were not overwhelming enough, he even sees a point to loving, a 'because', an echo of an argument used at a football match in London fog: 'Because they need me.'

EPILOGUE

The first snow had come and gone again.

I had read on the Net that a purchase option and the display rights for *The Calydonian Boar Hunt* had been sold at an auction in Paris. The buyer was the Getty Museum in Los Angeles, which could now exhibit the painting — unless in the two-year option period an owner appeared from out of the blue and laid claim to the property — and could take up the option and acquire permanent possession. There were a few brief sentences about its origins and the discussions that had raged about whether it was a copy or an original by a different painter, since there were no sources proving that Rubens had ever painted any Calydonian boars. But the experts were now agreed that Rubens was the artist. There was nothing about how the picture had come to light, the fact that the Norwegian state was the vendor or any mention of price.

Diana had realised that it would be difficult to run the gallery alone now that she was a mother-to-be, and had therefore — after consulting me — decided to bring in a partner who could take care of the more practical aspects, such as the financial management, so that she could concentrate more on art and artists. Our house had, furthermore, been put up for sale. We had agreed that a slightly smaller terrace house in a more rural setting would be a better place for a child to grow up. And I had already received a very high offer. It was from someone who had rung me the second he had seen the ad in the newspaper and asked for a viewing that very evening. I had recognised him as soon as I opened the door. Corneliani suit and geek-chic glasses.

'Not one of Ole Bang's very best perhaps,' he commented after racing from room to room with me in tow. 'But I'll take it. How much do you want?'

I mentioned the quote in the ad.

'Plus a million,' he said. 'Deadline the day after tomorrow.'

I said we would consider his offer and escorted him to the door. He passed me his business card. No title, just his name and a mobile phone number. The recruitment agency's name was written in such small letters that to all practical intents and purposes it was unreadable.

'Tell me,' he said on the doorstep, 'didn't you use to be king of the heap?' And before I could reply: 'We're thinking of expanding. We may ring you.'

We. Small letters.

I let the deadline pass without mentioning the offer to the estate agent or Diana. I didn't hear anything from 'we', either.

Since, on principle, I never start working before it is light, on this particular day I was — as on most other days — the last man to arrive in the car park outside Alfa. 'The first shall be last.' This is a privilege I have formulated myself and implemented, a privilege that can only be granted to the company's best headhunter. The position also implies that no one can take your parking spot even though, on paper, it is subject to the same first-come-first-served rule as other company parking spaces.

But on this day there was a car there nonetheless. An unfamiliar Passat, probably one of our customers who thought it would be fine to park there because of the Alfa sign hanging from the chain behind the space, a halfwit who did not have the capacity to read the large sign by the entrance directing them to VISITOR PARKING.

All the same, I felt a little uncertainty. Could it be that someone in Alfa had come to the conclusion that I was no longer . . . I didn't complete the thought.

While I was casting around for another spot, annoyed, a man strode out of the office building heading in the vague direction of the Passat. He had a Passat-owner gait, I determined, and breathed a sigh of relief. For this was definitely not a rival for the spot but a client.

I parked my car demonstratively in front of the Passat, waited and hoped. Perhaps it was a good start to the day after all, perhaps I could shout at an idiot. And, sure enough, the man tapped on my side window, and I looked into a coat at stomach height.

I waited a couple of seconds before pressing the window button, and the glass slid down slowly — yet still a little faster than ideally I would have liked.

'Listen —' he began before being interrupted by my studied drawl.

'Well, how can I help you today?' Without deigning to cast him a glance, I prepared to deliver a refreshing sign-reading lecture.

'Would you mind moving your car a bit? You're b-ocking my way out.'

'I think you'll find that *you* are blocking

my way *in,* my good —'

At last the atmospheric noises reached my brain. I peered out of the window and up. My heart almost stopped beating.

'Of course,' I said. 'Just a moment.' I fumbled manically for the button to close the window. But my fine-motor-coordination skills seemed to have vanished.

'Wait a sec,' said Brede Sperre. 'Haven't we met before?'

'I doubt it,' I said, trying to produce a calm, relaxed bass voice.

'Are you sure? I'm certain we've met.'

Shit, how could he have recognised the alleged third cousin of the Monsen brothers at the Pathology Unit? That version had been bald and dressed like a bumpkin. This one had luxuriant hair, an Ermenegildo Zegna suit and a freshly pressed Borelli shirt. But I knew I shouldn't be too dismissive, put Sperre into defensive mode and set his brain whirring until he remembered. I took a deep breath. I was tired, more tired than I ought to have been today. This was a day when I had to deliver the goods. Show that I could live up to the reputation I had once enjoyed.

'Who knows?' I said. 'To tell the truth there's something familiar about you, too . . .'

At first he seemed a little bewildered by this counter-offensive. Then he put on the boyish winsome smile that made Sperre so well suited to the visual media.

'You've probably seen me on TV. I hear that all the time . . .'

'Right, that's probably where you've seen me too,' I said.

'Oh?' he said, curious. 'Which program was that, then?'

'Must have been your program. Since you think we've met. Because the TV screen is not actually a window through which we can see each other, is it? On your side of the camera it's more like . . . a mirror maybe?'

Sperre looked slightly confused.

'I'm joking,' I said. 'I'll move. Have a great day.'

I activated the car window and reversed. There were rumours going round that Sperre was screwing Odd G. Dybwad's new wife. Rumours that he had screwed the old one, too. And — for that matter — that he was screwing Dybwad.

As Sperre was driving out of the car park, he stopped before turning, so that for two seconds we were sitting in our cars windscreen to windscreen. I saw his eyes. He was looking at me as though he had just been tricked and only realised that now. I sent him a friendly nod. Then he accelerated and was off. And I looked in the rear-view mirror and whispered: 'Hi there, Roger.'

I entered Alfa and roared a deafening 'Good morning, Oda!' and then Ferdinand came rushing towards me.

'Well?' I said. 'Have they come?'

'Yes, they're ready,' Ferdinand said, tripping down the corridor after me. 'By the way, there was a policeman here. Tall, blond and quite, erm . . . good-looking.'

'What did he want?'

'He wanted to know what Clas Greve had said about himself in the interviews he had attended here.'

'He's been dead a long time,' I said. 'Are they still investigating the case?'

'Not the murder case. It's about the Rubens picture. They can't work out who he stole it from. No one's come forward. Now they're trying to trace who he's been in contact with.'

'Didn't you read the paper today? Now they've started to doubt whether it's an original Rubens again. Perhaps he didn't steal it; he might have inherited it.'

'Bizarre.'

'What did you say to the policeman?'

'I gave him our interview report, of course. That didn't seem to interest him much. He said he would contact us again, if there was anything.'

'And you're hoping he will, I suppose?'

Ferdinand gave his squeal of a laugh.

'Anyway,' I said, 'you take care of that, Ferdy. I trust you.'

I could see how he rose and sank, how the responsibility made him grow and the nickname made him shrink. Balance is everything.

Then we were at the end of the corridor. I paused in front of the door and checked the knot of my tie. They were sitting inside, ready for the final interview. The rubber-stamping. For the candidate had already been selected, was already appointed, it was just the client who wasn't aware of it yet, who thought they still had some say in the matter.

'Then send the candidate in exactly two minutes from now,' I said. 'One hundred and twenty seconds.'

Ferdinand nodded and studied his watch.

'Just one tiny little thing,' he said. 'Her name's Ida.'

I opened the door and stepped inside.

There was scraping of chairs as they stood up.

'I apologise for the delay, gentlemen,' I said, shaking the three hands held out to me. 'But someone took my parking spot.'

'Isn't that wearing?' the chairman of Pathfinder said, turning to his public relations manager who nodded in vigorous agreement. The shop steward representing the employees was there too, a guy in a red V-necked sweater with a cheap white shirt underneath, undoubtedly an engineer of the saddest variety.

'The candidate has a board meeting at twelve, so perhaps we ought to get cracking?' I said, taking a seat at the end of the table. The other end had already been prepared for the man they would, in one and a half hours' time, happily agree would have to be Pathfinder's new CEO. The lights had been set up in such a way that he would appear at his most favourable, the chair was of the same kind as ours, but its legs were a bit longer, and I had laid out the leather briefcase I had bought for him, bearing his initials, and a gold Montblanc pen.

'Indeed,' the company chairman said. 'By the way, I have a confession to make. As you know, we very much liked Clas Greve after the interview he gave.'

'Yes,' said the public relations manager. 'We thought you had found the perfect candidate.'

'He was a foreigner, I know,' said the chairman, his neck coiling like a snake's, 'but the man spoke Norwegian like a native. And we said, while you were escorting him out, that in the final analysis the Dutch have always had a better understanding of the export market than we do here.'

'And that we might be able to learn from someone with a more international management style,' the public relations manager added.

'So when you came back and said you were not sure he was the right man after all, well, we were very surprised, Roger.'

'Really?'

'Yes, we were quite simply of the opinion that your powers of judgement were wanting. I haven't said this before, but we were considering withdrawing your commission and contacting Greve direct.'

'So did you do that?' I asked with a wry smile.

'What we're wondering,' the public relations manager said, exchanging glances with the chairman and flashing a smile, 'is how you could spot there was something amiss.'

'How did you know instinctively what we were utterly blind to?' asked the chairman, with a loud clearing of the throat. 'How can anyone be such a good judge of character?'

I nodded slowly. Pushed my papers five centimetres up the table. And slumped into the high-backed chair. It rocked — not too much, only a little. I looked out of the window. At the light. At the darkness that was on its way. A hundred seconds. The room was quite silent now.

'It's my job,' I said.

From the corner of my eye I saw the three of them exchange meaningful nods. And added: 'Besides, I had already begun to consider a candidate who was even better.'

The three turned towards me. And I was ready. I imagine that is how it feels to be the conductor during the seconds before the concert starts, feeling the eyes of everyone in the symphony orchestra glued to your baton, hearing the expectant audience behind you settle in.

'That's why I've brought you here today,' I said. 'The man you will meet is the new shooting star, not just in the Norwegian but in the international management sky. In the last round I reckoned it would be quite unrealistic to wrench him away from the job he had. He is, after all, God the Father, God the Son and God the Holy Ghost of the company.'

My gaze shifted from face to face.

'But without promising too much now, I think I can go so far as to say that I may have unsettled him. And if we should get him . . .' I rolled my eyes to suggest a wet dream, utopia, but nevertheless . . . And the chairman and the public relations manager had predictably and inevitably drawn closer. Even the shop steward who had been sitting with his arms crossed had placed them on the table and leaned forward.

'Who? Who?' whispered the public relations manager.

One hundred and twenty.

The door opened. And there he stood, a man of thirty-nine in a suit from Kamikaze in Bogstadveien where Alfa gets a fifteen per cent discount. Ferdinand had dabbed some skin-colored talcum powder on his right hand before sending him in because, as we know, he suffered from sweaty palms. But the candidate knew what he had to do, for I had instructed him, set the scene down to the last detail. He had dyed his hair an almost imperceptible grey at the temples and had once owned a lithograph by Edvard Munch entitled *The Brooch*.

'May I introduce Jeremias Lander?' I said.

I'm a headhunter. It's not particularly difficult. But I am king of the heap.

ABOUT THE AUTHOR

Jo Nesbø is a musician, songwriter, economist, and author. The first crime novel in his Inspector Harry Hole series was published in Norway in 1997, an instant hit, winning the Glass Key Award for best Nordic crime novel (an accolade shared with Stieg Larsson and Henning Mankell). He also established the Harry Hole Foundation, a charity to reduce illiteracy among children in the third world. He lives in Oslo. www.jonesbo.com

The employees of Thorndike Press hope you have enjoyed this Large Print book. All our Thorndike, Wheeler, and Kennebec Large Print titles are designed for easy reading, and all our books are made to last. Other Thorndike Press Large Print books are available at your library, through selected bookstores, or directly from us.

For information about titles, please call:
  (800) 223-1244

or visit our Web site at:
  http://gale.cengage.com/thorndike

To share your comments, please write:
  Publisher
  Thorndike Press
  10 Water St., Suite 310
  Waterville, ME 04901